I closed my eyes and offered a silent prayer: *Ancestors, grandfathers and grandmothers of the four sacred directions. This is your grandson, Rory. I come before you in a humble manner and ask you to be with me as I dance for the first time. Kinânskomitin.*

The emcee announced, "Host drum, you're up. Aho, aho! Junior Boys Fancy Dance. It's powwow time. Let's see what you got, boys."

With the first beat of the drum, I began to dance. I twisted, dipped, bobbed.

ANCESTOR APPROVED

Intertribal Stories for kids

EDITED BY
CYNTHIA LEITICH SMITH

Heartdrum
An Imprint of HarperCollinsPublishers

Heartdrum is an imprint of HarperCollins Publishers.

Ancestor Approved: Intertribal Stories for Kids
"What Is a Powwow?" © 2021 by Kim Rogers
"Fancy Dancer" © 2021 by Monique Gray Smith
"Flying Together" © 2021 by Kim Rogers
"Warriors of Forgiveness" © 2021 by Tim Tingle
"Brothers" © 2021 by David A. Robertson
"Rez Dog Rules" © 2021 by Rebecca Roanhorse
"Secrets and Surprises" © 2021 by Traci Sorell
"Wendigos Don't Dance" © 2021 by Art Coulson
"Indian Price" © 2021 by Eric Gansworth
"Senecavajo: Alan's Story" © 2021 by Brian Young
"Squash Blossom Bracelet: Kevin's Story" © 2021 by Brian Young
"Joey Reads the Sky" © 2021 by Dawn Quigley
"What We Know About Glaciers" © 2021 by Christine Day
"Little Fox and the Case of the Missing Regalia" © 2021 by Erika T. Wurth
"The Ballad of Maggie Wilson" © 2021 by Andrea L. Rogers
"Bad Dog" © 2021 by Joseph Bruchac
"Between the Lines" © 2021 by Cynthia Leitich Smith
"Circles" © 2021 by Carole Lindstrom

Library of Congress Control Number: 2020945305
ISBN 978-0-06-286995-1

Typography by Molly Fehr
23 24 25 PC/BRR 10 9 8 7
❖
First paperback edition, 2022

CONTENTS

In memory of Michael Lacapa
(Hopi/Tewa/Apache)

FOREWORD

Imagine you're attending an intertribal powwow.

Maybe it's your first time. Maybe your family has been on the powwow trail for generations.

You might make new friends or reunite with old ones. In line for fry bread, you could strike up a conversation with a vendor and buy a key chain from them later that day. From the bleachers, you could admire a dancer's shawl and, that night, recognize her wearing everyday clothes on the way home.

Through stories, poetry, and visual art, the contributors to this anthology coordinated their efforts—via phone calls, emails, texts, and an online task board—to reflect the interconnectedness of the powwow experience. We've filled this book with memorable characters . . . some of whom know each other, some of whom don't, and all of whom are pleased to welcome you.

WHAT IS A POWWOW?

KIM ROGERS

A powwow is
friends and family
gathered together to honor the Creator,
Kinnekasus, Man-Never-Known-on-Earth,
who watches over us.

A powwow is
a way to remember those
who've passed on,
even ancestors we did not know
who stay in our hearts
forever.
They are near us
always.

A powwow is
a place to show
our resilience
and strength.
We are still here
generation
after
generation,
into the future
and beyond.

A powwow is
drums and songs and dancing,
in jingles, feathers, shawls, and beaded buckskin
regalia
you and your family made
with love.

A powwow is
eating fry bread and corn soup
together,
selling or buying
artwork, jewelry, and T-shirts
that everyone would be
proud to take home.

A powwow is
prizes and recognition.
But community
is the best prize of all.

A powwow is
a place for belly-laughing late
into a sleepy night with your grandpa Lou,
then getting home after midnight.

A powwow is
where our hearts beat as one
to the thump *of the drum,*
together
so strong
where we belong.

A powwow is
healing
and soul-soothing
pure joy,
a circle of life
where the Creator,
Kinnekasus, Man-Never-Known-on-Earth,
smiles upon us.

FANCY DANCER

MONIQUE GRAY SMITH

Mom walked a bit lighter on the earth; my little sister, Suzie, giggled louder; and I—well, I gained a dad. Most people would call him my stepdad, but there's nothing "step" about him at all.

My father, the man whose genes run through me, had left two years earlier, when I was nine. One day, he just never came home from work. Mom tried to explain it to us, but we already knew that things weren't good between them. Kids know. Adults don't think we do, but we do.

What I didn't expect was that he never came to see us. He never even phoned. Ever. It was hard to see how much Suzie missed him. You probably think that as his son I must have been sad, but I wasn't. I was the opposite. You see, my father was not a kind man. Not to me or my sister and especially not to my mom. That was the hardest part of all. Watching how he hurt my mom. His temper was only one reason why I was relieved when he left.

When my parents found out they were pregnant with me, my father moved Mom far away from Saskatchewan and her family. While she kept in touch through email, I had never met my grandparents, aunties, uncles, or any of my cousins. No one had ever come to visit us. And we'd never gone to visit them.

I looked it up on a map once, and Saskatchewan, Canada, is pretty far from Ann Arbor, Michigan. My father never said it, but I'm pretty sure he hated that my mom was Cree. Why else would he forbid her to speak Cree in our house, or practice our ceremonies, or do anything at all that was part of our culture?

I do have one memory of my mom celebrating her culture. I was about seven or eight. It was the middle of the night, and I was thirsty, so I headed to the kitchen to get a drink. As I got close, I noticed a light flickering and music playing. The music was new to me, but the drumbeat was powerful. Like it was calling me closer. I peeked around the corner to see what was going on in the kitchen, and there was my mom, dancing. She stood tall, her head high, shoulders back, and her feet softly moved to the beat of the drum. In her hand was what looked like a bundle of feathers, and, just like her feet, she moved it to the sound of the drum.

I watched until the music stopped and Mom blew

out the candle. I made my way back to bed without her knowing that I had seen her dancing. That night I learned something really important. I had always known my mom was strong, but now I knew she was way stronger than I'd thought. In the middle of the night, she was keeping her culture, our culture, alive.

Nine years of living with my father meant I knew almost nothing about who I truly was. I'm pretty sure he was ashamed of us, or at least that's how it felt. He often told Suzie and me that we'd be better off in life if we had looked more like him and his Irish ancestors, but we didn't. There was no questioning we were Native.

I always knew Mom was proud of me, and that was all I needed. At least that's what I thought, until she brought Paul home.

Paul quickly became a regular at our dinner table and around our house. He's Cree like us, but from Treaty 8 territory in Alberta. He came to teach for a semester and loved it so much, he stayed. Paul and Mom both work at the University of Michigan; that's where they met. He came into the library looking for a specific book, and my mom, who is a librarian, helped him find it. They've been pretty much inseparable since then.

Not long after Paul came into our lives, Mom got back in touch with her family. Our family. Although we hadn't been able to go to Saskatchewan to meet them, we were using FaceTime a couple of times a week. I was liking getting to know everyone, and there were a lot of them! I liked knowing I was part of a big family and that I looked like them. I especially loved watching how Mom laughed with her siblings.

Now Mom walks every day just like she did that night I saw her dancing: head high, shoulders back.

A couple of months after Paul moved in, we were driving home from a good day of fishing out at Olson Park when he turned on the stereo. Out of the speakers came the same music that Mom had on that night I saw her dancing in the kitchen. The drumbeat went right to my heart. I could feel the rhythm, and my head began to move to the beat.

"You ever been to a powwow?" Paul asked.

"A what?"

"Guess that answers my question."

"What's a powwow?" I asked him.

"Only one of the greatest weekend events *ever*."

"And?"

"And?" He glanced at me and could see I really had no idea what a powwow was.

"Well, where do I begin? It's both a ceremony and cultural gathering, where we dance, sing, visit, and laugh. There's always a heck of a lot of laughing!" Paul chuckled. "Then there's the food. My mouth waters just thinking about the fry bread loaded with butter and salt. Oh, and can't forget the Indian tacos." He turned to me with a grin. "No powwow is complete without at least one Indian taco. Mmm, mmm, mmm." Paul wiped the back of his hand across his mouth. After a moment, he added, "But really, for me and how I was raised, powwow is a way of honoring our traditions, our families, and our Ancestors."

"Is it just us?" I asked. "You know, uh, Native Americans?" Our family had hidden who we were for so long that I wasn't sure what to call us.

"Mostly, yes. Native people travel from all over to go to powwows, but non-Natives are welcome too. That's part of the beauty of the powwow, the sharing of cultures." He turned his head toward me. "We have one of the biggest powwows in the United States right here in Ann Arbor. It's called the Dance for Mother Earth Powwow."

"Really?"

Paul nodded. "I noticed you dancing in your seat. I think you have the moves to be a fancy dancer."

"Okay, first of all, I don't even know what a fancy dancer is. And second . . ." My father's voice rang through my mind. *Hope you got some brains in that head of yours, 'cause you sure ain't got any hopes of being on any sports team.* He had laughed and then mocked me more. *Unless you plan on being the water boy, but you'd probably screw that up, too.*

I leaned my head against the window. "I'm not good at anything that requires coordination, like sports. So I'd probably suck at this fancy-dancing thing."

As we drove along Pontiac Trail, I watched the trees go by and wondered if I'd ever stop hearing my father's voice in my head.

We were almost home when Paul started talking again. "Your mom's told me some of the stories of how your dad treated you. How he treated all of you." He looked over at me for a moment and then back to the road. "I'm sorry that happened."

"Why are you sorry? You didn't do anything."

"You're right, I didn't, but I can still be sorry that you had to experience that. No child or woman should ever be treated like you, Suzie, and your mom were. It helps me understand a little bit why you think you wouldn't be any good at fancy dancing. But for what it's worth, I think you could be good. Dancing isn't just about being athletic, it's about telling a story to the drumbeat and revealing the strength that is in your heart." Paul was quiet until we pulled into our driveway. He put the truck in *Park* and turned to me. "There is a lot of strength in your heart, Rory. You can let the unkind things your father said define you. Or—"

"Or what?" I asked.

"Or you can define yourself. Including what you want to be good at. There are always going to be people who want to pull you down. That's the hurt in their heart. But it's up to you whether you let them succeed."

We sat in silence except for the powerful beat coming out of the speakers. Paul was using his thumb on the steering wheel to keep up with the drum. My upper body began moving to the beat again. This time my head bobbed a bit, forward and back and side to side.

"You know, Rory, I was quite a fancy dancer back in the day. If you wanted, I could teach you."

I turned to look at him. "Really?"

"Sure. I'd love to."

Hesitantly, I responded, "Okay. Might help if I knew what a fancy dancer was."

Paul laughed. "I suppose it would. That's what the first class will cover. Tomorrow night."

"Why not now? Or tonight?"

Paul laughed again and slammed the steering wheel with his hand. "See, I knew there was a dancer in there! Give me a night to clear out the garage. We're gonna need space for you to get your moves on."

"I can help you clean it."

"I was counting on that." Paul turned to me and tousled my hair. "Maybe we can get your mom and Suzie to help us."

After dinner, the overhaul from garage to dance floor began. We had to clear out all the winter and summer toys we no longer used, old paint cans, and bins of clothes that Mom had saved from when Suzie and I were little. The next night I had my first fancy-dance lesson. We started by smudging. At first, I didn't know what to do. Paul showed me how to take the smoke from the sage in my hands and run it over my head and then down my body. He explained it was like having a shower, but instead of cleaning my body, it cleaned my spirit. Paul said smudging would help me feel good inside, and he was right. There was something about the smell of burning sage that gave me a peaceful feeling.

When Paul turned on the music, he told me, "Just close your eyes. Let the drumbeat and the song wake you up. Notice your breathing. Breathe in through your nose and out through your mouth."

My body wanted to move, but I was afraid to give in to the urge. I was afraid I wouldn't do it right.

It was like Paul could read my mind. "It's okay, Rory. There's no right way, only *your* way." He put his hands on my shoulders and looked me in my eyes. "Your body remembers how to dance. Your ancestors have been dancing like this for generations." His hands moved up to cradle my face. "Trust yourself."

Paul dropped his hands and took a step back. "I want

you to start by moving your head. Feel the drumbeat move through you."

After a couple of months of practicing two nights a week, I could feel my whole body getting stronger. I loved both the dancing and the smudging, but especially the time with Paul.

It was an icy-cold January morning when I found it. Lying there in front of my cereal bowl. A flyer for the annual Dance for Mother Earth Powwow. On the flyer Paul had written, *I think you could be ready to dance at this, but it doesn't matter what I think. It matters what you think. Love, Paul.*

I shoved the flyer into my backpack and left for school. At lunch, I pulled it out as I began to eat my ham and cheese sandwich.

I could just imagine what my father would say: *How Indian are you trying to be, Rory?* Maybe he was right. But I felt different when I danced. More like me. It was all so confusing. I crushed the flyer into a tiny ball and tossed it into the garbage with the rest of my uneaten sandwich.

That night I pretended to have a sore tummy. I excused myself from dinner and my night of dancing with Paul. I was lying on my bed feeling sorry for myself when there was a knock at the door.

"Yeah?"

Paul opened the door a smidge. "Can I come in?"

"I suppose."

He came and sat on the side of my bed. "If you can't come to the garage to dance, then the dancing is going to come to you."

"I really don't feel like it."

"I know. That's why I brought some homework for you."

I rolled my eyes at the word *homework*.

Paul reached into his back pocket and pulled out his wallet. "If I'd had homework like what I'm about to give you, my life sure would've been different."

I watched as he opened his wallet, pulled out an iTunes gift card, and placed it beside me on the bed. "I want you to go online and download your favorite powwow music. That's the first of your homework."

I tried not to, but I couldn't help it. A smile crept across my face.

"Then I want you to practice standing on one foot at a time, up on your tippy toes. I want you to focus on your breathing, like I showed you. We have to get your mind and body believing in each other."

I gave him a *what are you talking about?* look.

"The song is the bridge between your mind and your body. But right now, your mind and your body don't trust each other. We have to build that bridge of trust. When you truly learn to believe in yourself, all of you . . . then that is the greatest gift learning to fancy dance will give you."

That night, as I practiced my balance, and then when I lay in bed listening to my favorite songs, I felt a determination I'd never felt before. I decided I was going to prove my father wrong. But mostly, I was going to prove to myself that I could do it. I was going to dance at the powwow. I was going to be proud of who I was.

The next morning, over a bowl of mush and blueberries, I announced, "Sooooooo. I'm gonna do it."

"Do what?" asked my sister as she shoved oatmeal into her mouth.

"I'm going to enter the Junior Boys Fancy Dance at the powwow."

"Yes!" Paul said loudly, and raised his fist straight up.

Mom reached over and hugged me. "Oh, my boy. I'm proud of you."

I had just over two months to get ready, and not just physically. Mentally, emotionally, and spiritually too.

A couple of weeks later, I found two boxes on my bed. One was large and the other was ginormous! I noticed the return address was my mom's home community in Saskatchewan. I opened the large one first and pulled out the most beautiful regalia. I had been watching fancy dancing on YouTube and hadn't seen anything quite like this.

It was turquoise, white, and black, and when I held it up to myself, I knew it would fit.

I quickly opened the ginormous box, wondering if maybe it had a bustle in it? Sure enough, wrapped very carefully in tissue paper, was a bustle that matched. At the bottom of the box there was a letter. I sat down on my bed and opened it.

Nephew,

I want you to have my regalia. Dance it proudly. Make it come alive again . . . just like I used to.

If the feathers got a bit squished, ask your mom to steam them. She'll remember how.

I hope to see you dance one day. Hey, you should come home for our powwow. I can teach you some of my moves.

It's gonna be a real good day when that happens.

Uncle Fred

Come home. Those words put tears in my eyes. I'd always thought of Ann Arbor as home, but I was beginning to wonder if there were lots of places to call home. I'd talk to Mom later about going home to the powwow. For now, I had to focus on the Dance for Mother Earth Powwow.

As the weekend of the powwow approached, Paul and I spent time going over how the judges would be scoring the dancers. Not that I expected to win or anything, but I needed to know what they'd be looking for so I could make sure I did my best. I wanted my family to be proud of me. To be honest, *I* wanted to be proud of me.

Paul had written out the judging criteria for me:

Dance style
Stopping (over/under step)
Regalia (authenticity, footwear)
Attitude (sportsmanship)
Judges' call on song quality
No points if any items dropped

"Regalia. This one you're going to rock," Paul said with a smile. I had to agree. My regalia was awesome! Just then, Mom came into the kitchen and placed a package on the table in front of me. "For you," she said, and kissed my cheek. "Open it."

"Okay." I pulled the white tissue off to find a stunning pair of moccasins. I looked at her. "For me?"

Her eyes glistened. "Yes, Rory. For you."

"Wow, Mom! These are gorgeous!" They were tanned moose hide. The tops were covered with white beads, with black beads in the middle to create an eagle with a turquoise circle around it. Around the ankles was white rabbit fur. I lifted them to my nose. "They smell sooo good! Where'd you get them?"

"I made them."

My eyes got big. "You made these?"

"Yes, I made them." A smile spread across her face.

I liked seeing her happy.

Paul pulled Mom in for a hug. "Lila, my love, you never cease to surprise me."

I stood up and squished myself into their hug. "Thank you, Mom. Thank you."

Mom pulled away and held my face in her hands. "I'm so proud of you, Rory. Now don't let me interrupt you two any longer." She turned to leave the kitchen. "I think you have some more strategizing to do."

"That we do," Paul said.

I sat back down, smelled my new moccasins one more time, and then put them on.

"Now you're really going to rock the regalia category." Paul smiled at me and looked down at the judging criteria. "Okay, next category. Attitude and sportsmanship."

Finally, the day we'd been preparing for arrived. I danced in the Grand Entry at the start of the powwow. I wasn't too nervous, because all of us dancers were part of it, but when it came time for Junior Boys Fancy Dance, everything changed.

I stood near the entrance to the Skyline High School

gym, and Paul adjusted my headpiece. "Ready?" he asked.

I shook my head. "I need more time." The other dancers looked calm, confident.

"Look at me, my boy." Paul took my chin between his thumb and forefinger. "Don't be comparing yourself to the other dancers. Uh-uh. When you walk out there, you breathe deep. Feel those Ancestors with you, and on that first drumbeat feel their love come alive in you."

I gave a slight nod.

"The first time I danced, I was afraid. Shaking so hard my feathers were jiggling. But I've learned that sometimes in life, you gotta be brave before you can be good. So that's what I want you to do, Rory." He motioned his head out to the gym. "Go out there and be brave. The good will come."

Just then, the powwow emcee announced, "It's time for the Junior Boys Fancy Dance."

I took the biggest deep breath I'd ever taken and turned to enter the gym.

"Rory," Paul called out to me.

I looked back at him and realized I never would've gotten here without him. Actually, so much of who I was, who our family had become and my life now, was because of him.

He smiled at me. "Kisâkihitin."

I smiled back at him and felt myself relax. "Kisâkihitin, Dad."

The arena director was motioning for me to keep moving. I took my place in the flow of dancers entering the gym. I shook my head, rolled my neck, lifted my shoulders, and planted my feet solidly. I leaned forward, trying to see past the other dancers to scan the bleachers for where my mom, sister, and Paul were sitting.

When I found them, I gave a nod and they all waved. I could see my mom wiping tears from her eyes. She put her hand on her heart.

I closed my eyes and offered a silent prayer: *Ancestors, grandfathers and grandmothers of the four sacred directions. This is your grandson, Rory. I come before you in a humble manner and ask you to be with me as I dance for the first time. Kinânskomitin.*

The emcee announced, "Host drum, you're up. Aho, aho! Junior Boys Fancy Dance. It's powwow time. Let's see what you got, boys."

With the first beat of the drum, I began to dance. I twisted, dipped, bobbed.

I felt alive. Proud. Cree.

FLYING TOGETHER

KIM ROGERS

The time on my smartphone read oh four hundred (0400). It was still too early for a rooster to crow. I'd been up the whole night thinking that if I stayed awake for that long, morning wouldn't come and Mom wouldn't be leaving again.

Grandpa Lou peeked his head into my room. The brightness from the hallway spilled into my eyes. I shielded them with my hand as I sprang upright in the blinding light.

"Oh good. You're up, Jessie girl," said Grandpa Lou in a singsong voice.

Grandpa Lou never had a problem getting up at any hour—joyfully. "I've made breakfast, if you're hungry. Get it while it's hot."

The smell of sausage and french toast wafted into

my room, trying to draw me out like a giant invisible "come here" finger, but it wasn't working. I hadn't had an appetite—ever since Mom told me the news.

Grandpa Lou closed the door. I threw off my covers. My feet felt like boulders dangling from the side of the bed. I wrapped a blanket around my shivering shoulders, then stumbled toward the window.

Stars still sprinkled the velvety Oklahoma sky. Maybe, just maybe, the sun wouldn't come up and Mom wouldn't have to go. And maybe today wasn't January 5, the day that I'd been dreading for weeks.

I got dressed and combed my messy hair.

In the foyer, Mom's overstuffed green duffel bags stood at attention, ready to march out the door.

I staggered around like a seventh-grade zombie girl, hoping I was dreaming.

Everyone else flittered frantically around the house. Grandpa Lou loaded the last of the breakfast dishes into the dishwasher at a rapid-fire pace. Our little dog, Fritz, zipped behind Mom from room to room, because even he knew. His metal tag jingle-jangled with his every step. It sounded like a sleigh at Christmastime, but this was no holiday celebration.

Mom, aka Captain Vanessa Stephenson, was going on another deployment to the Middle East. She was leaving me at home with Grandpa Lou and Fritz to fend for ourselves—

All over again.

Don't get me wrong. Grandpa Lou is the best grandpa ever. And Fritz is a great pup because he likes to cuddle with me when I'm sick or sad or even happy. He's the best doggie in the whole wide world. Well, except when he tinkles on the floor and makes Mom yell and she threatens to ship him off to the moon.

Before Mom's socks get soaked, Grandpa Lou usually cleans up Fritz's tinkles first. He made me an honorary member of the official pee patrol. Fritz is a good name for a dog like him. His bladder is definitely on the fritz 24/7. Even though he's technically still a puppy because he's not yet one year old, we're hoping he'll get an A in potty training soon.

Besides Mom, Grandpa Lou is my superhero. He came to live with us after my parents got divorced and Grandma Grace passed away. He helps me and Mom and keeps us company, and we do the same for him. We all stay less lonely that way. Plus, he gives me hugs and makes me laugh.

One time he made me laugh so hard that Dr Pepper flew right out of my nose. That stuff burns like fire. I so wish that I'd been drinking milk that day. My friend Dylan Jones said that Kool-Aid isn't so bad coming out your nose either, but only if it's not red. "Red stuff coming out your nose will freak your mother out," he'd said.

Grandpa Lou makes the best fry bread in all of Indian Country; it's my great-grandma's recipe. He's teaching me how to make my own. It requires no measuring cups. "Just eyeballing it," he says.

We like to eat our fry bread with ham hocks and beans or, our favorite way, with powdered sugar like a giant doughnut. Sometimes Grandpa Lou pokes a hole in the middle of the dough before he fries it.

"Like a real doughnut," I told him.

He winked. "Yeah, a Wichita doughnut."

Grandpa Lou and I always laugh and eat. Fry bread. Fry bread. Fry bread. Mostly while Mom is working late. Powdered sugar sprinkles our shirts like fresh-fallen snow. Fritz even gets a bite or two of Wichita doughnut and licks the snowy sugar off the floor.

Grandpa Lou is a big kid in disguise. Mom said he never grew up. Grandpa Lou is six foot two, with wavy salt-and-pepper hair. He takes me to places like the amusement park, then he rides the roller coaster with me and makes me sit up front, where he screams the loudest. Everyone stares, but he doesn't care.

Like Mom, he served in the military. Grandpa Lou was a sailor in the US Navy, where he says he sailed the seven seas. Sometimes he sings a silly song about it.

But there's something I haven't seen him do in a while: Dance at a powwow.

"I'll just watch," he always says as he stays stuck to his lawn chair at our Wichita Tribal Dance each August. Mom can no longer get him to dance the Veterans' Song.

"My legs are too old," he says.

"Excuses, excuses," says Mom, shaking her head. "You're not *that* old."

"We Elders aren't spring chickens. I'm more of a winter chicken."

"A fall chicken," Mom says.

But Mom and I both know that age isn't the *real* problem.

In a few months, Grandpa Lou is taking me to the University of Michigan powwow in Ann Arbor. Mom graduated from U of M and had hoped to visit with a few old friends who live in town. We'd planned this trip long before we knew she was deploying.

I'll be dancing in the Fancy Shawl competition for the first time at this powwow without Mom to cheer me on. I've only competed at the Wichita Dance. But my other mission is to get Grandpa Lou to dance. He just doesn't know it yet. I'm sad that Mom won't be there to see it.

"Hey, Jessie girl," said Grandpa Lou, grabbing his travel coffee mug. "You ready?"

We were headed to Tinker Air Force Base to drop

Mom off for her deployment.

Grandpa Lou was wearing his Thunder·team baseball cap, a black T-shirt, and faded blue jeans. I guess you could say he was one hip grandpa. Not the kind who wears black socks with shorts to the grocery store.

Mom came rushing down the hallway in her tan flight suit—the one she wears when she's deploying overseas. Stateside flight suits are green like her duffel bags. Her ebony hair was braided in a tight bun, just above the collar as per air force regulations.

"Jess, do me a favor, please, and let the dog out," she said. She slung one of her bags over her shoulder and hurried out the front door.

Grandpa Lou grabbed the other bag and followed her to his king cab truck, closing the front door behind them.

"Okay, little dog. Time to go outside. You can't leave tinkles on the floor, even with Mom going away. It's not nice."

But Fritz wasn't listening. Even wearing his warm sweater, he wasn't a fan of going outside on wintry mornings. He jingle-jangled over to the window near the front door and peeked out at Mom and Grandpa Lou in the driveway. He cocked his ears to the side and whimpered.

"Oh, you stop that right now, Fritz. She'll be back before you know it," I said, trying to convince myself.

Fritz's whimpering had turned into a bark. It echoed

through the house. I looked around. The house was already so empty, and Mom hadn't even left the driveway. Her Wichita and Affiliated Tribes mug sat on the kitchen countertop—empty too. I wasn't sure how I could get through another three months without her.

Mom being late wasn't an option, and I'd had it with that little dog. I put on my coat and gloves and marched him right into the backyard. He ran to the fence, where he stood peering through the slats, sniffing and snorting like a miniature bull as Mom and Grandpa Lou finished loading the truck.

"Get to it, mister," I said, jumping up and down, trying to generate heat. Then I went back inside so that I could give him some privacy and unthaw my frozen toes.

Ten seconds later, I heard a scratch at the back door. *Did he really do his business that fast?* Goofy dog.

As we left our neighborhood in the Oklahoma City sub-urbs, porch lights glowed while everyone else was still sleeping.

On the highway, we passed lit-up fast-food restaurants, frost-covered trees, then Frontier City Theme Park. Under an inky morning sky, the Ferris wheel was all aglow in flashing changing colors. Red. Blue. Green. Yellow.

But there were no signs of human life anywhere, except for one SUV that sped past Grandpa Lou's truck.

"The only people out at this hour are medical people," said Grandpa Lou.

"Yeah, and military members," said Mom.

She had to be right. There were many early mornings when she had to be at Tinker to fly an "out and back"—military talk for a daylong mission. I imagined all the people in scrubs and uniforms driving the highway every morning before dawn—real-life superheroes like Mom and Grandpa Lou.

All three of us yawned in unison as we passed the twinkling skyline of downtown Oklahoma City.

When we got to Tinker Air Force Base, we stopped for a security check. The military policeman saluted Mom; then we drove through the gate.

In a base parking lot, Grandpa Lou tried to help Mom with her bags, but this time she insisted on carrying them all herself.

A bus puttered nearby. The exhaust made it look like a snarling dragon in the dark. Through the illuminated windows, I could see several uniformed people boarding and some sitting in seats. The bus would take airmen to the flight line. (Even women are called airmen.)

My mom is a pilot, and she would be flying an AWACS plane from Oklahoma to the Middle East with a full crew.

Mom set her bags on the pavement, and we hugged and kissed her goodbye. But I wasn't about to let her see me cry.

I bit my lip as she hurried toward the bus. Grandpa Lou put his arm around me. Then Mom stopped for a moment.

"Hey, Jess, I can't wait to eat some of your fry bread when I get home. You'll make some for me, right?"

I nodded.

Grandpa Lou gave me a sideways glance. "It will be your turn to fly solo soon."

I wasn't ready for all this flying solo stuff. Not with fry bread. Not at a powwow. Not getting Grandpa Lou to dance. Not doing all that without Mom.

As we were leaving Tinker, the sun hadn't even come up yet, and Mom was already gone. We drove back to a lonely house, where a giant puddle greeted us in the foyer.

"Fritz!" Grandpa Lou and I both yelled.

The months before the powwow flew by faster than I'd imagined. Grandpa Lou and I kept ourselves busy.

My weekdays were filled with school and way too much homework. And in front of Mom's oversize dresser mirror, I practiced the Fancy Shawl steps Cousin Nora had taught me, worried that I'd mess up come powwow time.

Grandpa Lou's weekdays were filled with adding more beadwork to my moccasins, watching his sci-fi shows on Netflix, and taking lots of naps.

Weekends were busy, too, but sometimes sad. One

Sunday we drove to Anadarko, Oklahoma, and visited Grandma Grace's grave, where we left her favorite yellow daisies for her birthday. Another time we drove there just because.

I missed her so much.

I also hung out with my best friend, Rachel Ramirez, watching horror movies and scarfing down pizza. Sometimes Grandpa Lou watched those movies along with us, always hiding his face behind a throw pillow during the really scary parts.

We kept in touch with Mom on Skype. She said she was keeping busy flying missions and that she missed us, even Fritz. We didn't tell her that he was still getting an F in potty training.

Grandpa Lou continued giving me fry bread lessons. Then one Saturday he said, "It's all you now."

I got five handfuls of flour and added this and that, poured in hot water, mixed and kneaded, let it rise, and fried up the dough. He took a few bites. No smiles. No response. Only the sound of sizzling oil cooling on the stovetop.

Then he finally said, "Your great-grandmother would be proud."

I exhaled, hoping Mom would feel the same when she got home.

Then the day came for Grandpa Lou and me to leave for the powwow. I packed a suitcase with some clothing, my favorite pj's, and my colorful Fancy Shawl regalia. I ran my fingers over my newly beaded moccasins. Grandpa Lou was one talented grandpa. I hoped he would teach me to bead soon.

On the way to the airport, we dropped off Fritz at the kennel. I narrowed my eyes at him. "You be a good pup." But he was so excited, he tinkled everywhere.

At Will Rogers World Airport, Grandpa Lou left his truck in the long-term lot. He grabbed a cup of coffee after our security check. "I need something to keep me awake," he said. When they called for boarding, he chugged it down as fast as he could.

On the plane, Grandpa Lou snored the whole way to Michigan. And I mean snored. Drooled big and everything. I had to wake him a few times because even people on the ground probably heard him. He has a thing called sleep apnea and usually wears an oxygen mask to help him breathe while he's sleeping. It makes him sound like Darth Vader.

When he fell asleep again, I took a quick pic to send to Rachel on Snapchat. I captioned it "Snoozin' Grandpa."

Right before we landed in Detroit, I shook Grandpa Lou awake again.

On the ground, I hit send to Rachel. She responded

with five smiley emojis with some hearts and zzzz's.

Grandpa Lou drove our rental car to the hotel. Later that night, he picked up on his snoring where he'd left off on the plane. I woke him and made sure he put on his Darth Vader mask.

It wasn't until after midnight when I finally caught my own z's.

From the free breakfast, Grandpa Lou had saved me cereal and a cinnamon roll so I could sleep in, and he went downstairs to read the paper.

After I ate a late breakfast and Grandpa Lou sipped his coffee, a brilliant blue sky greeted us on the way to the powwow.

Squinting at the puffy clouds, I thought of Mom somewhere above, flying sorties that kept the US and our Native Nations within its borders safe.

When we arrived at the gym, a few dancers were slipping on regalia over their shorts and tees behind open car trunks and SUV hatches. The cold air gave me goose bumps, so I decided to head to the girls' locker room. On my way there, a little dog wearing a T-shirt that said *Ancestor Approved* greeted me. He rolled over, and I gave him a good ol' belly rub. I wondered how tinkling Fritz was doing at the kennel.

When I came out looking for Grandpa, the gym echoed with all the familiar sounds of a powwow—*tink, tink* of jingles, *clink, clink* of bell bands, and *buzz, buzz* of excited voices.

Grandpa spotted me. "Let's go!" he said. "It's about to start."

We bolted to the registration table. Dancers were lining up, ready to enter the arena. Before I could blink, the announcement came for Grand Entry.

The drum *thumped, thumped, thumped.*

The drummers sang, "Hey yah. Hey yah. Yah hey. Yah hey."

I took my place behind the other dancers. When the song started, I danced into the arena, scanning the crowd and wishing that somehow Mom would be there.

Afterward, I took a seat next to Grandpa Lou in the bottom bleachers. He leaned over. "Nature calls. I'll be right back. Too much coffee."

The Veterans' Song started to play, and an invitation was announced for all those who'd served our country to come to the arena. I sank in my seat. Grandpa Lou would miss it.

Men danced in street clothes and regalia. Women danced in regalia, and street clothes with fringed shawls.

But the song played long, and Grandpa Lou was back.

"Now it's your turn," I said. "Let them honor you."

He shook his head. "I'm too old."

"No way," I said. "Look at all the Elders out there. You

can do it, too. What do they have that you don't?"

"Energy."

My eyes watered because I thought he'd never dance again.

But Grandpa Lou saw how sad I was.

A huge grin spread across his face. "For you," he said. Then he got up and entered the arena, where he danced with all the other superheroes just like him.

For the rest of the day, he didn't stop smiling.

"Did you see me?" he said.

I nodded, trying not to laugh.

I knew the *real* reason why Grandpa Lou didn't want to dance. All this time he was still grieving. One year of sitting out had turned into almost three.

"Grandma Grace would be so proud," I said, then gave him a side hug.

Grandpa Lou's voice cracked. "I know she would."

When the announcement came for Girls Fancy Shawl, my heart raced and sweat trickled from my temples to my beaded earrings. "I don't think I can do this. What if I get the steps wrong? I don't think I'll win. I've only done this a few times. I . . . I . . . I can't do it without Mom."

"Breathe," said Grandpa Lou. "You got this. If a winter chicken can dance with these old chicken legs, surely you can dance with your spring ones. It's not about winning. It's about flying."

Grandpa Lou always knew the right thing to say.

Calm washed over me, and I knew I could do this. I even felt Grandma Grace with me. I'm sure Grandpa Lou felt her, too. I stepped into arena with the other dancers to await the drum song.

With all my heart and soul, I danced. Even though Mom wasn't there, I danced. Even if I wasn't going to win, I danced. Even though I was scared, I danced.

I twirled and swirled my shimmering shawl round and round like a beautiful butterfly to the beat of the drum. In Grandpa Lou's beaded moccasins, I stomped my feet like Cousin Nora taught me.

Flying solo didn't feel so lonely after all. We were really *flying together* in spirit. One spirit.

When the dance ended, I headed back to Grandpa Lou, trying to catch my breath.

"I knew you could do it!" he said.

"And I knew you could do it, too. If only Mom could have seen us flying." I sighed.

We watched the next few categories, the gym *hum-hum-humming* with dance and song, and both of us still grinning.

Then I heard a familiar voice.

"You'll make me some fry bread when we get home, right, Jess?"

"Mom!"

Grandpa Lou and I leaped from our seats and ran to her. She was dressed in her flight suit, arms open wide. We all embraced in one family-size hug. Mom and I cried while Grandpa Lou just laughed.

"What are you doing here?" I asked, wiping tears.

"Our deployment was cut short. We came back on commercial flights. Couldn't miss being here. I'm just sad I missed your category, Jess."

"You missed the best part." That's when I told her all about Grandpa Lou.

"Your grandma Grace would be proud," she said as she winked at Grandpa Lou.

Then she gave him another hug.

Now the three of us were grinning.

Dancers stomped and swirled in rainbows of colors as we watched the rest of the powwow together—one happy family.

Well, except for Fritz. But we'd all be home together soon. In the kitchen, powdered sugar would be sprinkled all over our shirts from the fry bread I'd make Mom and Grandpa Lou. We'd give Fritz a few bites of our Wichita doughnut, and he'd lick the snowy sugar off the floor. And someday he'd finally earn his A.

WARRIORS OF FORGIVENESS

TIM TINGLE

I've had a lot of really weird conversations in my life, and I'm sure you have, too. Yes, I'm talking to *you*. But this morning's talk with Mom was just about the weirdest ever. Here's how it went:

"Luksi, you know how you always want to parade in and dance at the Choctaw Powwow every Labor Day? Well, you can this year!"

"Really, Mom? Oh, yakoke, thank you!" I shouted, and gave her a big hug.

But I'm old enough to know better. Totally unexpected good news always carries something behind its back. My first warning came when Mom was a little too quick to change the subject.

"Now, what would you like for lunch?" she asked.

"Whatever's on the table, Mom," I said. "Why are you asking me? And when did you decide to let me dance in the powwow this year? You know Labor Day is six months away."

"Hoke! Well, we can have chili-cheese hot dogs or pizza—your favorite pepperoni, of course. Which will it be, Luksi?"

"How about cherry pie with peanut butter ice cream, Mom-who-refuses-to-stay-on-the-subject?"

"Great! Pizza it is!" she shouted.

When I rolled my eyes exaggeratedly, she finally said something that made sense.

"Oh, Luksi, if you're going to dance in front of the Choctaw chief and the council members, you need to practice. There's a powwow this coming weekend in Michigan, and I thought you could practice there."

"Are you kidding me? Michigan? Last time I looked, we lived in Oklahoma. Do you know how far Michigan is from Oklahoma?"

When *she* rolled *her* eyes, *I* finally said something that made sense.

"Hoke, Mom. I'll sit down and shut up and you can tell me the whole story."

Hoke, I'm talking to *you* again. Are you listening? I am interrupting the narrative for a brief explanation of Luksi, my name. Sounds weird, huh?

That's because it's the Choctaw word for "turtle," and my full name is Luksi Bob Bryant. Not Luksi *Robert* Bryant, but Luksi Bob. And all through school I've been answering to the name Luke, so my friends wouldn't make fun of me. Most of them aren't Choctaw, and when we were in kindergarten, they'd play dumb peek-a-boo games every time they said my name.

Look Seee! Look Seeee!

Can you see me, Look Seeee?

So I told them my name was Luke Carl, and some people just called me Luke C.

Hoke, so when anybody calls me Luke, you know they are not Choctaw. Got it?

Now, back to the story.

While I munched on delicious cheesy pepperoni pizza, Mom sipped her iced tea and talked.

"The truth is never simple, Luksi. And this morning, we have two truths. Truth Number One: You can practice powwow dancing in Michigan."

"Not in jeans and a T-shirt," I said, dripping cheese on my chin.

"I've already taken care of that," Mom answered. "Your dad's old powwow outfit, from when he was a young boy, is already packed in your suitcase."

"My suitcase! When are we leaving?" I asked.

Mom glanced at the wall clock. *Not good*, I thought.

"When your uncle returns from the Choctaw Senior Center. He is driving the bus to Michigan."

"The bus! Hoke, let's hear Truth Number Two."

"You are such a smart little boy, Luksi," Mom said, blinking her eyelashes like a Hollywood starlet. "Your uncle has agreed to carry a busload of Choctaw Elders to the Michigan powwow."

"Mom, Uncle Lanny is the one Choctaw I know who does not like taking care of old people. Why would he agree to do that?"

"He already drives the school bus, and somebody thought he'd be perfect for the job," she said. "And Truth Number Two? You are going to the powwow to make sure your uncle Lanny behaves. Choctaw Elders deserve respect, and you will make certain they get it."

I chewed and swallowed a mouthful of pizza and took a sip of lemonade, trying to make sense of what I'd just heard. "So, I am going to Michigan to dance in a powwow, but really to keep an eye on Uncle Lanny? Mom, let me introduce myself. I am twelve years old."

"And very mature for your age," Mom said.

I plopped my chin on my chest and shook my head.

Just then a loud honking sound shook the walls.

"That must be your uncle Lanny," Mom said. "Are you ready to go?"

Ten minutes later, with my suitcase loaded on the bus, we pulled away for a three-day trip to Michigan. I sat behind

Uncle Lanny while twenty-four Choctaw Elders stared out the windows and chatted away.

Uncle Lanny spoke over his shoulder to me, not even caring if anybody heard.

"No, I still don't understand why I took the job," he said, "driving twenty-four Choctaw Elders all the way to Michigan. I hate this! When it's time to stop and eat, I might just bury my face in the plate in front of me."

I said nothing, and Mom's words started rolling around in my head. *Choctaw Elders deserve respect, and you will make certain they get it.*

"You know, your mom got me into this," Uncle Lanny said, reading my mind. "Since I drive the local school bus, she volunteered me."

Surprise, surprise! So *Mom* was the somebody who volunteered him. *Truth Number Three*, I'm thinking.

"Here I am," Uncle Lanny continued, "driving a busload of Choctaw Elders from Durant, Oklahoma—the capital of our Choctaw Nation—all the way to Michigan!"

"At least you are not alone," a familiar voice answered. It was Susan Fellabush, and she stood up and tapped him on the shoulder. Susan worked at the nearby Choctaw Cultural Center and had agreed to ride along and help.

She was maybe twenty-four years old, and very detail-oriented. Every Choctaw knew she was the one person who never freaked out, no matter what happened.

When the crazy lightning-filled thunderstorm hit our Labor Day celebration in 2016, with twenty thousand Choctaws sleeping in tents, she talked the tribal council into keeping every building on the grounds open twenty-four hours a day. So the thousands of Choctaws camping out in tents dragged their sleeping bags to the huge cafeteria or museum and were served free meals till the storm passed.

And for this trip, Susan had already booked rooms for everybody at two hotels along the way. Many rooms.

"Luksi," Susan said, "I'll walk to the back of the bus every thirty minutes or so, checking on everybody. Don't be alarmed when I get up. And don't worry, on these bumpy roads I know to hold on tight."

"Hoke, no problem," I said, just as the bus hit a *big* bump, causing the older lady right behind me to *squeal!* and spill her hot cup of coffee down my back.

"Yikes! That's not how I like my coffee," I said, rocking back and forth as the burning liquid flowed down my spine and across the seat.

"Let me get a towel," said Susan. "Do you need Lanny to pull over?"

"No, I'll be fine."

"I am so sorry," the elderly lady said.

"Don't worry, Mrs. Chukla," I said, gritting my teeth. "I needed the wake-up call."

"Oh, Luksi, you are so funny," she said. "I just wish

I hadn't wasted my coffee." The whole bus exploded in laughter at that.

"I can take care of you," Susan said. "I have a gallon jug of coffee under the seat."

"What's a little burn on the back when you've got coffee for everybody!" shouted Jay MacVain from the rear of the bus.

"An eighty-year-old Choctaw comedian, that's all we need," said Uncle Lanny.

"Uh, Susan," I whispered, "maybe we wait till we come to a stop to pour more coffee."

"Of course, Luksi," she said as she wrapped a towel over my shoulders.

Forty-five minutes later, another Elder, Mrs. Simmons, called softly from the rear of the bus. "Miss Fellabush, can you help me?"

Susan leaped from her seat and scrambled to the back of the bus. She must have guessed what the problem was, because she leaned over and they whispered.

"Lanny," she shouted, pointing to a convenience store coming up on the right. "Time to stop."

"The beginning of one long restroom stop," Uncle Lanny muttered to himself, slowly pulling over.

Susan hurried to the front of the bus. She turned to face our Elders as Lanny parked beside the store. "If anyone needs to go to the restroom, now's the time," she announced. "Please let Mrs. Simmons go first."

I watched as Mrs. Simmons gripped the back of the seat in front of her and struggled to stand.

Uncle Lanny slapped his forehead, impatient as usual.

Jay stepped back and allowed her to pass, but he wasn't finished. He followed her down the aisle to make sure she didn't fall. And as she hesitated at the door, he sucked in his belly and stepped around her. Once on the ground he reached up for her.

"I'll be your escort," he said as she stared at her feet and lifted her legs one at a time, carefully moving down the steps. Jay took her hand and guided her to the pavement.

"Yakoke," she said with a smile.

By now the aisle was full of Choctaw Elders, all taking their much-needed restroom stop. I stood up and looked for anyone else needing help. "Is everybody hoke?" I shouted.

"We will be in a few minutes," Mrs. Minger said, "if everybody will get outta my way!"

No one moved, but everybody laughed, for that's the Choctaw way. If it's not funny, it's not living. With so many elderly Choctaw men and women on the bus, the line was long. Like in most corner store restrooms, there was only room for *one at a time*. One went while everyone else waited.

Mrs. Simmons had been widowed for almost ten years. Her husband of fifty years had died of a sudden heart attack. Before his death she was outgoing and friendly, always inviting folks over to enjoy her pork steaks and pashofa corn chowder.

But once her husband passed on, she seemed to change overnight. She only left the house on Sunday mornings for church.

When the final Elder had passed me, I jumped into line and followed them from the bus into the store. I watched as Mrs. Simmons wandered about and picked out a few snacks; a cherry fried pie, chocolate chip cookies, and a 7UP soda pop. She plopped her purse on the counter and raked everything out, looking for money.

"See if this works," she said, handing a card in payment to the cashier, a teenager who kept his head down, never looking at her.

"Sure thing, " he said, bagging the snacks and running her card through the machine.

"Is that enough money?" she asked. "My grandson gave it to me."

"That's plenty, ma'am," said the cashier.

I turned away. Soon Jay followed her to the bus and helped her up the steps.

"Why don't you sit here, behind Lanny," he said. "I'm sure Luksi won't mind you sitting next to him."

"Oh, that is so sweet of you," she said, and Jay took her by the elbows and eased her onto the seat. He then turned and helped a dozen other women onto the bus.

I enjoyed watching Susan try to stop herself from hurrying everyone. Once, after helping an older man with a cane, I saw her step back and wrap her hands around her chin. She took a deep breath and smiled.

When everyone was settled and in their seats, we took off in the direction of Tulsa. Michigan was still a thousand miles away. "Nice of your grandson to give you the credit card," I said to Mrs. Simmons.

"Yes, he is a very sweet boy. He gave it to me for the trip, and it was just the right amount of money."

"What do you mean?" I asked.

"The nice boy at the cash register didn't ask me for any change. He said the card was exactly enough."

"That's good," I said, and put my arm around her.

"Susan," Uncle Lanny said. "I'm gonna drive a loop around Tulsa before we have to stop again. Maybe we'll make it to Missouri."

"I think you're dreaming," she replied.

"That's why we gave ourselves two days plus," Jay said, from his seat right behind me.

"Jay, weren't you in the back of the bus?" Susan asked.

"I *was* in the back of the bus," he said. "But when a lady as pretty as Mrs. Simmons needs help, a true Choctaw gentleman stays close by."

I looked at Susan and we shared a nice smile.

The next twenty miles passed quickly. The road twisted through the western edge of the Kiamichi Mountains, surrounded by trees sprouting the first signs of early spring leaves.

As we drove by a grove of pine trees, a fat pine cone popped against the window next to me—and a thought popped into my head.

The nice boy at the cash register didn't ask me for any change.

That's what she said.

"Mrs. Simmons?" I asked.

"Yes?"

"Did the nice boy at the cash register give you the credit card back? After you bought the snacks?"

"Why, no, he didn't," she said. "I bought the snacks with the card and he said it was enough."

My jaw dropped and my eyes grew big in disbelief. "Jay, are you listening to this? Susan?"

"Give me a minute," Susan said. "I have family phone numbers for everyone. Maybe I have her grandson's number." She scrambled through notes on her phone.

"What is your grandson's name?" she asked Mrs. Simmons.

"Gabe, his name is Gabe Simmons."

In less than a minute, Susan had him on the line.

"Hello, Gabe. This is Susan Fellabush. I'm helping out on the trip to the Michigan powwow. Yes, she's fine," she said. "I'm calling about the credit card you gave her for the trip." There was a brief pause. "Oh," she said, with tension in her voice, "it was a *debit* card. How much was in the account?"

Another pause, and the bewildered look on Susan's face told me everything I needed to know. The "nice boy" had stolen the debit card, and the only question was *how much did he steal?*

Susan tucked away her phone and turned to me. "Four hundred dollars," she whispered.

"We can't let him get away with it!" I shouted.

"What should we do now?" she asked.

"I know what the Choctaw Lighthorsemen would do," Jay said. "He'd be arrested before sundown."

How can you not love these old Choctaw folks! They know our history, our survival stories! The Choctaw Lighthorsemen were the only real law in the old Oklahoma west, for half a century.

"Well, Jay," I said, "we're not the Choctaw Lighthorsemen, but we can't let him get away with it. Uncle Lanny," I said, leaning over him, "it's time to turn this bus around."

"Oh, sure thing, Luksi," Uncle Lanny said. "My job is to do everything you say."

I didn't know what to do, but Jay MacVain did. He stood up and spoke in a serious voice. "Lanny, maybe it is time for you to hand the wheel over to someone who understands and cares about these Choctaw Elders."

"Maybe me," Susan said, standing up beside him.

I wasn't about to be left out of this ceremony.

"Maybe me," I said, squeezing between them.

Jay started it first, a soft little Choctaw laugh, and soon Susan joined him, then Mrs. Simmons, and finally everybody on the bus dove in! A louder, funnier Choctaw laugh I've never heard!

"Hoke, all right already," Uncle Lanny said, joining in the laughter. He pulled the bus into a shopping center parking lot and turned it around.

"Now what do we do?" he asked Susan.

"Drive back to the store, and hurry!"

Trees sped by and road bumps bumped and soon we arrived.

"Let me take care of this," Uncle Lanny said. I saw him clench his fists as he stepped from the bus. *I would not want to be that cashier*, I thought.

Susan went online and found the number to the sheriff's department. She called and reported the theft of the card. "And please call and let me know whatever you find out about the cashier," she said before hanging up.

I slipped through the open bus door and was about to follow Uncle Lanny to the store, when something caught my eye. A beautiful hawk flew from a huge old oak tree beside the store. I felt a soft breeze on my neck, and I knew that somebody was trying to tell me something.

"Yakoke, thank you," I whispered.

I walked beneath the tree and saw the cashier climbing down the tree trunk. I waited. I expected him to see me and run away. Instead, he approached me with his hand outstretched.

"Please take this and give it to the lady," he said. He opened his palm and there lay the debit card. I took the card and waited for him to speak.

"Yakoke," he said, which told me he was Choctaw.

"Why?" I asked him. I could have told him, *The card was a gift from her grandson*, or *She is a Choctaw Elder. How could you do that?* But the simple word *why* seemed to be enough.

"I made the worst mistake of my life," he said. I watched as he closed his eyes and his chin sank to his chest.

"*Why?*"

"College. I am flunking out of college. I don't have enough money for books. It's spring break now. I'm working full-time at two different jobs. But I still don't have enough money."

He waited for me to reply, but I said nothing.

"I made a terrible mistake," he said. "What should I do?"

"If you want to face what you did," I said, "take the card back and give it to Mrs. Simmons."

He met my eyes and slowly nodded.

"I'll get her if you return to the store," I said.

"I can't go back there," he said. "I've already called in sick, and somebody is on their way to replace me."

A sudden blaring sound of sirens came from the front parking lot. *WHIRRRRRRRRRR.*

"Sounds like things just got a little more complicated," I said. "The cops have arrived."

"Time to confess," he said. Then he turned to me, and with a sad smile said, "My name is Jimmy."

I handed him the debit card and he walked from the tree to the front of the store. Uncle Lanny was standing between two policemen on the sidewalk.

"There he is," he said, pointing to Jimmy.

Mrs. Simmons, aided by Jay MacVain, stepped down from the bus. "Oh, there is that sweet young man," she said.

Soon we all gathered in a tight circle, surrounding Mrs. Simmons and Jimmy. "I want to return this to you," Jimmy said, handing her the card.

"Yakoke," she said, batting her eyelashes and turning her head to smile at the cops.

"Do you want to press charges, ma'am?" an officer asked. "Just say yes and we'll take him to jail."

"Take this young man to jail! Why would you do that?

Maybe you need to learn some manners," Mrs. Simmons said.

"Looks like you lucked out this time, young man," said the officer.

I pulled Susan aside and told her what Jimmy had said. She nodded and turned to the officers. "We're fine here," she said. "Everything is under control."

"If you're certain, then we'll be on our way," said the lead officer. Glancing at Jimmy, he added, "But we're never far away, and you've got our number if you need us." The policemen then climbed into their patrol car and sped away.

"Let's get back on the bus!" shouted Uncle Lanny.

"Not just yet," said Susan. "Jimmy, we need to talk. Follow me."

She led him to the base of the oak tree, just as a shadow passed over me. I looked up and saw the hawk land on a limb high overhead.

I had no idea what Jimmy said to Susan, but they talked for a long time. Finally, Susan grabbed her phone and waved what looked like a friendly finger at him.

The strangest day of my life had only just begun!

Susan returned to the bus with her arm wrapped around Jimmy. "It's all arranged," she said, "and the Choctaw Nation has approved it. Jimmy has been hired to travel with us, to help Lanny and me care for our passengers."

"Yes!" I shouted.

Uncle Lanny gave me a hard stare. "I hope you know what you're doing," he said to Susan.

"Sir, I will be the hardest-working young Choctaw you've ever seen," Jimmy said. "At least I'll try to be."

Even Uncle Lanny had to smile.

Jimmy leaned over and whispered in my ear. "The tribe is also paying for my books, and I'm going to apply for a scholarship."

In half an hour we were once again on our way to Michigan. To the Michigan powwow!

Two days later, after a dozen restroom stops and two laughter-filled nights of Choctaw Elders wandering about hotel lobbies and asking, *What room am I in?*, we pulled into the powwow parking lot.

We arrived four hours later than we'd planned. It was already eleven o'clock in the morning, and I knew I had to hurry to make the Grand Entry. I dashed from the bus with my clothing bag slung over my shoulder.

The dressing room was crowded, of course, but I'm a skinny little Luksi. I don't need much room. I scrambled out of my jeans and jumped into my dad's white leather britches, pulling tight a blue-and-yellow beaded belt. I dove headfirst into his old Choctaw shirt with rattlesnake diamonds on the sleeves. With deerskin moccasins on my feet and a bright red feathered headband, I felt ready to go. The drums sounded so powerful and strong, booming through the walls.

> *Follow the kid in front of you,*
> *Follow the kid in front of you,*
> *Just follow the kid in front of you,*

I whispered to the beat of the drum.

I stepped and stomped to the beat of the drum. As I neared the entrance to the arena, I saw a throng of Choctaw Elders smiling and clapping. They had formed a hallway of Choctaw Elders, plus Susan, to give me strength before I entered the arena!

At the head of the line stood Uncle Lanny, and across from him our newest Choctaw friend, Jimmy. And they were chanting a new song—to welcome me.

> *Luksi achukma, halito,*
> *Welcome Little Turtle!*
> *We are Choctaws,*
> *We are one,*
> *Warriors of Forgiveness!*

"We are warriors of forgiveness," Uncle Lanny whispered in my ear as I danced past him.

"Warriors of Forgiveness," I sang to the rhythm of the drumbeat. "Warriors of Forgiveness."

I knew our lives would never be the same—Jimmy, Mrs. Simmons, Jay MacVain, Susan Fellabush—our lives would never be the same.

Uncle Lanny and Jimmy were our new leaders, our Warriors of Forgiveness.

BROTHERS

DAVID A. ROBERTSON

Aiden enjoyed drives like this one. Not city drives. On the highway, toward anywhere far away. Where he and his foster parents were going now, there wasn't much to look at, not at first, but it wasn't all about scenery. It was being away from so many cars, and traffic lights, and signs, and houses, and people. They were headed south, then southeast, on their way to Michigan. Until Wisconsin, the land was flat and wide, the sky endless and enormous. As ceaseless as the prairies.

It was sixteen hours from Winnipeg to Ann Arbor. The flatlands and open skies would accompany them for at least seven hours of the trip. Aiden did only a handful of things during the long drive, which was broken up by bathroom and gas stops, and a quick hotel stay about half-way to Michigan.

The one constant was reading. He had a stack of books at his side, along with a water bottle and a bag of snacks his foster mother had prepared for him. His foster parents had their own water and snacks at the front of the car.

The thing he did during the first hours of the drive each day lasted only as long as his device's battery life. He had been permitted to download a few games onto his iPod, and to play those games for as long as his battery lasted. This was how his foster mother monitored his screen time: He started each day with the beautiful sight of 100 percent battery life, but once the iPod was dead, it was dead. There was no going back. Aiden thought it was unfair.

This meant that for a good five hours on the first day, all he had to do was read, because after not too long the prairies were boring, even the sky. You could only make clouds into so many shapes.

But once the car got deeper into Wisconsin on the second day, as the prairies were left behind, it was like they were in a whole other world. There were actually things to look at. Like, the land actually had contours. Hills. There were more trees, fewer farmers' fields. So during the last hours, even before his iPod died, Aiden traded time between staring at a screen or, later, the page of a book and staring out the window. And his mind wandered while he took in the pretty new landscape. Aiden's foster parents, who were white, were taking him to a big powwow, and he kept thinking about the life he'd missed, but still might be able to find.

A few months earlier, he'd been connected with his birth parents. They lived in a Cree community in Northern Manitoba. Aiden found out that he had an older brother named Vince, too. They messaged together for weeks, and then one day Vince invited Aiden and his foster parents to the place they were headed now. Along with being a computer nerd, a fellow sci-fi enthusiast, and a lover of all things eighties and nineties, Vince was an accomplished Grass Dancer. This was going to be Aiden's first powwow. He'd only just started to take lessons in the city after finding out Vince danced, and had only seen the different kinds of beautiful dances, the vibrant clothing worn by Indigenous people while performing them, on YouTube. Vince said that he'd taken part in so many powwows that he couldn't even count them; he was seventeen, five years older than Aiden. Vince had told Aiden lots of things over text, about their home community, their birth parents, what life was like there, and dancing. Aiden was most excited to see his older brother.

They finally pulled up to their hotel. It was late in the afternoon, and everybody was tired. They checked in, ate a quick meal in the restaurant, and turned in for the night. Aiden's foster parents were asleep almost as soon as their heads hit their pillows, but Aiden had trouble falling asleep. He was really tired but kept thinking about the same things he'd thought about in the car. They weren't driving anymore, but his mind was still racing. He had a new window to stare out of: the hotel room window, where even though it was night, the streetlights outside painted the curtains orange. Aiden stared until his body and his brain gave up, and his thoughts turned to dreams.

Aiden devoured a free continental breakfast in the hotel lobby the next morning. The good kind. There was the regular: bagels, bread, cereal, bananas, apples, instant oatmeal. But there were also waffles, omelets, and sausages, and nothing was safe from his stomach. While eating (his foster parents described it as inhaling, not eating), he noticed how many Indigenous people were lining up to get food and sitting at the tables. This must have been where people from out of town going to the powwow were staying. Aiden had never been around so many people like him before; there weren't a lot of Indigenous people in his community or at his school. He started to imagine them later on in the day, when many of the breakfast-goers would be in regalia.

Aiden hadn't brought anything special to the powwow himself. He'd never owned regalia. When he took lessons, it was just in regular clothes. He'd asked his foster parents to buy him an outfit, or else what was he going to dance in?

But they'd flatly refused, telling him only, cryptically, that he wouldn't need anything from them. So after breakfast he put on sweats and a sweater, and they were off from the hotel to the powwow.

There was a parade of cars heading from the hotel and around the outskirts of the city toward the powwow, like they were in some kind of procession. Aiden spent the drive checking out license plates to see where everybody was from, because the scenery wasn't all that exciting. There were churches and schools and farmland on the left, nothing different than in the country around Winnipeg, and more of the same on the right. Nothing much changed until they drove through a residential area before pulling up in front of Skyline High School, where the powwow was taking place.

It was a huge school, a building constructed out of metal and glass and brick, and Aiden couldn't think of a bigger school in Winnipeg. But still, as he looked around and all he could see were the parking lot and the school, something didn't seem right.

"Hey, aren't we going to a powwow?" Aiden asked.

"We are," his foster father said. "This is where it is."

"Is there a field behind the school or something?"

With such a big school, he supposed that it wouldn't be surprising if the school had an equally big field. The only other times he'd been to the States, it had been to play hockey, and the hockey arenas were all supersized too.

"No, Aiden," his foster mother said. "The powwow's *inside* the school, in the gym."

"Inside the school?" Aiden repeated.

That didn't sound right at all. All the powwow videos he'd seen were in fields. Not in gyms. He was in a gymnasium almost every day for phys ed. For basketball. For volleyball. For beep tests. Floor hockey. Ultimate. All those things, but not powwow dancing.

They had arrived with lots of time before the Grand Entry at noon, so after going through the admissions gate, they decided to walk around the vendor floor to see all the things that people had for sale.

"When am I supposed to dance?" Aiden asked as they walked from the front of the school to the back, where the vendors were.

There were two times for intertribal dancing on the first day of the powwow. One started right after the Grand Entry, and Aiden did *not* want to dance that early. He was already nervous and was convinced that if he had to dance in front of all the people in the gym right away, the big breakfast he'd eaten wouldn't stay in his stomach for long.

His foster mother looked sympathetic, probably because Aiden looked as sick as he felt. "At one thirty p.m."

Aiden's heart started to thump. He checked his iPod for the time. "That's right after the Grand Entry!"

"Yeah, but the Grand Entry takes a long time. It starts at noon. You won't be so worried. Give it time," she said.

"Plus going first, it's like ripping off a bandage!" his foster father said.

"You're telling me two different things!" Aiden said.

"Aiden," she said. "Look, once it's over, you can just relax."

"I'm *not* relaxed."

"I know you're not, but—"

"Vince will be in the Grand Entry, so you can watch for him from the stands," his foster father added. "That'll help pass the time. Oh, wait . . ."

"Stop trying to make me feel better. You guys suck at it."

"I thought you wanted to come," his foster mother said.

"I did. I do. It's just . . ." Aiden took a deep breath. He'd seen videos of Grand Entries, too. They *were* long, and looked cool. There was a drum group playing songs, flags at the front, and so many dancers after that. So many dancers in so many different types of regalia. Finding Vince among the dancers in all those colorful outfits would be like playing Where's Waldo? So maybe his foster father was right. Just watching for Vince in the stands, trying to spot him, might be fun, and a good distraction. And his foster father wasn't always the best judge of what was fun. In the car, he'd wanted to play I Spy with Aiden. That was early on in the trip. There was so much of the same thing on the prairies, and no colors, and that would have been super boring. This would be at least more fun than that.

The vendor floor felt like an event all its own. Aiden had been to career fairs before, with big rooms filled with lots of tables arranged in what felt like a maze. This room was like that. There were gray tables, side by side, aligned in row after row, and as he and his foster parents walked along the side of the vendor floor, the rows looked like they went on forever. With all the tables and all the vendors selling their merchandise at those tables, there were so many different things to look at.

There were tables with bracelets and necklaces and dream catchers. There were tables with clothes, like sweaters and shirts and vests and jackets. There was a dog modeling a shirt that read *Ancestor Approved*. There were pendants and blankets and staffs and hats and masks, and it all made Aiden feel dizzy. What he noticed most of all were the beads on almost every table, and he thought, as they walked by table after table, that there were probably as many beads in the room as there were stars in the sky.

There was one table, near the end of their long, zig-zag trip through the vendor floor on the way to the gymnasium, that Aiden stopped at. Before then he'd just window-shopped like you do at the mall, and slowed down once because he came across a big group in the aisle: Elders walking with a young woman, a middle-aged guy, and a kid. The table he stopped at was full of regalia; the same sort of outfits he'd seen on YouTube and, in particular, for the dance that he was learning to do. The dance Vince did. The Grass Dance.

The regalia for Grass Dancers was different, because it didn't have feathers. Instead, the outfits were bright and colorful, with fringes made of yarn or ribbons. Aiden looked over all the outfits on display at the table until he found one that he thought was perfect. One that he might even dance in, no matter who was watching him, no matter how shy he felt. He picked it up and turned it around in his hands, admiring the yellows and blues and greens and reds. His foster parents had given him money to buy something on the vendor floor, and this was the only thing that he wanted.

"Can I get this?" he asked.

"Oh . . ." His foster mother sighed and shook her head.

"Do you know how expensive these are?" his foster father asked him, what felt like rhetorically.

Aiden really didn't know. He hadn't priced out the regalia on the internet, just looked at the dances and the outfits, and he hadn't looked at pricing here either.

"We gave you enough for maybe one of those dream catchers, Aiden. We just don't have money for that."

"What am I supposed to dance in, these sweats?" Aiden asked.

"I'm sure we can figure something out," his foster mother said.

"Like what?"

"You just never know," was all his foster father said.

Aiden looked at the price then, and that, too, made him feel nauseated. They were right, but he was still furious. All that practicing and nothing to wear. He put the regalia back on the table and stormed off toward the gym.

"I'm not dancing!" he shouted en route, with his foster parents trailing behind.

As mad as he was, Aiden felt confident in this decision. He might not have even danced in the beautiful outfit he'd picked out. Now he wasn't going to dance at all. Sitting in the stands suited him just fine.

Aiden forgot how mad he was for a moment when he walked into the gym just before noon. The stands, which had been pulled out from the sides of the gym, were packed. It was like there was a big basketball game happening. He'd never considered powwows a spectator sport, but he guessed he'd watched tons of them on YouTube over the past month and not because anybody made him. Wouldn't it be even better in person?

"Do you want to sit?" his foster father asked.

At his voice, Aiden remembered that he was mad. Begrudgingly, arms crossed, he followed his foster parents up the stands to one of the few spots left available.

There were people from all cultural backgrounds in the stands. It wasn't just an Indigenous event for an Indigenous crowd. Aiden people-watched, while everybody waited for the Grand Entry to begin. There was a hum of excitement in the crowd. There were even people selling stuff here, away from the vendor floor. He could see a few musicians hawking their CDs, and in a sectioned-off area right near Aiden, there was a girl about his age and a woman.

The girl was selling raffle tickets, and it didn't take long to see what they were raffling off: a beautiful turquoise belt buckle and a blue shawl with intricate yellow ribbon work. The belt buckle was all kinds of awesome. Aiden didn't even have a belt for a buckle; he just wanted to put it on the shelf in his bedroom beside his Star Wars action figures. Before the girl and woman approached them, he'd decided to buy a ticket. He knew he could afford at least that.

The girl and woman were a team. Mabel (Aiden heard the woman introduce herself) concentrated on his foster parents, gave them what she said was a mental health screening.

The girl, who looked about twelve like Aiden, sat beside him.

"Hey," she said, "I'm Maggie."

"I'm Aiden," he said.

"Where are you from? Who's your family?" she asked.

"Uhhh . . . Winnipeg?" He pointed at his foster parents

to indicate his family. "But my brother's in the Grand Entry."

"No, I meant your home community. Like, where are you from, what tribe?"

"Oh, Cree." He felt flushed. He'd never told anybody at school that he was First Nations. "And my brother . . . my family . . . is from Norway House Cree Nation."

"Cool," she said.

"What about you?"

"Cherokee," she said. "Not the jeep."

"Funny."

"So, wanna buy a ticket?"

"Yeah, for the buckle. It's awesome."

Aiden bought a raffle ticket, and the kids waited while Mabel finished doing her screening with his foster parents. When they were done, Maggie and Mabel kept moving through the crowd.

"See you around, Aiden," Maggie said before leaving.

"Yeah, see you."

Not long after Aiden had bought the raffle ticket, the Grand Entry started, and the crowd, which had been murmuring constantly like white noise, settled down. The drum pounded like a heartbeat, breaking the silence with three heavy thuds. Aiden could feel it resonate through the room, right through his feet and up across the rest of his body. Then, with a steady beat and singing, the Grand Entry began.

An announcer named Sheldon Sundown—over the rhythmic song that Aiden could feel in his chest—started telling the crowd who was coming in. But Aiden, rather than try to listen to Sheldon over the beat of the drum and the power of the singers, just watched.

The eagle staff came in first, and after that, a series of flags, followed by dignitaries and Elders. Everybody's feet were shuffling to the song, and even the oldest Elders showed a well-timed movement. The younger dancers were really moving, dancing like they were already involved in the competitions.

When the Grass Dancers stepped onto the waxed hardwood floor, Aiden paid special attention to them, appreciating how intricate and colorful their outfits were and lamenting that he hadn't gotten to buy regalia like theirs. The delicate beadwork that must've taken weeks, the ribbons that hung and swayed in the air as though caught in a breeze, and how even the headbands were amazing.

In the middle of this line of dancers, Aiden caught eyes with Vince. Aiden waved. Vince waved back without breaking stride. They both smiled broadly at each other. Just dancing in the line, he looked better than Aiden had ever danced in the lessons he'd been taking when he'd felt brave enough to actually try, and not stand to the side. Vince looked powerful and beautiful and confident. How was Aiden going to look in his baggy, viciously ugly gray sweats, in the middle of the gym, with everybody staring at him?

Before they could do much more than wave at each other, Vince had moved on, more dancers kept coming in with the Grand Entry, and Aiden felt alone. More than that, as time went on, he felt panicked. His pulse was racing, and he felt sweaty and shaky. He could hear his foster mother telling him that he was supposed to dance right after the Grand Entry. *No way.*

"I've got to go to the bathroom, okay?" he said.

"You don't really have to go to the bathroom, do you?" his foster father asked.

"Yeah, I do."

"It's okay to be nervous," his foster mother said. "Really. I know this is difficult and weird."

"But we know how hard you've been working, and you'll do great," his foster father said.

"I told you," Aiden said while he walked away, "I'm not dancing."

He didn't go to the bathroom at all. Instead, he found a good place to hide until after the intertribal dance took place. He'd miss his turn, but he wouldn't embarrass himself. Some Cree kid who'd never really been or felt Cree, trying to act Cree in front of a million people. That was how Aiden felt, anyway.

There was nobody else under the stands. Just some

litter that had fallen through the cracks. Drink cups and chip bags and things like that. Aiden found a spot in the middle of the empty space, where he'd be out of sight but would still see some of the Grand Entry, and could feel the song through his body. He did like that feeling. It made him feel less panicked. Like the drums were working hard to keep his heartbeat steady.

Aiden figured that he'd only have to wait until the intertribal dance started, until it was too late for him to join in. Then he'd return to the stands, say he got lost or something (the school was big; getting lost would be easy), and oh well, they could just watch for the rest of the time and have supper with Vince later.

The Grand Entry gave way to a welcome address, and Aiden kept hiding. It was just after one p.m. and there wasn't much to see now, so he turned around, sat on the floor, and buried his head and waited.

"Tansi," a voice said, not more than a few minutes after he'd made like an ostrich.

Aiden felt a nudge on his shoulder. He looked up to find Vince standing over him, his regalia still on, a suit bag slung over his shoulder.

"Oh, hey." Aiden stood.

They'd texted almost every day, had video-chatted too, but this was the first time he'd seen Vince face-to-face, up close.

"That's 'hi' in Cree," Vince said. "Tansi."

"Yeah, I figured."

"How's it going?" Vince gave Aiden a hug, patted him on the back. "It's good to see you."

"You too," Aiden said. "How'd you"—he looked around at the barren space underneath the stands—"find me?"

"I went up to see you, and your foster parents said they saw you duck under here," Vince explained.

"Oh, they did?"

"Stage fright?"

"I don't know," Aiden said. "I guess."

"What else do you guess?"

"It's just . . . I thought when I came here maybe I'd feel more at home or something, but I feel just as different here as I do at school in Winnipeg. It's like I don't belong anywhere."

"What do you mean that you feel different? What's wrong with that?"

"I just want to feel like I belong."

"But Aiden, you do belong. And everybody's different. It's not on *you* to feel the same, it's on others to accept you because you're not," Vince said. "It's on *you* to be okay with being different."

"That's super confusing," Aiden said.

"We're all a community, that's what I mean. And

everybody's here from all over, and they all come together to do this as a big family."

"I just wanted to see my real family."

"Me too," Vince said. "But you'll find out, if you keep coming to things like this, that your family's even bigger than you think."

"What about them?"

"Your foster parents?"

"Yeah."

"They're family, too, aren't they? They hooked us up together, right? They'd be welcome in our circle."

Aiden felt the anger pressing up into his chest again. "*Maybe*. But they wouldn't even get me an outfit to dance in. That's *mostly* why I'm hiding."

"They didn't get you an outfit"—Vince brought out the suit bag he'd been carrying over his shoulder—"because they knew I was going to give you this."

Vince handed Aiden the suit bag. Aiden just stared at it at first, like the gift was the bag.

"Well, go ahead and open it." Vince laughed.

Aiden unzipped the bag to reveal a Grass Dance outfit. It was bright lime green, with blue, black, green, red, orange, and yellow ribbons connected to the arms and legs and chest. On the legs and arms and chest were designs that looked like flames. They were outlined in black and layered with colors: orange, then yellow, then red at the center of each design.

"This is amazing!" Aiden said. "The flames are so cool."

"Look closer at them," Vince said. "They look like flames, but they're animals."

Aiden did look closer and saw that Vince was right. He could see an eagle on each leg, its wings rising upward and turning into flames. On the chest, the flames were squirrels, Aiden thought, the tails becoming flames, like the eagles' wings.

"Is this really for me?" Aiden asked.

"I mean, it's too small for me," Vince said. "Yeah, of course it is, brother."

The drums, which had fallen silent since the Grand Entry had ended, started up again.

"That's us!" Vince said.

Minutes later, Vince and Aiden were standing in the middle of the gym, Aiden's feet pressed against the hardwood floor. In the middle of the dancers, in the middle of the huge crowd of onlookers, Aiden felt like everybody was watching him. He was nervous, but with the regalia on that Vince had gifted him, he was proud, too. The song was playing, and Vince was moving his feet, trying to encourage Aiden into movement.

"Come on," Vince said, "you can do it. This is where you should be, trust me."

Where he should be. He looked into the stands, at the crowd, and found his foster mother and father. Then he kept moving his gaze closer and closer, until he found himself scanning the gym floor carefully, just like when he'd stared out the window of the car. This would have been the best view.

Vince was right. All the outfits were so different, from one dancer to the next, and even their movements were different. Each person danced to the song in their own way, with their own passion, even though it was the same song. They were a big community, and each one of them in the community was their own person. They dipped and swayed and moved to the song, dancing with grace and power and pride.

Maybe, after all, this was somewhere he could belong.

Maybe it was somewhere he did belong.

He looked at Vince, the brother he'd just met, and saw him moving more now, his legs stomping on the ground, then rising, his heels kicking back into the air, his body lunging and straightening, his arms keeping balance, extended out from his body. Aiden started to move his feet, then his knees, then his body.

Aiden started to dance.

REZ DOG RULES

REBECCA ROANHORSE

While there were many things that Ozzie appreciated about being a Rez dog, there were exactly three that were the absolute best:

1. No masters. It was a provable fact that Rez dogs, by definition, had no masters. In fact, one of the defining qualities of the *Canis Liberatus Reservatus* (as he and his kin were known in Latin) was a lack of human-imposed rules. Ozzie was his own dog, and the only laws he followed were those of nature, who told him to when to eat, when to sleep, and when to lift his leg on a convenient tree. Ozzie was as free as any living creature could be. Sure, it was lonely sometimes, especially on rainy nights when all the humans and their pets were warm and cozy inside and Ozzie was stuck outside, making do with whatever shelter he could find. And he sometimes wondered what his life would be like if he lived in one of those houses with four

walls and a roof and warm cuddles from a human child. But overall, he was content, because he knew nothing was as warm and comforting as freedom. He was a canine majestic and untamed, and he preferred it that way.

2. No leashes. It would logically follow that a dog who would abide no master would also not tolerate a leash. Ozzie was proud to say that he had never succumbed to the tyranny of wearing a leash, a harness, a gentle lead, or any other human-created restricting device. He firmly believed in unencumbered movement. Ozzie went where he wanted, when he wanted. Mostly on four feet, but it was not unheard of for him to catch a ride in the bed of an old pickup truck when he had to get across town in a hurry. He imagined himself roaming the mesas like his ancestor, the wolf, and he felt proud of his heritage.

3. Mrs. Cruz's back porch on Sunday afternoons. While it was true that Ozzie would never wear a leash and had no human he called master, he was very fond of Mrs. Cruz. She was by nature a kind and generous woman and the best human Ozzie knew. She had raised three children and many more grandchildren in the little adobe house on the southern edge of the Pueblo of Ohkay Owingeh in New Mexico, the place Ozzie called home. Mrs. Cruz's house had passed down through her family for generations. It was filled with a lot of pride and laughter. It was also occasionally filled with fried chicken. And Mrs. Cruz, never one

to waste, would often give any leftover fried chicken she had to Ozzie, along with any other scraps of tamales, refritos, pastelitos, and calabacitas, if he showed up on Sundays just after the children and grandchildren had been stuffed full of Sunday lunch and piled into their cars and trucks to head back to their own homes. He and Mrs. Cruz would sit together on the back porch watching the setting sun as she picked the bones out of the chicken and fed him the meat by hand. It was, in a word, heaven.

So it was quite worrisome to Ozzie when, from his perch on the back patio just outside the kitchen screen door, he overheard Mrs. Cruz talking to her eldest grandson, Marino, about having to give up the house. They were sitting at the kitchen table enjoying a late cup of coffee and eating the last of the prune pastelitos. "Maybe it's time I pass it to your father," Mrs. Cruz said, sadness tingeing her voice.

"No, Grandma," Marino said, distressed. "This is your home. Dad would say so, too. It wouldn't be the same if you weren't here."

"But this house needs so much work," Mrs. Cruz said with a heavy sigh. "The roof leaks, the foundation needs fixing, and I need to have someone take a look at the well. I think it's going to run dry soon."

"I can help fix things around the house," Marino said. He took a sip of his piñon-flavored coffee. He was a nice grandson and Mrs. Cruz's favorite. He was short and wide, only a few inches taller than his grandmother, with a thick thatch of black hair and mischievous brown eyes. Ozzie knew he was always quick to offer someone a ride to town in his old truck or to haul wood for the Elders, and he had never heard an unkind word spoken about the young man.

"Oh, Marino," Mrs. Cruz said, "I wish you could. But what I need is a bit of money." When she spoke, Ozzie could hear tears in her voice. "I don't even think I can afford my electric bill this month."

"I can make some money," Marino volunteered eagerly. "I make T-shirts. I can sell them and raise enough money so you can keep your house."

Marino had a silk-screening T-shirt business, where he made a variety of clever T-shirts that celebrated Native identity and culture. Ozzie couldn't actually read what they said, but he did remember that at the last summer street fair, he had sat quietly under Marino's vendor table watching people come up, peruse the T-shirts, laugh, smile, and finally hand over the twenty or thirty bucks to own one for themselves. Marino came home that night with his pockets full of money and bought his grandmother a new stewpot. Mrs. Cruz was so happy she made green chile stew and even sneaked Ozzie a bowl. Ozzie had wolfed it down (pardon the expression) and then sat in the dusty backyard out under the stars, content. Selling T-shirts sounded like a fine idea to help Mrs. Cruz. Ozzie barked a supportive *woof!* from his side of the screen porch.

Marino smiled at Ozzie through the wire door, but Mrs. Cruz was shaking her head. "But where would you sell on such short notice? I need the funds for the electricity bill by next Friday." Next Friday was less than two weeks away. Marino would have to find a place to sell quickly if he was going to help.

"My friend Eli told me about a powwow that's happening this weekend in Ann Arbor, Michigan. She already has a vendor license and a booth. I can set up with her."

"But it's all the way in Michigan," Mrs. Cruz complained, sounding concerned. "Do you really think your old truck will make it from New Mexico?"

"Ah, don't worry about me," Marino said. "Me and that old truck have been everywhere. Maine to San Diego. I'm sure we'll make it to Ann Arbor."

"I don't know." Mrs. Marino wrung her wrinkled hands. "I don't think you should drive alone."

Ozzie had no idea where Ann Arbor, Michigan, was, but he knew he wanted to help. He pawed gently at the screen door, letting out a very restrained whine. Mrs. Cruz looked up from the table. "Why are you crying, Ozzie? You're usually such a good boy."

Ozzie was indeed a good boy. But today he was a good boy with an ulterior motive. He whined again, and this time he added the pièce de résistance: puppy-dog eyes.

Mrs. Cruz's whole body softened. Her shoulders dropped, her hands settled around the coffee mug she was holding, and a smile spread across her wrinkled face. "Hey, why don't you take Ozzie?" she suggested.

Marino looked back over his shoulder. Ozzie gave him the full puppy-dog-eyes effect, and he added a little excited jump to show just how much he wanted to go. Marino looked thoughtful. "Huh," he said. "I hadn't thought about it, but maybe."

"You told me that he was so well-behaved at the summer street fair," his grandmother reminded him.

"He was," Marino admitted. He leaned close to the screen door. "What do you say, Ozzie? Want to go to Michigan?"

"Bowwow!" said Ozzie, which sounded a lot like "powwow," and the Cruzes exchanged a look of surprise.

"Did he just . . . ?" Marino asked, awed.

His grandmother grinned and gave Ozzie a thumbs-up. "I think so."

"It will take three days to get there, so we'll leave on Wednesday. Can you be back and ready to go on Wednesday, bright and early?" Marino asked Ozzie. Ozzie usually slept in the doghouse out behind the old gas station, because there were more people coming and going from there and the chances of getting fed were quite high. Of course,

Cheetos and beef jerky couldn't match Mrs. Cruz's cooking, but he made do. But he had no qualms about giving up his coveted gas station spot for a few days on the road trip.

Ozzie gave another bark.

"Well, okay then," Marino said. "Let's go to a powwow!"

The drive to the Ann Arbor powwow was long, but Marino kept it fun by playing all his favorite music on the truck's old radio, which he had hooked up to his phone. There was one particular song that Ozzie really liked, and each time it came on, he made sure to sing along, his voice matching the high notes in a series of *arooooooo*s and *wroooowww*s.

Marino laughed. "This is the Northern Cree Singers," he told Ozzie. "They sing a style called Northern Drum. They're my favorite, too."

Ozzie *arooo*'d again.

They stopped for dinner, and Marino fed Ozzie three delicious ninety-nine-cent fast-food burgers. "Don't get used to it, Ozzie," he playfully warned his canine companion as Ozzie munched a double meat with cheese, no onions. "This is a special occasion. And besides, our travel money is running low."

"Woof," said Ozzie, appreciative of the burger but worried about what Marino had said about money. If Marino didn't sell his T-shirts at the powwow, would they even have enough money to get back to Mrs. Cruz's?

The pair pulled into Ann Arbor early Saturday morning. Marino checked his GPS for the location of Skyline High School and pointed his old truck in the right direction. Ozzie stuck his head out the window, snapping at the cold wind and smelling a hint of rain in the air. They pulled into the parking lot, and Ozzie could see that it was already busy with vendors bringing in their wares and dancers in bright, colorful regalia. He barked happily. He knew they were there to try to earn money, but the powwow looked like so much fun!

Marino parked the truck, a look of consternation on his face. "Eli said she'd meet me in the parking lot, but I don't see her anywhere. I'm going to have to go in and find her," he told Ozzie. "Do you want to come?"

What a ridiculous question. Of course Ozzie wanted to come. Before Marino could ask again, Ozzie wiggled out of the open window and leaped to the ground. Marino climbed out of the driver's seat, stretched and yawned, and then headed for the gym, Ozzie on his heels and ready for adventure.

Ozzie could see the problem immediately. Eli and Marino's booth was in the very last row in the very farthest corner, about as far away from the main dance floor and the food and drink concessions as possible. The only good thing was that the booth was close to the area designated for health services, and Ozzie had spotted a very friendly-looking girl setting up a table to sell raffle tickets. He would definitely say hello to her later, as she looked good for a pat on the head and perhaps a treat. But right now he was focused on Marino and Eli and their terrible T-shirt-selling spot.

"What are we going to do?" Eli moaned. "No one's going to see us way back here."

"Don't be negative, Eli," Marino said, setting a box of T-shirts on the table. "We'll just have to think of something." He scratched his chin. "Maybe we can make a sign with a big red arrow that points people back to our booth."

Eli perked up. "That's not a bad idea."

Marino opened the box and started laying out the T-shirts on the table for display. He even hung some on the wall behind them so people could see them from farther away. "And maybe you can walk around and pass out flyers telling people about our booth."

"Now that's a great idea," Eli said. "There's only one problem. We don't have any flyers."

Marino braced his hands on his hips. "Hmm. Good point. Well, we'll think of something. My grandmother needs this money, so I'm not giving up before we even get started."

Speaking of getting started, Ozzie could hear the noise picking up near the front of the gym. The deep bass of the drums, the higher, brighter sounds of the accompanying singers, the jingle of bells, and the rhythmic thump of dozens of dancing feet.

"Woof?" he said to Marino.

"What's that? Oh yeah, you can go see what's going on. We're going to finish setting up."

"And pray someone notices us," added Eli, looking morose.

Ozzie pressed his wet nose against Eli's hand to tell her everything would be okay, and she patted Ozzie's head in appreciation before he headed out to explore.

The powwow was a riot of color and noise and happy people. He saw people representing so many different Native nations of all ages and skin tones and traditions. It was very exciting, almost too exciting for a Rez dog who spent most of his time in the wide-open country. But he was getting used to the crowds. If only Marino and Eli had a way to get all these people to notice their booth way back in the corner.

Ozzie had an idea. Maybe Marino and Eli didn't have flyers, but they did have a four-legged friend who could be a walking billboard.

Ozzie ran back to the T-shirt booth, where Marino and Eli sat, faces glum. The T-shirts were still piled in neat stacks on the table, looking like no one had come to buy them yet. "Still no customers," Marino said, "but

I'm sure someone will come soon."

A lot of someones would come if Ozzie had anything to say about it! He perused the T-shirts, looking for just the right one, finally settling on a black shirt with white lettering that said *Ancestor Approved*. He casually pulled it down from the table while the two friends weren't looking. Using his front paws and teeth, he wiggled his head into the T-shirt. His body followed. His front legs came out of the arm holes. Voilà! Ozzie was wearing a T-shirt. Now he had work to do.

He started at the admission gate. There were people still milling about, waiting for friends and holding blankets they would lay down later to save their seats. He wound his way through the crowd, making sure they could all see his T-shirt. Finally a young girl wearing bright purple leggings and an oversize pink hoodie noticed him. "Hey, check out that dog in the cool shirt!" she said to the two friends who were standing next to her. "I wonder where he got that?"

Ozzie paused long enough for the girl's friends to admire his shirt before he woofed a *follow me*.

"I think he wants us to follow him," the girl's friend in the black baseball cap said.

"I think you're right," said the pink hoodie girl. "You all want to go see where this dog got his shirt?"

"Sure!" said the boy in the cap.

"Why not?" said the other friend, a girl wearing red sneakers.

And Ozzie had his first potential customers!

Next, he trotted through the gym over to where the dancers who had just finished dancing were lounging on the bleachers, the girl in the pink hoodie and her friends trailing him. He walked back and forth in front of a jingle dress dancer, who was laughing and leaning in very close to a boy in beautiful green-and-white fancy dance regalia. They didn't notice him. He would have to think of something else to get their attention. Just then a drum started up, playing a northern-style powwow song. Ozzie recognized the style from the songs Marino had played on the drive to Ann Arbor. It made him want to dance, and he did a little high-stepping to the beat of the drum.

"Whoa, is that dog dancing?" he heard a voice ask. It was the fancy dancer.

"How cute!" said the jingle dress girl. "Hey, that's a pretty great shirt, dancing dog. Where did you get that?"

"Woof!" said Ozzie, and the two dancers exchanged a look.

"Might as well," said the boy, and they both stood up to follow Ozzie.

More customers! Ozzie pranced toward the concessions, the girl in the pink hoodie, the boy with the black cap, their friend in the red sneakers, the jingle dress dancer, and the fancy dancer all following.

The concessions area smelled wonderful. Ozzie's mouth watered as he smelled fry bread and corn soup and Navajo tacos and hot dogs with lots of ketchup and mustard. But he was on a mission and refused to be distracted. He spotted a long line of people and strolled past slowly enough for everyone to get a chance to read his shirt. Sure enough, people started talking about the funny dog with the cool T-shirt, and when a few people moved out of the line to ask where he had gotten such a great shirt, he knew they would follow him. And follow him they did. So that when he came back to Marino and Eli's booth moments later, he was leading a parade.

Eli noticed him first. She looked up from a comic book she was reading, her eyes going wide.

"Uh, Marino . . . ?"

Marino lifted his chin and his jaw dropped. He stood up. "What in the world, Ozzie? Where did you find all these people? Wait . . . are you wearing a shirt?"

Ozzie woofed happily and high-stepped up to the table where the T-shirts were displayed. Soon the crowd was so big and so busy that he had to squeeze under the table to get some relief. He could hear Marino and Eli explaining their shirts and unpacking the sizes people requested, and most importantly, he heard people say, "I'll take one!" and once he heard a woman say, "I'll take four!" And Ozzie figured he'd helped out pretty good.

The powwow went on for another day, and Ozzie made sure to make his rounds and tell people about Marino's booth again, this time with a T-shirt that said *Rez Dawg*, which he was pretty sure Marino had made with Ozzie in mind.

This time, by the end of the day, Marino and Eli were sold out.

"We couldn't have done it without you, Ozzie!" Eli exclaimed, giving Ozzie a hug around the neck.

"You're the greatest!" Marino said. "Give me a high five!" Ozzie knew this trick and lifted a paw to slap against Marino's open palm.

"Goodbye, Ozzie," Eli said. "You were the hit of the powwow. You and Marino have to come back next year!"

"Definitely," Marino assured her, and Ozzie barked his agreement. Marino bent down to rub Ozzie's ears. "Okay, Ozzie, time to pack up and get back to Ohkay Owingeh and Grandma's house."

And so they did.

The drive took three days, and once again Ozzie feasted on cheap cheeseburgers and sang along to Marino's music. (Northern Drum was his new favorite.)

They pulled into Mrs. Cruz's driveway late Wednesday

evening as the sun was setting across the distant mountains. Ozzie hopped out first. The air smelled like fried chicken and fresh bread, and as much as Ozzie had enjoyed his trip, he was happy to be home.

Home! Ozzie had always thought himself a free-range dog with no particular home. But seeing Mrs. Cruz's eyes light up as she hugged Marino and watching as tears ran freely down her cheeks as her grandson handed her an envelope full of enough money to fix the house and get the well checked and pay her light bill, Ozzie had to reconsider.

Perhaps he was free, and perhaps he would never wear a leash or call anyone master, but Ozzie decided right there and then that he had been wrong. There weren't just three things that were the absolute best about being a Rez dog, there were four:

1. No masters.

2. No leashes.

3. Mrs. Cruz's back porch on Sundays, and the occasional Wednesday.

And . . . 4. coming home.

SECRETS AND SURPRISES

TRACI SORELL

"Shhh. Come in here and shut the door."

I hear Nimaamaa's lowered voice urging Imbaabaa into their room. My parents whisper a lot these days. I gently rest my ear on their closed door.

". . . Powwow . . . Don't think we can . . . No, no, that won't work!"

Can't what? What won't work?

Tomorrow we're leaving for the powwow. We're going to drive all the way down to the University of Michigan in Ann Arbor. We'll celebrate my cousin Wenona's upcoming law school graduation. They're going to honor her along with other graduating students at the powwow. She is the oldest grandchild, daughter of Daddy's oldest brother, Makwa. She's also the first person from Daddy's family to go to law school.

We live in Sault Ste. Marie, Michigan, on St. Marys River. Everyone knows everyone here in "the Soo."

Our tribe is proud of Wenona.

Nimaamaa has an aunt who is a lawyer. That side of the family lives way over on the Turtle Mountain Rez in North Dakota. It's close to the Canadian border, like we are. We mostly see Mama's relatives in the summer.

"Whatcha doin', Amber?" River's voice rings out behind me.

My back stiffens, and I pull my ear away from the door, quick.

"Nothing," I mumble, and head down the hall to my room.

"Looks like you want to hear what they're saying," River accuses me.

I give my younger sister side-eye as I shut my bedroom door behind me. My poster of A Tribe Called Red flaps. I need to put a new piece of tape on it.

Louise Erdrich's book *Makoons* falls out of my backpack as I belly flop onto my black-and-purple bedspread.

Makoons and Chickadee, the twin brothers in the book, are always included in what *their* Ojibwe family does. Unlike me.

My family used to include me. When River had leukemia and had to have all those treatments this past year, my parents kept me in the loop. I helped them so much.

River's better now. Actually, that's why we're able to drive all the way to the university for this powwow. Lately, though, they've been acting weird and have secret conversations all the time.

River's voice and my parents' voices mingle in the hall of our two-story house.

"Amber!" Imbaabaa calls out from what sounds like downstairs. "Heading over to Nizigos's for a bit. Back by eight."

Then I hear the door to the garage close.

Again! Pulling back the curtain, I watch the SUV's taillights wind their way through our neighborhood filled with high-pitched roofs for the long winter. They turn right and drive north past Kewadin, our tribe's casino. They've been going over to my nizigos Rain's house at odd times the past few weeks—without me.

Racing past the family photos lining the hallway, I plop onto my parents' bed. Nookoomis must know what's going on. I punch number two on the speed dial to call Grandma.

"Boozhoo," she answers.

"Boozhoo, Nookoomis. You at home? I want to come over."

Nookoomis lives only one street over from us and teaches our Ojibwe language at the tribal school. When she's not at work, I never assume she's home. She's out with someone in our family, at the casino with her friends for dinner and shows, or teaching language classes at the Ojibwe Learning Center and Library for community members. She's on the move.

"No, no. . . . I'm out right now. But I'll see you tomorrow when we head down south," she responds.

I swear I hear River in the background.

"Are you at Nizigos's?" I ask.

Nookoomis responds a bit too fast. "Need to go, love. Busy, busy. See you tomorrow." She hangs up fast.

What is going on around here? Why is everyone at Auntie Rain's house?

Mama, Daddy, and Grandma already have everything loaded the next day when they swing by early to pick up River and me from school. All our dance regalia and the stuff for Wenona's giveaway are packed inside duffels and bins, filling every space.

"Come on, girls. Let's roll," says Imbaabaa as he puts some powwow music on low. River plugs her headphones into the portable movie player. Nimaamaa sits next to Daddy, crocheting a baby blanket for her coworker in the tribe's transportation department. I lean my head on Nookoomis's shoulder while she reads a book on her tablet.

At times like these, I wish I had my own phone so I could watch videos or text my cousins who are on their way to the powwow too. But "no phones until sixth grade" is the rule in our house, no matter what any other cousin, friend, or kid my age has. In a couple of months, fifth grade will be O-V-E-R. I can't wait!

"Here we are!" Mama calls out as we pull up to the toll booth at the Mackinac Bridge.

"Aanii," the Ojibwe man working in the bridge toll booth calls out with a big smile.

"Aanii," Daddy responds as he hands him the money, and then we start across the Mackinac Bridge. Everyone gazes out their window.

The bridge connects Michigan's Upper Peninsula, where we live, with the lower part of the state. It's a five-mile drive across the suspension bridge where two Great Lakes—Michigan and Huron—meet in the Straits of Mackinac.

Our Ojibwe people have lived here forever—fishing, trading, and being out on the water. On the east side of the bridge is Mikinaak Mnishenh, which means "Turtle Island" in Ojibwe. It's called Mackinac Island in English. We'll get the best view of it on the way back home.

"Noozhishenh, wake up," I hear Nookoomis whisper to me and feel her pat my knee.

I open my eyes, see the Saginaw exit and know that we're way down the Lower Peninsula, so I must have been out for a while.

Everyone climbs out at the gas station for a break.

Mama's phone buzzes. She heads inside to talk. I roam the candy aisle with River, looking for chocolate. Daddy fills the tank while Nookoomis waits for us by the register.

After we've piled back in, Mama announces that Auntie Niibin, Daddy's older sister, and her family have landed in Detroit. She works in Washington, DC, helping veterans from tribes all across the United States. I can't wait to see our two cousins! River and I dance Jingle Dress at powwows and so do they. The rest of the trip is filled with one story after another about past powwows and who and what we're most excited about for this one we're attending for the second time.

"I know what I'm most excited about," says River. "It's giving—"

I see Nookoomis touch River's knee, which makes her stop talking.

Nimaamaa glances back at River, while Imbaabaa looks in the rearview mirror.

River starts again. "It's giving hugs to all my cousins."

Okaaay, that's cool. But was that what she was *really* going to say? Ugh! So frustrating. Even River is keeping secrets. No one wants me to know anything in this family anymore.

I face the window as this long drive winds down.

I hope things get better tomorrow at the powwow. I haven't felt this miserable since River got sick and we spent so much time at the hospital. We weren't sure if she'd get well. I'm not sure if I'll ever feel like a real part of my family again.

Finally, it's powwow weekend! We eat a quick breakfast at the hotel and then head to the Skyline High School gym. Back when Auntie Niibin went to school at the university, they hosted the powwow on campus in the Crisler Center, where the women's and men's basketball teams play. But a few years ago, they moved it off-campus.

My auntie and her friends definitely miss the big arena. They describe it as filled with dancers from Native Nations across the United States and Canada. I kinda like it here, though. The elevated track that circles above the gym floor where we dance is cool. I like the big locker rooms where we can change into our dance outfits.

It looks like today's crowd will fill the gym. The parking lot is already really full. Luckily, we find a spot, but others will have to take the shuttle from the university.

I reach into the back to grab the black garment bag, but Daddy pulls out camp chairs for me to carry instead.

River smiles as Mama takes the garment bag and hustles us all inside. Again, they are all being weird.

Nookoomis decides our family should set up to the right of the emcee's table at the far end of the gym. She announces that she knows Sheldon Sundown from her days on the powwow circuit, long before we were born. He's Seneca, and his Tribe's Reservation is in New York at the opposite end of Lake Erie from us here in the Lower Peninsula. Hope he's funny!

River and I smooth out a large folded blanket across the bleacher to hold our space. We decide to explore while Daddy places stadium seats for the grown-ups on the floor-level bleacher below ours.

We pass through the concessions area, where we'll get blanket dogs and corn soup later on. We enter the larger area to see what the vendors have for sale. River always looks at the beaded barrettes. But I want to see Nimi-shoome Makwa's art on this year's powwow T-shirt.

Wow! Way before I even get to the table, I can see his colorful design with the woods, lake, plants, and animals from our Ojibwe lands up north. He works at Kewadin, but his heart is in his art. Some of his artwork hangs in our school and in the tribal offices where Mama works.

"Amber, come here! Look!" River calls from across the room.

I head over to see what she can't wait to show me.

"Isn't this one beautiful?" Her finger presses on top of the glass lid of the display case, pointing to an eagle feather design barrette with rainbow-colored beads around the edge and stem of the feather.

"Yes. Do you know how much it costs?" I ask.

"That one's forty-five dollars," replies the woman, in a bright purple blouse with a large beaded floral barrette in her shoulder-length hair.

It seems like a more than fair price. Indian price, actually. The barrette is covered with small, cut beads which are way harder to bead and expensive to buy. I've watched Nizigos bead with those.

Just then Imbaabaa's phone dings in my pocket. He gives it to me when we're out somewhere. The message says, **Come back**. I want to explore more, but that'll have to wait.

"We gotta go, River," I prod.

"Miigwech!" River says to the woman as we leave to walk back to the dance arena. "I'm gonna have to work on Nimaamaa to get that barrette."

"Yeah, she gave you a great price," I offer.

River smiles. Her light brown hair's almost shoulder length again since she finished the treatments. She's twisting it around her finger. I see her mind going over how soon she can get Imbaabaa to the booth to have a look.

As we approach the chairs, we see that Nizigos has joined Grandma, Daddy, and Mama. Everybody has a weird grin on their face as we walk up. Something is definitely up.

Mr. Sundown's voice booms through the gym. "Dancers, time to get ready. Grand Entry is less than an hour from now." The master of ceremonies keeps everyone on track at the powwow and shares good jokes and stories.

"You girls need to head to the locker room," says Mama.

"We're here, we're here," Auntie Niibon proclaims as my DC cousins run up and give River and me big hugs. Everyone puts their stuff down next to ours. They start talking to River, complimenting her on how healthy she looks and how they can't wait to see her dancing today.

Normally she and I always dance Jingle Dress alongside our cousins, but she couldn't dance at all this past year.

The Jingle Dress dance is used in ceremonies for healing and is also danced at powwows. Each time River couldn't dance, our cousins and I danced with her in mind and for everyone who needed healing. To have her beside us today is the best. I do kinda wish I could get a word in on their conversation, though.

Nookoomis motions for us to gather around her. She prays for us to have our hearts and minds in the right place as we get ready to dance at the powwow.

Both Mama and Daddy pick up the garment bag with our jingle dresses and other regalia inside. "Miigwech to everyone for all you've done, especially to Nookoomis and Nizigos, and to River too," Nimaamaa says. "It's been a difficult year. We're so happy to be here today to celebrate Wenona's graduation and see all our girls dancing."

Okay, major confusion. Why is Mama thanking the group? What's going on?

"We are so grateful for all Amber did this past year to help us," I hear Nimaamaa say.

Wait, what? I stop twisting my long braids together and look up.

Auntie Niibin puts her hands on my shoulders.

"We all worked together to make you this new dress and accessories," Mama finishes.

Imbaabaa unzips the garment bag, but I can't see anymore. The pools in my eyes make everything blurry. My cool hands feel good against my searing-hot cheeks. I can't believe this. I thought they didn't want me around whenever they took off to Nizigos's house without me.

"Do you like it?" River's voice breaks through my haze.

I wipe my eyes and see the dress for the first time. It's the vibrant royal-purple material I adored at the fabric store months ago when I went with Nizigos. The beaded collar, wrist bands, and leggings have silver, black, and purple beaded accents. Everything is so beautiful. I know Auntie Niibin and my cousins helped with making those too.

I can't stop crying. The heaviness within me is gone, but I feel a new kind of awful. How could I think that my family didn't want me around? Sure, we don't always get along. But they love me—always.

"I love all of it. Miigwech, everybody," I finally reply, taking a deep breath. "I couldn't figure out why you all kept having secret conversations and going off to Nizigos's without me. Even Nookoomis, who always tells me everything, wouldn't share anything! It made me start to wonder."

Nookoomis's arms reach around me, squeezing me tight. "You're too smart, Noozhishenh. We had to be extra careful to keep it from you." She laughs.

Then everyone laughs. They're right. I'm always the one who guesses a surprise or finds out things before anyone else.

"Now, you girls go get ready. We're excited to see some beautiful dancing today," says Nookoomis.

Mama and Daddy each hug me tight.

"Nookoomis is right. We can't keep hardly anything secret from you," Imbaabaa whispers in my ear.

We head into the gym locker room to change. I keep looking at my beautiful jingle dress, sparkling and bright in my favorite colors. No wonder Daddy wouldn't let me carry the bag. I thought we brought my yellow-and-blue dress. But that one was getting a little small. I can't wait to step and turn, always keeping one foot on the ground while dancing.

"Everybody line up for Grand Entry," says Mr. Sundown as we exit the locker room.

We put our bags by our parents' seats and get in line.

First the warriors line up—veterans and active-duty service members, who dance into the arena carrying the eagle staff and various flags. Those will be posted by the head table where the emcee and arena director sit.

The Head Man and Head Woman dancers who will start out each intertribal and special dance today follow them, along with special guests like tribal leaders.

After them, the men line up according to age (Elders are always first) and the type of dance they do.

And finally, the women and the kids do the same behind them. So we stand in the very back, behind the boys.

With so many Ojibwe families here, there are lots of girls dancing Jingle Dress. Competition for prize money will be fierce today.

As the host drum begins the song that draws us into the arena, I look at River and my cousins, saying my own small prayer that we'll dance well for Gchi-Manidoo today. I feel the beat and begin to lift my heels off the ground as we wait our turn to enter. I see Cousin Wenona rush in and join the women farther up in line.

As the emcee, Mr. Sundown announces who comes into the circle as we all dance into the arena. Grand Entry takes a while. Once we're all in the arena, the different drum groups take turns playing a flag song, a veterans' song, and other honor songs.

After the colors are posted, he officially welcomes everyone and introduces special guests, including tribal leaders and university officials.

Us cousins are excited to dance together and celebrate Wenona's graduation during the Student Honor Song after the intertribal dancing. And once Grand Entry ends, we head back to our chairs. We all hug Wenona. She tells us how law school has worn her out. "Less than two months to go, but then I have to study for the bar exam this summer."

"Studying in summer?" I ask. That sounds horrible. It's the opposite of what summer is for.

"Yep, I won't even be able to come home. I'm staying here and working part-time at a law firm so I can study in their law library and in my apartment. I have to pass the Michigan bar exam to be able to practice law. It's not easy," Wenona explains.

We all look at each other wide-eyed. Us cousins look forward to summer adventures together, when everyone comes to stay with us or Nookoomis for a month before River and I head over to Turtle Mountain to hang out with Mama's side of the family. I'm glad I'm not an adult yet. Seems to be more work and less fun the older you get!

We take turns dancing and walking through the hallways to eat, shop, and find all the freebies. I take a purple stress ball from the Detroit urban Indian health clinic's table.

Lots of Ojibwe people and folks from other tribes live and work in Detroit. Many of them come to this powwow.

Soon, Mr. Sheldon's call rings out. "Time to honor our Native students—those at the university, here at Skyline, and elsewhere who are graduating or worthy of honor for their good grades."

He calls out students' names to come and stand in front of the head table, so everyone can see who we will honor when the host drum sings the honor song.

There are two Native law students called before Wenona—one from Saginaw Indian Chippewa Tribe of Michigan and the other from Grand Traverse Band of Ottawa and Chippewa Indians. The words Chippewa and Ojibwe refer to the same people.

Then we hear, "Wenona LaPlante, Sault Ste. Marie Tribe of Chippewa Indians," and we watch as she joins the other two in front of the table. There are a few more graduate students and almost two dozen undergraduates who are called to join them.

Then Mr. Sheldon mentions that he'll call up those on honor rolls. He names several kids. Then I hear, "Amber LaPlante, honor roll at JKL Bahweting School, Sault Ste. Marie Tribe of Chippewa Indians."

I jump up from my chair and look at my family. Mama and Daddy both have big smiles, and River claps and squeals. They are all *super* sneaky.

A second surprise? Again, puddles fill my eyes. For a powwow that was supposed to be about celebrating Wenona's graduation, seeing River dance again, and enjoying time with our family, I end up honored.

Wow, not what I expected today.

I pull River up and make her come stand beside me. She would have had good grades if she hadn't missed so much school because she was sick. We plant ourselves next to Wenona as the drummers begin to sing. All of us follow the Head Man and Head Woman around the arena.

Miigwech, Gchi-Manidoo. Miigwech, family. So many good surprises today at the powwow. And we still get to compete in Jingle Dress later!

WENDIGOS DON'T DANCE

ART COULSON

As he stepped from his bedroom into the dark hallway, Jace noticed the flickering light before he heard the muffled laughs and tinny music coming from his uncles' room one door down. He poked his head in the half-open door.

"Is this how you guys spend every night? Staying up late watching Bigfoot videos?"

Jace stood in mock anger, hands on his hips, imitating his mother's voice.

His uncles turned to look at him over their shoulders. Their eyes were wide and faces blank, like deer standing along the roadside.

They knew they'd been caught. Then they both chuckled.

"Wendigo," Uncle Mutt said.

"Windy what?" Jace raised an eyebrow.

"Wendigo videos, not Bigfoot this time," Uncle Jeff said. "Wendigos are spirits that live in the forests up there in the Great Lakes. We have to get ready for our trip to Michigan tomorrow. Wouldn't want to head over there unprepared."

Uncle Mutt nodded. His face was serious, but he couldn't hide his smile for long.

Jace's uncles had an unusual hobby. On weekends, they liked to hunt for Bigfoot, both in the forests of northern Minnesota and back home in Oklahoma. Many nights, they retired to their room after supper to watch Bigfoot videos online. They kept a big loose-leaf notebook filled with their observations, sketches, locks of hair, and grainy photos of old tree stumps and large, snowy footprints— did Bigfoot really wear hiking boots?

Jace must have missed that fact in science class.

"Well, you should both be in bed. We have a long trip tomorrow and it's just you two driving," Jace said. "You know I can't get my learner's permit for another two years and nine months."

Not that he was counting or anything.

"We know, we know. But this isn't our first road trip, little man," said Uncle Jeff. "Mutt and I have this down to a science. You got the sausage and cheese in the cooler, right, big brother? Thermos filled with coffee? Corn nuts? Bologna sandwiches?"

Mutt checked off each item with a flourish on an imaginary list on the palm of his hand. "Hawa! We're all set," he replied. "Now back to our video, already in progress."

Man, Jace's uncles could be annoying.

"Well, you should try to get some sleep. I don't want you all tired at the powwow and teasing to go back to the hotel for a nap at lunchtime." Jace felt like the grown-up in the room when his uncles were together. You'd think they were six years old instead of pushing sixty. They still shared a bedroom, after all. It was a wonder they weren't still sleeping in bunk beds.

Besides hunting Bigfoot, his uncles traveled the country telling stories at schools, powwows, and festivals.

This weekend, his uncles were traveling all the way from Minneapolis to Ann Arbor, to the University of Michigan's annual spring powwow, where they planned to visit with old friends and tell stories.

Jace was an unwilling chaperone. Jace's grandma wanted him to go along with her younger brothers to keep them out of trouble. Jace would much rather stay home and hang out with his friends. Plus, he was missing a day of school on Friday. Pizza day in the cafeteria. It was just unfair.

Once again, he'd be stuck in the back of the car on an endless road trip. Jace would have to listen to his uncles as they swapped stories, remembered every place they'd ever stopped for food (and what they had eaten), and counted every deer between Minnesota and Michigan.

Despite his uncles' vow to be ready for the trip first thing in the morning, they didn't get their ugly avocado-green station wagon loaded and on the road until almost noon.

"Your chariot awaits," said Uncle Jeff to no one in particular as he slammed down the rear hatch. Jace worried that the cracked rear window would finally give up its grip and fall out of the car entirely, but it held on. Maybe it was the *Indians Discovered Columbus* bumper sticker that held it magically in place.

Pure stubbornness, more likely.

"You using your GPS, Jeff?" Mutt asked. He pronounced it "gipps." Jace wasn't sure if that was intentional or just a sign of his uncle's old age.

"Nah, once we get on 94, it's a straight shot to Ann Arbor," Jeff said as he slid into the driver's seat. "In fact, we'll barely have time for you to finish one of your stories before we get there. Maybe you can just boil it down to the interesting parts."

Jeff grinned. Teasing his brother was his favorite pastime.

Jace napped most of the trip, waking only when they stopped for gas or when one of his uncles reached across him to fish around in the cooler for a sausage or hunk of cheese.

When they pulled into the Ann Arbor Holiday Inn parking lot just before midnight, Jeff shook Jace awake.

"We're here, neff. Time to wake up and start gathering your stuff. We also need help hauling in the cooler and gear."

They tossed their duffel bags on the floor of their room, rolled out Jace's sleeping bag, and jockeyed for position at the lone sink as all three tried to brush their teeth at once.

"No snoring," Mutt said, looking over at his brother.

"It'll be like I'm not even here," Jeff said. He had a weird look on his face, but Jace just chalked it up to the long drive. Maybe all the spicy sausage Jeff had scarfed down on the trip was biting him back.

They all lay down and Jeff reached over to turn out the light between the beds.

Once his brother and nephew were asleep, Jeff left them a note, and then quietly slipped out the front door of the hotel and into the parking lot. He rubbed his hands together and puffed out a steamy breath.

"It's good to see you again, Jeff. How's Mutt? Is he coming with us?"

The short, thin woman closed the door of her idling

SUV and leaned in to give Jeff a peck on the cheek. She was wearing jeans, a Pendleton jacket, and white fleece ear warmers that circled her long, dark hair. Her eyes sparkled in the brightness of the parking-lot lights.

"Nah, I'm letting him and my nephew catch up on their sleep. Just the two of us tonight."

Helen Peacock smiled. Her ears turned red, but Jeff couldn't see them under the ear warmers.

"I'm staying in a yurt up at Green Lake, in the Waterloo Recreation Area. It's only a half hour away, but you feel like you're camping in the wilderness. Great to sit on the deck under a blanket and watch the Northern Lights over the lake."

"And look for wendigos," Jeff added.

Helen looked at Jeff and slowly shook her head. That man could wring the romance right out of a Lifetime movie. No wonder he was still a bachelor.

Helen and Jeff had known each other for more than twenty years, but she still couldn't get used to his odd hobby. Or his even odder sense of humor.

Helen was the reason Jeff had jumped at the chance to come to Ann Arbor to tell stories and attend the powwow. Helen—Dr. Peacock to her students—taught math at the Saginaw Chippewa Tribal College on her Reservation, two hours north of Ann Arbor. She attended the University of Michigan powwow each spring.

"Skoden. We need to get started if I'm going to have you back here before breakfast," she said, opening the driver's door.

The sound of running water and the smell of coffee woke Jace before any light peeked in around the room's heavy flowered drapes. He rolled over in his sleeping bag and ran a hand through his long hair.

Uncle Mutt was moving quickly and methodically in the dark, singing an old Cherokee song under his breath as he prepared to meet the day. He was trying not to wake anyone.

As Jace gradually traveled from dreamland to the here and now, he sensed something wasn't quite right. After more than ten hours in the car and a less-than-comfortable night's sleep on the floor, he wasn't sure of much. But he *was* sure of one thing: when they'd gone to bed, there had been three people in the room. Now there were only two.

"Uncle Mutt?" Jace said.

"Siyo, Jace. How'd you sleep?"

"Where's Uncle Jeff?" Jace said, without answering the question.

"He's right over there in his bed. Where do you think he is? He's going to sleep the whole day away—if the cannibal ghosts don't carry him away."

Jace shivered, remembering the stories his grandmother

had told him about the water cannibals who snuck into homes at dawn and carried away the souls of children who stayed in bed too late. Yeah, no fluffy bunnies and happy puppies in his grandmother's stories.

Uncle Mutt flipped on the light switch next to the sink and squinted to get used to the sudden brightness.

"Hmm, you're right. We seem to be missing someone. Jeff must have snuck out early to be first in line at the breakfast buffet. That boy sure does love his bacon."

Jace stood up and stretched. He could almost touch the ceiling. He'd grown almost a foot in the last year alone. He reached into the pocket of his shorts and drew out a hair tie. As he pulled his hair back into a loose ponytail, he saw a note on the table between the beds.

"There's our explanation," Uncle Mutt said as he crossed the room, carefully stepping around the duffel bags, comic books, and cracker boxes.

> Gone to look for wendigos with Helen. I'll be back in time for breakfast. Don't eat all the bacon.
> —ᎤᏣ

Jeff had signed his note with his Indian name, Totsuwa, or Redbird. Jace's grandma and his uncles usually called each other by their Cherokee names, especially when they were speaking their language.

When he was younger, Jace—Jayson when his mom was mad—had been curious about his uncle Mutt's name. He went to his grandma, figuring she would tell him the truth. Uncle Mutt would probably make up some far-fetched story about how he had gotten his unusual name.

"Elisi, what's Uncle Mutt's real name?" Jace had asked her one day.

"What do you mean?" she replied.

"I mean, Mutt is his nickname. What's his real name? Is Mutt short for Matthew or Mathias or something?"

"No," his grandmother said. "Mutt *is* his real name. Our parents named him and your uncle Jeff after two guys on an old radio show."

Grandma didn't say what kind of music they played on that old radio show. Probably country and western, if he knew his family.

Uncle Mutt coughed, bringing Jace back into the present.

"Well, he could have said something before we all went to sleep, so we didn't worry," Mutt said, taking another sip of his coffee and shaking his head. "But that's my brother—Mr. Responsible."

Jace frowned. Uncle Jeff's note said he'd be back before breakfast. So where was he?

"I bet he's already down at the buffet waiting on us. Get dressed and we'll meet him down there." Uncle Mutt was already dressed for the powwow in a pair of black jeans, handmade boots, and a denim shirt. A red bandanna was fastened around his neck with a silver slide. His graying hair was pulled back in a loose ponytail. He slipped on a dark blue blazer and grabbed his white cowboy hat to complete what he called his "Official Storyteller's Uniform."

Jace pulled on a pair of jeans before sitting on the edge of Jeff's bed to put on his boots. He grabbed a flannel shirt from his bag and slid it on before announcing, "Let's go."

But Uncle Jeff wasn't at the breakfast buffet.

Jace and Mutt went through the short line and sat at a small table near the window. The dining area was full of Indian people of all ages. The room was loud with excited conversation and laughter. Powwow mornings were always like that.

But Jace was having a hard time getting in the mood.

Uncle Mutt shoveled eggs and toast into his mouth, pausing only for the occasional breath and sip of black coffee. He pushed his tinted, silver-framed eyeglasses back on his nose with the index finger of his right hand and looked over at his nephew.

Jace just pushed his eggs and hash browns around with his fork. He looked down at his plate in silence. "He'll turn up, Mutt. Jeff and Helen are probably already over at the school watching them set up for the powwow. We'll head over after breakfast and give him a hard time for disappearing on us."

Hours earlier, the SUV had jolted through the pine forest along a dark road as Jeff and Helen drove toward Green Lake. An occasional snow flurry spun in the beams of the headlights. The cool air blowing through the SUV's vents smelled fresh and crisp, like pine needles, with just a hint of woodsmoke. Jeff loved early spring, when the whole world started anew.

Helen pulled off the road, parked the SUV at her yurt, and turned off the engine. The night was dark, and their eyes were slow to adjust. "We're here," she said, looking over at Jeff. She kept her eyes on him as he unbuckled his seat belt and adjusted his baseball cap. "Hope you'll be warm enough. Want to see the lake before we head into the yurt?"

She and Jeff walked toward the lake, holding hands.

"Let's hit one of the trails, see if we can find any sign of the wendigo," Jeff said.

"We don't have a flashlight or a trail map," Helen said. "This isn't a good idea." She followed Jeff up the dark trail anyway. "And what about bears?"

"What about them? I'm more worried about encountering a wendigo in the wild, to be honest. They look kinda mean on YouTube."

"Then why in the world are you looking for them?" Helen asked. "Besides, you know they're not real, right?"

"How can an Ojibwe woman say that? They're *your* stories—you mean you don't believe 'em?"

"Do you believe every Cherokee story you've ever heard?"

"Sure do. Well, except for Mutt's. He lies a lot."

They walked on in silence, with the occasional sound of an animal in the underbrush or the crack of a branch to keep their hearts beating fast.

"Didn't we pass this dead tree already?" Helen asked, worry creeping into her voice.

"Hmm. Not sure. You think we doubled back on ourselves?" Jeff stopped and looked around them in the dark. It was hard to make anything out more than a foot or two away.

Helen gasped. "What's that?" She pointed off in the distance. Her hand shook.

Jeff's eyes grew wide. Fingers of flame danced along the tops of the trees.

"Wendigo," he said.

As they walked in the front doors at Skyline High School just after eleven a.m., Jace darted ahead of his uncle. He ran past the gym, straight to the back of the building, where the vendors were set up. He walked quickly from table to table, asking the people at each if they had seen a short Indian man who looked really tired.

"Sure, a lot of them," said the woman working at the fry bread stand. "I'm surrounded by short Indian men. And they're always acting tired when I have work for them to do."

She held out her hand. "My name is Maisie. What's yours? If I see your friend, I'll tell him you're looking for him."

Jace introduced himself. "It's my uncle Jeff. He's missing."

"He's got short gray hair and wire-rimmed glasses. And he's probably wearing a polo shirt and his Native Pride baseball cap," Jace added hopefully. "He's kind of short and round. And he laughs a lot."

The woman shook her head and said, "Sorry, hon. I haven't seen anyone like that recently. You might ask one of the security guards or call the police before the powwow gets going." She went back to kneading her dough.

Jace didn't want the police looking for his uncle. Besides, there were plenty of people here from the community he hadn't spoken with yet. Maybe one of them had seen Uncle Jeff. He was hard to miss.

"Or," Maisie said, "you could ask the young woman who stopped by here earlier, Tokala. She's a detective, you know. And you're in luck—that's her across the way at the jewelry table now." Maisie tilted her head and pointed with her lips.

Jace walked up to the girl, who was just finishing her conversation with the jewelry vendor.

"Excuse me, Tokala, maybe you can help me? I need to find my uncle Jeff. He's missing and I'm really worried."

Tokala turned to look at Jace. "I'd be happy to help you, but I'm working on a mystery of my own at the moment. Have you looked in all the places he could be? They're holding the storytelling in the school theater later. Have you checked there?" At Jace's nod, she added, "Are you staying at the hotel? Have you looked there?"

"Yes, my uncle Mutt and I have looked everywhere. He's really missing."

Tokala's eyes narrowed at the mention of Uncle Mutt, but she didn't let the unusual name faze her. "As soon as I solve the mystery I'm working on, I'll find you and help search for your uncle, if he hasn't turned up."

"Thank you," Jace said, holding out his hand. "I'm Jace, by the way. I'm glad to meet you. I've never met a real-life detective before."

"Pleased to meet you," Tokala said. "Hope you find your uncle soon."

Jace walked back to Uncle Mutt, a worried look on his face.

"Uncle Jeff's not here either." Jace flopped down on the

floor with his back against the wall. He didn't want to cry like a little kid, but his frustration and worry were causing his eyes to fill with tears.

Just then Jace felt a warm, slobbery kiss on his cheek. He jumped a little and quickly turned to find a short, stocky black-brown-and-white dog with its tongue hanging out of its brown-and-white face. The dog looked like something Grandma and her sewing kit might have pieced together from bits of mismatched dogs. It was wearing a T-shirt that read *Ancestor Approved*. He had to smile as he reached out to pet the dog.

"Heh. See, even the four-leggeds want you to stop worrying," Uncle Mutt said, reaching down to scratch the dog behind its ears. Just then, a large group of Elders walked past, talking excitedly and laughing. The dog glanced up and then trotted after them, wagging its tail.

"Jeff will show up soon. I just know it," Uncle Mutt said.

But, truth be told, Mutt was worried about his kid brother, too. No matter how old they got, Jeff would always be his little brother. And it was Mutt's job to look after him. "If he doesn't turn up by lunchtime, we'll call your grandma back in Minnesota and see if she's heard from him."

The night before, as Jeff and Helen approached the clearing where they had seen the odd light dancing on the trees, they heard voices. They could just make out a flurry of activity through the trees ahead.

They stopped at the edge of the trees. Helen gasped when she saw men unloading cargo from muddy ATVs and hauling it toward the trees across from where she and Jeff stood. A small fire burned in the middle of their makeshift camp, throwing fingers of light on the trees that surrounded them. So the odd fire they'd seen hadn't been a wendigo after all.

The men in the camp moved quickly, unloading deer and hauling them up side by side into the trees by their back legs. There must have been two dozen deer altogether. Large and small. Buck and doe. One of the hunters, a short, bearded man wearing coveralls and work gloves, dressed each deer, one after another, working quickly and quietly by the light of the lanterns that sat on the ground near him. He'd obviously done this before.

What were these guys doing? It wasn't hunting season.

Poachers!

Jeff signaled for Helen to stay quiet and backed away from the edge of the clearing.

"If we ever find our way back, we'd better get one of the rangers out here," he said.

"Yeah, that's not gonna happen," said a man's voice out of the darkness. Helen and Jeff jumped as they heard someone rack a shell in a shotgun.

"You're staying here until we're done. Then we'll decide what to do with you."

The man gestured with his shotgun for Jeff and Helen to sit down. Helen cried softly as she and Jeff sat with their backs to a large tree. Their captor tied their wrists together with a rough length of rope he pulled from the pack on his back.

"Now sit there and be quiet and let us get our work done," their captor snarled. "Don't make me haul you up in that tree like one of them deer."

After the man returned to the clearing, Helen and Jeff sat in silence, afraid to speak. Their shoulders and arms ached. The chill of the ground was working its way up their bodies. They could see the man with the gun talking to the others and gesturing back toward where they sat at the dark edge of the woods. After a brief, excited conversation, the poachers got back to their work.

"What are we going to do?" Helen asked in a whisper.

The forest around them was quiet. They could see the stars above them through the tops of the trees. Helen sniffled. Jeff felt a knot in his stomach and began to shake.

Neither of them could think of a way out of this. And the night was growing colder by the minute.

Just then, a plump, scruffy raccoon waddled out of the underbrush and sat up on its haunches. It tilted its head and looked at Jeff and Helen. It chattered and squeaked at them.

"What's that you say, gvli?" Jeff said to the raccoon. "vv—halisdela! Yes—help us!"

The raccoon chattered at them some more. She quickly licked and bit both front paws before turning and wandering back into the bushes.

"You don't think she understood you, do you?" Helen asked Jeff.

"I don't know why not. My mom always told me that all animals speak Cherokee. That raccoon had a bit of an Ojibwe accent, but I caught the drift of what she was saying. She's going to get help."

Despite their predicament, Helen had to smile.

A shiver ran up her spine as she heard coyotes yipping and howling off in the distance.

A moment later, they heard the call of a whip-poor-will.

"See, they're passing the word," Jeff said.

"Shhh," Helen said.

"What?"

"Shhh, I said! Don't you hear that?"

Footsteps were moving toward them in the darkness. They both strained their eyes as they scanned the dark woods. The footsteps weren't coming from the direction of the clearing where the poachers continued their work.

They were coming from the deeper part of the woods.

Helen's voice rose. "Do you think it's a bear?"

Just then a tall, thin, shadowy figure stepped from behind a tree and moved swiftly toward them. Neither could see it clearly or tell whether it was animal or human. It made no sound. Both Helen and Jeff let out a surprised gasp. Before they knew it, the ropes slid from their wrists. They got to their feet, but their rescuer had vanished!

"What the—?" Helen said.

"These ropes weren't cut," Jeff said, looking at the pieces in his hand. "It looks like someone burned them. Where did he go? Did you see where he ran off to?"

Helen didn't answer. Instead she pointed to the top of the trees, where flames leaped away from them.

Jeff nodded. "Wendigo."

Helen didn't argue with him. She just said, "Let's get out of here," as she grabbed Jeff's arm and pulled him away from the clearing and into the welcoming darkness of the forest.

"Excuse me," the deputy said that Saturday afternoon, stepping into the doorway of the gym and stopping in front of Tokala, who was typing away on an iPad Mini. "I'm looking for a man and a boy. Mutt and Jayson Mills?"

"Never heard of them," Tokala said, pausing her typing and looking up at the deputy with narrowed eyes.

"Well, if you should see them, please let them know we're looking for them. We've found their missing relative, Jeff Mills."

"Oh, you must mean Jace. I met him earlier when he was looking for his uncle. That's him over there with his other uncle, standing by the fry bread stand."

The ride out to the University of Michigan Medical Center in the back of the deputy's car was the longest ride Jace had ever taken. Flurries danced around the car. The sky was darker than normal.

"But they're all right, aren't they?" Uncle Mutt asked the deputy.

"Yes. They're tired. Cold. A little hungry. But they'll be fine once we have them checked out by a doctor," the deputy said. "It's just a precaution. Neither of them was hurt."

Jace ran into the room and threw his arms around his uncle, who was sitting in the bed nearest the door. "You had us so worried." Then he noticed Helen sitting in the other bed, looking at him.

"Hello, young man."

Jace walked over and shook Helen's hand. She pulled him down into a hug.

Jeff was starting to get uncomfortable with all the emotion in the room.

"Quite the matching outfits we have on," he said. He and Helen wore thin hospital gowns, white with small blue flowers.

Helen sat up straighter in the bed and struck a pose.

"You were supposed to be at the powwow with us, not hiking in the woods and chasing bad guys," Jace said, his voice rising. "What were you thinking, Uncle Jeff?"

"I told you I wanted to look for a wendigo. I wasn't going to find one at the powwow," Uncle Jeff said matter-of-factly. "Wendigos don't dance."

"The police told us that some poachers had you tied up in the woods. By the time the police got there, the poachers had cleared out. All they found was an abandoned camp and some tire tracks," Mutt said. "How did you two ever get away? You're not exactly Houdini."

Jeff used the controller to raise the back of his hospital bed a bit higher.

"You see, it's like this," he began. "It all started when a clever raccoon told a wendigo about our predicament . . ."

Mutt and Jace groaned.

Mutt picked up a pillow off Helen's bed and tossed it at Jeff. "Shouldn't you save the stories for the powwow?" he said. "If we leave now, we might get back before they run out of fry bread."

INDIAN PRICE

ERIC GANSWORTH

"It'll be fun," my mom said, which meant, for sure, it wouldn't be. We're small-time Indian craft vendors, setting up at powwows and socials in Upstate New York, Ontario, and Quebec. In addition to regular beadwork items like key chains and glasses cases, my mom makes whatever wild thing her imagination offers. My dad makes ribbon shirts and breechcloths. Owners like custom details, but he always brings samples. We're good enough that we can usually count on nearly empty bins coming home to the Rez, just outside Niagara Falls.

Lately, we've requested "Golden Booths," with a view of dancers and close to food vendors and bathrooms. Partly it's because we do well enough, sales-wise, but we also do it so my dad doesn't have to walk far. We keep quiet about this, but we know, and worse, he knows.

When my mom told me we were going to Michigan, I thought we'd be staying at a hotel. Hot tubs are good for my dad, and when white people see us coming, they usually decide they don't need to enjoy it anymore and go back to their own rooms.

My dad says they're scared of the scars on his legs, but even at thirteen, I know better. They're afraid our ethnic germs are gonna throw off the chlorine and sneak up on them.

Turned out we were staying with my mom's brother. Uncle Dave worked custodial at the high school where this powwow was held. He said he'd lucked out on his first workday. His boss, a guy named Mike, amazingly was also Indian. Turtle Mountain Ojibwe. It might seem like a small thing, but there aren't a ton of us around once you move off the Rez. Uncle Dave's wife, Florence, worked at the university, a *professor*, my mom always reminded me. Florence and their boy, Potter, used to come when Uncle Dave visited our Rez, where my ma and Uncle Dave were raised, but they gradually stopped, and no one speaks of it.

"Now remember, call her *Auntie* Florence," my mom said once we got on the road. On the Rez, you call women auntie who you aren't even related to. It's the ones who act like your real aunties when they aren't even, telling you secrets your parents don't want you to know, embarrassing you at a party, just to show they can. Lately, when the Rez aunties see me, they make a big show of putting their cigs and lighters in their beaded purses and clutching them. As if I'd steal their nasty Rez-brand smokes. They know I don't smoke. They're just telling me: *No Wampum Incident repeats!*

"Did you take inventory before we left?" my dad asked.

"I'll take it again," I said, so he would hear: *I'll remember to call her Auntie.* It was going to be challenging enough to call my cousin by his name. Who names their kid "Potter," anyway? It would be like me being named Roofer (or ex-Roofer).

See, Uncle Dave paid the bills with his custodian job, but he was also a potter, making traditional open-pit-fired clay pots. He even had pieces in museums that didn't want our work.

Whenever Uncle Dave talked my mom into applying for fellowships and they told her no thanks, they said her work didn't fit into categories. It's not traditional enough to be "folk art," and it's too traditional to be "contemporary." Or like my dad says: *If people can understand it when they first look, they think it's not sophisticated enough. It never even occurs to them that it's just the doorway into the bigger ideas. And if it doesn't look like a Pendleton blanket, then they think the designs aren't Indian enough.*

Like a lot of brothers and sisters, they've argued this for so long, they sometimes can't remember which side they're on. Uncle Dave thinks she should make work that's harder to understand, and then he backs off, saying it needs to be more basic. His stuff sells better because it doesn't cost as much, and he puts in enough obvious signs that say *INDIAN ART HERE*, and people know what it's supposed to be, right away. He says if white people are purposely shopping for Indian stuff, your stuff better include lots of feathers and geometry, if you hope to make a sale.

"What the heck is this?" I pulled up a long, narrow gift box hidden in a folded Pendleton blanket we used as a table cover. It was shut tight with my mom's signature fancy ribbon ties.

"Just leave it," my mom said. "And when we get there, put it in Potter's room." She was being cagey.

My parents believed I should know the whole business: inventory, hang-tag pricing, the change box, and the secret change box underneath, where we kept bigger bills.

The one thing I had the hardest time mastering was Indian Price, the most important part of being a powwow arts-and-crafts vendor. This was the slightly lower price you gave to someone you knew was definitely Indian, but this rule took me forever to understand.

◈

At Uncle Dave's, my parents stayed in the "guest room," a room where only dust bunnies lived. The whole house was decked out in "authentic Indian art," from vendors with tribal proof for the Indian Arts and Crafts Act. My mom says this law means you can't call something for sale "Indian made" if it wasn't actually made by an Indian. A law about not lying, I guess. Most powwows enforced it. I said all it took was eyes to tell we were "authentic Indians." My mom reminded me that not everything is that simple.

"We thought you might want to stay with Potter," *Auntie* Florence said. "He and his friends are in your uncle Dave's 'man cave.' They're dancing tomorrow and want to practice."

Potter was going to dance? Maybe he'd made inroads with the Indians that Uncle Dave says are scattered around Detroit. "Or you can stay in his room. You're old enough to make your own decisions now," she said, smiling. She *definitely* knew about the Wampum Incident.

At least she wasn't going to act like the Rez aunties. Maybe instead, she was just going to make sure their valuables were away in a giant safe.

Potter was seventeen, so he wouldn't want some middle school kid hanging around. I chose his room. It also had crafts everywhere, but his stuff seemed to come from a ton of territories. Like a bunch of Indians from around the country had exploded in this room.

I snuck my mom's fancy ribbon off that mystery gift. Years of practice left me able to peek without anyone knowing different. Inside was a loop of hide, like Chewbacca's bandolier. Weird. My mom rarely worked white hide leather. The beadwork was unusual, too. A foot-long single arrow, solid red glass beads, with the point at the top.

An included note card had a turtle on it, like you see at any powwow vendor area. Generic "Indian designs." Feathers and geometry, like my dad says. Customers often sent a card with payment so my mom could seal it in before doing her ribbon magic. This card was someone else's privacy, but I had to know.

> Congratulations on your election to the Order of the Arrow and your successful call-out and Ordeal! We are so very proud you stuck to this! We know it wasn't easy.
> Love, Mom and Dad

This commission was a gift for Potter from my uncle and auntie. But Order of the Arrow? What could that possibly be? I was also curious about how you could get "called out" successfully. Being called out for the Wampum Incident was definitely not a happy time for me. It must mean something different to the Arrow Order guys.

Someone bounded up the stairs and knocked.

I laid my bag on the box as Potter opened the door a crack.

"Hey, Dalton," he said, just visible. "Mind if I come in?"

"It's your room," I said, hearing my own grumpiness. "Nyah-wheh for letting me use it."

"Sure, but you're welcome to join us," he said. His hair was longer than two years ago, touching his shoulders. Still, it was as pale as corn silk. "Just Xbox and junk food. Some guys in our troop think being a Scout means being perfect all the time, always doing something for others, but sometimes you just wanna hang with friends."

"Troop?"

"You didn't stick with Scouts?" When I signed up for Cub Scouts, the Rez leader switched our meetings from Wednesday nights to eight o'clock Saturday mornings. That killed scouting on the Rez.

"Anyway, we're getting in the hot tub if you wanna join. Just five of us. Plenty of room. Loosen our muscles." I told him I had stuff to do, but he set out a pair of Crocs, a towel, and a set of trunks he'd outgrown, in case I changed my mind. A while later, he and his friends were laughing, and my need to be an Indian and join my group was too strong, even if this wasn't really my group.

The air was sharp, though I had a towel around my shoulders. Potter and his friends slid the hot tub cover off and jumped in. Indians come in a big range of colors and looks, but his four friends looked pretty strictly white. I had the feeling I was the only actual Indian here, with Potter as a close second.

"Man, this is worse than my Ordeal," one named Craig said, and the rest laughed, a private joke. "Come on up, Little Man," Craig said, moving. It felt weird to wear someone else's trunks, but if you had to, it was best they belonged to your cousin.

The water was hot, and the wind blasted sharp air, each half of me getting a different extreme signal. I settled in, just my head and neck above water.

"Harry, you didn't turn the jets on?" Craig asked, and Potter stood. These guys seemed to like each other fine, but clearly Craig was the one they looked up to.

"Harry?" I asked. "I'll do it," I said, climbing out. Even after a minute underwater, I felt insulated. The air wasn't as painful. I turned the timer dial on the deck and hopped back in.

"H-A-I-R-Y," Craig clarified. "Since your cousin grew his hair out, that's what we call him." *Hairy Potter*, I thought, *almost a Rez-worthy nickname.*

"You sure *are* a red man, now, Little Man," Craig added. Apparently, nicknames were his thing. My blood had rushed to the surface in this March air, making my brown skin look like a very ripe peach. I gave Hairy Potter a sideways eye snap.

Potter raised his eyebrows in the center, like keyboard accent marks, silently asking me not to sass. His house, his rules. Two of the others started practicing their secret greeting, but Craig cleared his throat and they stopped.

Like *I* cared and was going to quick run out and tell the world.

A few minutes later I left, saying I had to get ready for tomorrow. I didn't want Potter trying to get me alone to say his friend didn't really mean anything by that comment, how he was treating me like one of the guys.

Just before we slipped out at sunrise for early setup, I saw Potter and Craig sitting in the hot tub, steam rolling into the orange sunlight. I wondered if all five were like my cousin, at the fringes of our community. I knew some pasty Indians, so I knew it was possible.

"Maybe you can use that tonight," my mom whispered. "If you ask Uncle Dave, nicely."

I didn't explain that I was just watching two friends spending time together. Potter and his friends seemed close, and I didn't have any friends like that since the Wampum Incident. I hung with Rez cousins, but they acted like they were being forced. Would I hang with a jerk if he liked me enough? If I didn't have any other choices?

"Did you put that box on Potter's bed?" my mom asked as we headed to the powwow.

"What's Order of the Arrow?" I asked as we got into the van, knowing I shouldn't have.

"Still being an elephant, huh?" she asked. Big ears, listening, long nose in everyone else's business. Her business this time. Some custom requests were strange. But if it didn't violate ceremony, she was willing. If someone wanted a beadwork Elsa with a beadwork Lion King on a medallion, that was the customer's business. Those commissions generally paid four times regular price. But something about this one bothered her. If it hadn't been for a family member, I'm guessing she might have turned this one down.

"I just wanted to know. If it's so special to him . . ."

"You wanna try a crack at this?" she asked my dad.

He'd been the one to give me a Rez version of the *Now You're a Man* talk: mostly that I had to wear deodorant and shower *thoroughly* every day. The basic version.

"It's a thing he does," my dad started. "*You* have cousins around all the time."

Lucky me. Some older cousins had filled in blanks left from my dad's sketchy "man" talk.

"Potter doesn't have that, but his dad grew up with us, and . . . he wants to belong to an Indian community."

Potter and I each had one enrolled parent, but because

of the way our Nation dealt with enrollment, I'm legally Indian, and he isn't. Uncle Dave knew, when he married a woman who wasn't enrolled, that his kids would never be considered Indian. But you don't get to say who you fall in love with.

"You gonna tell him?" my mom asked, trying to get my dad to tell me something she didn't want to deal with herself.

"It's *your* brother's kid. I think it's yours to do," my dad said.

Suddenly, this got more interesting. Ever since the accident two years ago, my dad usually did anything my mom asked. Our lives were forever changed when he fell off a three-story roof. He called disability insurance his "imaginary friend": it's there, but don't expect much from it when you're really in a tight spot.

When they x-rayed his feet, the doctor said they looked like shattered lightbulbs instead of feet. There weren't any bones to set. It was a long recovery, but he can walk now. Roofing, though, forget it.

"Potter and his . . . friends. They're gonna dance today." I knew this. My mom paused. "Just round dance at the intertribal. His friends aren't Indian."

"That's what intertribals are for, isn't it, though?" I said. "So anyone can dance."

"That's right," she said, "but it's like . . ."

My dad laughed a little. She joke-smacked him and he laughed harder.

"Just show him on your phone," she said.

He typed *Order of the Arrow* into an image search. As I scrolled past that red arrow, the other previews freaked me out: pictures of pasty white boys dressed in confused Indian outfits, like they'd yanked clothes from giant bags labeled *Expensive Indian Costume*.

Some guys even looked spray-tanned an identical color. A few wore black braid wigs and headbands. Almost everyone had bone breastplates. Everyone wore that same arrow bandolier.

Each picture looked like a ridiculous Indian mascot convention, rows and rows of preposterous headdresses and animal-skin hats with giant bull horns attached to the sides. And enough feather bustles that these guys might take flight on a windy day.

"Why are you showing me these weirdos?" I asked. The results reminded me of pictures you see around Halloween—shapely women in tiny fringed bikinis and headdresses, outfits called "Sexy Princess Deluxe." My dad was watching a TV show about something called Burning Man, where I saw wasted-looking people in similar outfits. "And how come no one says anything?"

"People do," my dad said. "Order of the Arrow says they're just honoring Natives and that we should be happy about their love."

"That's bull," I said, and stopped. Suddenly, Potter's room flashed into my mind. On the way here, we had five ribbon shirts, but right now, one was missing: the exact red of the bandolier, with white ribbons. I could see clearly what my parents were telling me, like when steam fades away from the mirror.

We set up at the school and started doing brisk business. My parents silently did Indian Price for certain customers, and I got better at seeing it. No one asked for it, and the only acknowledgment you got was a tiny quick smile. Then that person might bring a friend, who'd also buy something, even just a couple of Jitterbug Men, you know, little men made of big beads and some beadwork wire, guaranteed to hold together as long as you didn't play with them like toys.

Potter and his friends swept through before Grand Entry. He wore the red ribbon shirt and the beaded bandolier. The breechcloth he wore over leggings had a huge arrow pointing up. My parents would *never* put an arrow there, no matter the commission. Uncle Dave said Potter and his friends wanted to have good spots in the stands.

They moved in arrow formation like Canada geese, Craig leading in the center, with two red handprints painted onto his cheeks. Were those Potter's hands? All five crossed their arms rigidly in front of them.

Mostly, they were dressed like the guys on my dad's phone, a mash-up of traditional clothes from a range of Indian nations. One guy's shirt had so many ribbons, it looked like he'd hiked a hula skirt up to his chest. They looked like they'd spray-tanned together before coming. I wondered how that worked with a hot tub. A couple of men followed behind them, in matching khaki outfits, both wearing that bandolier. A third man was dressed in regular clothes. They were following too close to be strangers, so I guessed they were the dads of Potter's friends.

Seeing non-Indians dressing up and participating in intertribals was part of what you signed up for on the circuit. Powwow culture was partly a welcome to all who were interested. But it still felt like someone was putting on a costume of you. Particularly when they sprayed their faces. I'm not sure why that bothered me the most, but it did. Potter's group headed in.

The Plain-Clothes Dad told my mom he'd be back to talk, but he didn't return. We usually heard this when someone wanted to leave the booth without buying something.

The host food vendors cater a big meal on the Saturday for vendors and dancers, but we skipped out so we could spend time together as a family. That's what I was supposed to say, but I couldn't help thinking that it felt like staying with strangers.

I helped set the dinner table. Uncle Dave had planned traditional corn soup ahead, doing the hard prep before we got there. He'd twisted the dried kernels from the cobs, cooked them in wood ashes, and rinsed and rinsed. My mom helped with final steps, adding meat and kidney beans for taste. We'd brought pig knuckles from our butcher. A lot of non-Rez Indians called that poor-people food and used tenderloin, to be fancier, but it never tasted right.

After dinner, Potter and Craig and I cleared the table, and they asked if I wanted to join them in the hot tub again. I ran up to Potter's room to change. His regalia was nowhere in sight. He must have hung it up somewhere else when he switched back into regular clothes.

"Little Man, did you enjoy your first time at the pow-wow here?" Craig asked once we'd settled into the tub. That *Little Man* bit was getting old quick.

"Sure," I said. "It's like some others we go to. They're not all alike, but my mom says a whole bunch have popped up around colleges where Indian kids regularly go."

"So you do this all the time?" he asked eagerly, leaning forward.

"Not *all* the time," I said. "Gotta go to school, get my homework done, and travel to powwows. Sometimes I stay home." I gave a side glance to Potter. He scooped foam, flinging it out. No eye contact.

The whole family knew about the Wampum Incident, and that I hadn't been *allowed* to stay home this time.

"Did you enjoy *your* time at the powwow?" I asked Craig back.

"Sure," he said. "My dad's been taking me most of my life. It's one of the best things we do together. Some of my costumery was my dad's. He jokes that he's too fat for it now. I'm honoring his legacy by wearing it. He didn't stay an Arrowman through the Vigil, but he's encouraging me to stick to it." He scooped foam too.

The foam had brown flecks, like dirty wash water. Craig stood, and his belly and forearms were several shades pinker than his chest and face. They were flicking Tan-in-a-Can flakes that the chlorine had washed off.

"We're gonna have to spray again tomorrow morning," Craig said. "Just in case I decide to go breechcloth only." He grinned. "I'm just kidding, Little Man," he said, climbing out of the tub. Laughing, he yanked up the back of his trunks, giving himself a gross wedgie. "No amount of Savage Tan is going to get rid of these ghostly butt cheeks."

"Get going," Potter said, laughing. "Your dad's expecting you."

"He just wants to show me his OA dance moves," Craig said, rearranging his trunks.

"Promise is a promise," Potter reminded, but not pushy.

"Okay. Seven early enough so we're not rushed?" Potter nodded, and Craig headed in.

"You can go with him," I said. "I'm old enough to stay here alone."

"Never leave anyone alone in a hot tub," Potter said. "We aren't supposed to stay in too much longer anyway."

I started to climb out, but he said, "Wait. Not yet. I wanna talk man to man."

"Don't you mean 'Man to Little Man'?"

"No," he said. "Look, I know Craig can be a lot to take."

I said nothing.

"But you have an entire Rez to hang with. Cousins, non-cousins, all knowing Rez life. I don't have that. My dad talks about his home Rez and my mom talks about hers, and I'm never going to have that. Even when they take us for visits, it's not like I really fit in."

I had to admit, people from home didn't warm up to strangers that fast, even if they knew the stranger had relatives from the Rez.

I also had always thought that because his mom was not enrolled, she'd grown up as a City Indian. Guess I had gaps in family knowledge.

"Neither Rez will ever feel like home to me. OA isn't perfect, and I'm maybe one of the only real Indians in it," he added. I could not stop picturing those spray-tanned boys with face paint, headdresses, and arms folded dramatically across their chests in front of giant bonfires. He sighed, then mumbled, "But it's all I have."

I was surprised he'd had to face homecoming visits on two Reservations, and not surprised that he hadn't found much comfort in either place. Maybe I could make a difference.

"You have me," I said. "We could be a Rez of two." It sounded dumb and I had questions, but mostly, I wanted my cousin to feel like he was home, even if just for a little while.

"And on Sunday, you'll go home and won't have to think about everyone around you not knowing what it means to be Indian." I'd been going to powwows my whole life, and I'd never thought about what it meant for people like Potter.

"But these guys don't know what it means *at all*," I said.

"It's what I've got. If I need someone, they have my back. Know what I mean?"

I did, even though that wasn't even always true at home.

"You know about the Wampum Incident, don't you?" I said.

He sat still for a minute, then looked down at the water and nodded.

I got caught at last summer's National Picnic with a stolen hank of wampum beads. "Well, I'm going to tell you something no one else knows. *I* didn't do it."

Potter looked at me like *oh, sure*. Does anyone ever believe someone they think is a thief? "My friend Garth and me, we were walking the circuit, and he asked me to carry them 'cause his pocket had a hole. I left a little loop visible, so I wouldn't forget. An hour later, the guy who *really* owned the hank was grabbing my arm, accusing me of being a thief. He was even madder 'cause we're both vendors."

"Pretty sure your friend's pocket didn't have a hole," Potter said.

"Gee, I guess you got your Detective Work merit badge," I said, and we laughed. "Garth had stolen the hank off the table."

"Duh. So then what?"

"I claimed I wanted to show my mom to see if she had anything we might trade."

"Well, no one believed that," Potter said.

"I'm thirteen, and for real, pretty honest. Guess I wouldn't get my Lying merit badge."

"They don't have a merit badge for good lying," he said. "*Or* detective work."

"I know. Sorry," I said. "Anyway, the guy didn't believe me, and neither did my mom. She offered him almost anything from our table to trade and forgive. He chose one of her originals, like three times the price on the wampum hang tag, and I'm banned from his booth."

"A jerky move on his part," he said.

"Well, some Indians can be jerks, like anyone else. We're not lugging around noble savage batteries in those high cheekbones we're all supposed to have." He laughed.

At an event like this, they must hear a thousand white people tell about the Indian princess ancestor they found on RoyalHighCheekbones.com. "Anyway, that's part of my punishment."

"Part?"

"When I refused to explain, my mom hung the wampum beads around our booth sign. So now, at every event, I'm reminded. She says I can have the hank when I tell her why I did it. I quit hanging around Garth, but I still can't tell. His family's fierce. She might think she was being a good Rez auntie, telling his parents. But if he was busted, he might really get it."

"Even if he doesn't have your back, you still have his," he said.

"Somebody's gotta," I said. "I kinda see why you hang with Craig . . ."

"But?" he said.

I was so terrible a liar, he could hear my pause. "But *you* don't need spray tan," I said.

"Sometimes you do things for the other person's benefit," he said, like I hadn't just told him about Garth. "Even with costs." I nodded and stood up. Potter suggested that we could both crash in his room, but I volunteered to stay in the man cave, so he could have his room back. The regalia wasn't in the cave, either. He must have hung it somewhere I didn't see. Too bad. I was hoping to secretly try it on.

As the sun rose, my mom was chatty, laughing about things she and Uncle Dave had caught up on. Our inventory was pretty wiped out already, so we were going to have a light day. You'd think we'd break down early, but the only times we did that were when we'd sold out entirely. Then we just enjoyed the powwow. Today, we set up our Plan B for Light Tables. My mom kept examples of her custom work that no one at powwows bought, but that showed her skills. She also had nice-quality photos of other pieces.

As we guessed, not many people stopped at our table. People don't like waiting for things. The powwow T-shirt fundraiser stand was doing great business. The shirts had the powwow logo and dates, and the vendors were smart enough to know some Indians come XXXL. People bought them to support the event and saved them for future birthdays or emergency clothes.

I'd overheard a couple people talking about a *Rez Dawg*

shirt at some other booth. I bet it was way popular, so I might have to settle for a bigger one when I track it down. We lived on Dog Street, so I was a for real Rez Dawg. Made me wish I was still friends with Garth. He'd like that. Maybe I could get him one and be hopeful. It's not like either of us was going to move away. We'd be friends again at some point. You just didn't know when.

Potter and his group showed up before Grand Entry, Craig in the middle again, with the same dads trailing behind. The guys checked out my mom's photos, and our last two ribbon shirts, too small and too big for any of them. They were cream colored, with two purple collar and cuff ribbons, and across the chest, two short streaming ribbons.

This Two Row Wampum design was popular at home. It documented the treaty that maintained us as Nations separate from America. Here, it probably didn't mean much to anyone.

"I like your work," the Plain-Clothes Dad from yesterday said, flipping pieces around and putting them back. My mom nodded. This was part of the dance for him. If the beadwork had tires, he'd kick them. "You do custom work, I see," he added. He then put his arm around Potter's shoulder and brought him closer. "Like Potter's sash here. Beautiful."

"Thank you," she said, curt for her.

"Normally, that's a restricted item," he added. There was always more coming. "Arrowmen may only purchase one from the Scout Trading Post with proof they're Arrowmen."

"Yes," she said. "His parents purchased one. They sent it to me, so I would know exactly the dimensions and details."

We could hear that he was really saying she had no right to use their official patterns without paying for the use. Bead workers flirted with the law of other people's images all the time, like cartoon characters or Batman, hoping no Hollywood lawyers hung out at powwows.

"What's going on, Dad?" Craig said, wandering back from the next booth over.

"Just complimenting Potter's aunt for her crafting skills," the dad said. "Would you like a sash like Potter's?"

"What Arrowman wouldn't wear it with pride?" Craig said. "From a *real* Indian crafter?"

"What would something like that cost?" Craig's dad asked.

Craig hadn't heard the first part of the conversation. "I know it wouldn't be Indian Price," the dad added, which really meant: *I think you should offer me Indian Price.* There was only one way Craig's dad would know what Indian Price was. As before, Potter would not make eye contact with me.

"Are *you* an Arrowman?" I asked Craig's dad. I was no Boy Scout, but this didn't seem like very Scouty behavior to me.

"No, no, young man," he said. I remembered Craig saying something about his dad not finishing some aspect of the process. "We met your uncle and aunt right here at the powwow. Potter and Craig were in Cubs, and I recognized your uncle as a real Indian. We'd never met one in person before, and I thought Craig'd get a real kick. Is it true you live on a Reservation?"

"You gonna round dance with us?" Potter asked me suddenly. You didn't have to wear regalia during intertribals, so I could. But whenever I tried to dance, I wound up one step off. If I paused to catch the rhythm, the person behind me would plow into me, like in a winter car crash.

Potter was giving me subtle Indian Price face signals. He was trying to get Craig's dad to move along before he could begin the dance of angling to lowball my mom.

In return, I bugged my eyes, which you didn't need to be Indian to read as: *I am absolutely not going out there.*

"Only way you learn something is to do it," Potter added. In powwow culture, even the Tiny Tots, little pre-K kids, get familiar with competition by going out in full regalia, and each one gets a token prize from the judges for being brave enough to step into the arena. It was a few bucks, even if they just stood and cried. No matter, it was the beginning of them understanding owning our culture. Moms and aunties ate it up like the ghost bread sweetness it was. Tiny Tots was the only reason some folks came. Getting their dose of cute kids.

"I couldn't teach him when he was younger 'cause of my feet," my dad started. I didn't want him to have to retell that story, particularly in front of strangers.

"Sure, I'll go," I said, getting them out of an awkward situation by placing myself in one.

"Wait," my dad said, reaching for the small ribbon shirt. (We wouldn't be able to sell it if I wore it out there. It would be *used*.) "You won't be alone. I'll be with you in this shirt."

"You'll be with family," my mom added. "We'll be in the stands, watching." She covered our table and put out her *Sorry! Closed* sign to shut down a negotiation she'd feel pressured to lose. "Excuse us," she said to Craig's father. "We have some celebrating to do."

I added up all we were losing. The shirt, the custom job for Craig's dad. Did my family think it was worth it? How often did they have to make decisions about when to walk away, when to compromise to pay the bills, when to accept loss, and when to stand?

"Auntie?" Potter said. "Could Dalton wear that wampum string?" He pointed to the Incident hank.

Thanks a lot, Potter! I thought. "They're meant to

commemorate, right? They could commemorate Dalton's first powwow dance. My mom's got a hank of white ones. Maybe we can make Dalton a string." Potter was doing what he could to help.

"I suppose," my mom said. "Sometimes they come to be known for something different from what they used to. Part of their beauty." Finally, she was maybe thinking about forgiveness.

"Seems like a good change," my dad added as she slid them over my neck.

"Sometimes, a treaty only needs two people," Potter whispered to me as we got to the main floor, flanked by his friends. He reached for my hand. Some powwow round dances involved hand holding. If I took his, I'd also have to take Craig's. I looked at Craig's open palm, where spray tan didn't penetrate.

"You ready, Little Man?" Craig asked as announcements were being made.

"Hang on," I said, and ran to ask my dad if he'd track down that *Rez Dawg* shirt, in large, too big for me. He smiled when I said it was for Potter. I asked him not to take Indian Price. I wanted to pay in full for this little piece of our shared home.

"Ready," I said to Craig when I got back to the floor. "It'll be fun. Let's do it, Pinky."

He frowned, maybe hearing how I didn't like the name

Little Man, but then the frown faded as he repeated his new name, clasped my hand, and we began.

Potter led us into the people to his left, and Craig closed the circle behind us, framed by their other friends, as our families disappeared into a blur of smiling faces in the distance.

SENECAVAJO: ALAN'S STORY

Brian Young

Alan was practicing his dance for the upcoming pow-wow in Michigan on the only basketball courts in Navajo, New Mexico. Although his backyard had more than enough space for his moves, he didn't practice there because his three dogs never got the hint to leave him alone. Inside, there was too much furniture. His knees had many bruises to prove it. But the main reason he didn't want to practice at home was this: two weeks ago his parents told him that he wasn't enrolled with a tribe. They wanted him to choose which tribe he was going to enroll with. His mother explained that through her, he was half-Navajo and could enroll with the Navajo Nation. His father also said that because he was enrolled with the Seneca-Cayuga Nation, Alan could enroll as well. He already knew which nation he wanted to enroll with. But telling his parents the decision was sure to break his mother's heart.

Focusing on his powwow footwork took his mind off his conundrum. His mom wasn't very interested in powwows, but his father was and took every opportunity to immerse Alan in the community. When Alan danced, the drum synced with his heartbeat and he felt his footwork fitting into the footprints of his Seneca-Cayuga ancestors. Not like the Navajo ceremonies that he had been to, where he felt like he didn't fit in.

An older-looking boy stepped onto the other side of the court. Alan did his best to ignore whoever it was. The person walked right up to him, clumsily slapping a basketball in an effort to dribble it. It was Kevin, the jerk in his sixth-grade English class. Kevin had a growth spurt over the summer and became the tallest kid in the grade. He was so tall that he was mistaken for a high schooler—an ugly high schooler. His limbs, however, had outgrown his ability to control his own body, and as a result he was very clumsy.

Kevin mumbled something and stood for an awkward minute before Alan pulled out his Bluetooth earpieces. Alan grumbled to him, "What?"

"Get lost," Kevin responded.

"Use the other side of the court. I'm using this one," Alan said.

Kevin said, "Tough break, Braids. I'm using this one."

Alan put his earphones back in and went back to dancing. Meanwhile, Kevin, in all his derpy glory, couldn't control his limbs and tripped over himself playing on the side of the court. Alan chuckled at how stupid Kevin looked. Enough of that. Alan had to focus, time for freestyle.

At the end of the social song it happened. Kevin slammed his shoulder, intentionally, right into Alan's belly. There was so much pain that Alan's vision went dark.

"Seriously?" Alan yelled. He teared up.

"Ain't my fault you got in my way, Braids," Kevin said, smirking. "Oh, come on. You gonna cry?"

"No!" Alan said. Which was true; his eyes were already drying.

"You gonna be a crybaby?" Kevin said, his buck teeth showing through his smile. A pimple was growing on his forehead.

"Man, forget you!" Alan said. He wanted to say something more adult, but his father had taught him that the best way to deal with bullies was to ignore them. So Alan dusted himself off and left. He could move some furniture around in his living room. Up until the day he and his father left for Michigan, Alan awkwardly danced around the living room and around the topic of his tribal enrollment with his parents.

Alan was nervous the entire drive from his house to Albuquerque and the long flight from Albuquerque to Detroit. His mother thankfully decided to stay at home to feed the dogs. His father didn't once ask about enrollment during the drive from the airport to Skyline High School. Broad-leaved trees branched out like green umbrellas, and wind created ripples on the dark blue lake on the side of the highway. A few tall skyscrapers emerged from the green and blue, indicating where downtown Ann Arbor was. By the time they got to Skyline, Alan was certain that his father wasn't going to ask, and he was able to calm down.

His father parked their rental car in the vast parking lot. Alan and his father put on their regalia in the boys' locker room. His father's regalia had colors of the medicine wheel (black, red, yellow, and white), while his own were electric blue and green. Alan put on his turquoise moccasins, which matched his regalia. They navigated to the hard-floor gymnasium and passed other dancers. It felt so great to be back on the dance floor. Here, no one teased him for his long, braided hair or rammed their shoulders into his gut.

He put on his favorite playlist and practiced his dance moves at the outer edge. He sat down, exhausted, and drank a sports drink. Four fancy dancers, about his age, who Alan had noticed out on the floor approached. Alan sighed. There were bullies everywhere, he assumed.

"You got moves," said the oldest-looking. Facial hair poked out of his chin.

The one with the newest regalia playfully slugged his shoulder. "Hope I'm not competing against you."

"I don't see you on the circuits!" another said, his braids touching his skinny shoulders.

"What's your name?" the last, with short spiked hair, asked.

"How long you been dancing?" the oldest asked.

It felt like for every question he answered, five more were asked. They told one another what tribes they were, and like Alan, they came from multiple tribes. But they had been enrolled when they were born. *It must be nice to already be enrolled*, Alan thought. The stress of his enrollment status constricted his throat.

He told them he was from Navajo, New Mexico, and that he got into powwow competitions with his father, who was originally from Oklahoma. The boy with spiky hair came from Maine! The others, like his dad, were Oklahomans. The oldest was named Jordan. Alan didn't catch the other names.

"Noticed you don't have dance bells. Wanna borrow mine?" Jordan asked.

"What? Ah, shoot! I left them in the car. Where are you guys sitting?" Alan said.

"Over there." They pointed. "We'll keep a seat for ya."

Alan smiled. "Cool." He ran to his father to grab the rental car keys. He wanted to get back quickly. He was making friends.

Alan searched high and low, in between seats, in the trunk, and in the glove compartment for his ankle bells. He hoped he hadn't forgotten them at home. Last place he decided to check was underneath his seat. Lo and behold, he heard jingling and felt the smooth exterior of the bells. He squeezed them in his hands, shot up, and locked the rental car. He hurried back to the gymnasium. The bells jingled loudly as he navigated through the lanes of trucks and cars.

Suddenly, someone shouted, "Hey!" and ran right into the back of his shoulders. Alan tumbled down onto the pavement.

"Braids! Seriously?" a familiar voice said. Alan immediately knew who it was. How in the world was this jerk here? He wondered what deity he had pissed off to deserve this.

"Ugh, it's just you," Alan scoffed, getting up.

"Watch where you're going!" Kevin snapped at him. Since Alan had last seen Kevin, a volcano-size pimple had popped up right smack in the middle of his right cheek. Served him right.

"Whatever," Alan said, turning his back to him.

"Hey, I'm sorry about running into you," Kevin said.

Alan raised an eyebrow. There was only one reason why Kevin was being nice to him. "What do you want?"

"What are you talking about?" Kevin said. The fakest of smiles spread across his face. It was uncomfortable to look at.

"I ain't helping you," Alan said.

"I need your help, Braids. Please, you're the only person I know here."

Alan waited a few seconds before he said no. He wanted Kevin's hopes up so that it would hurt that much more.

"I'll do anything," Kevin said.

"Anything? Like leave me alone at school?"

"Won't even look at you," Kevin said.

Making new friends and getting Kevin to leave him alone at school; could this powwow get any better? "Fine. What do you need me to do?"

Kevin smiled and told Alan about accidentally selling a really expensive bracelet to a pretty jingle dress dancer for cheap. If he didn't get it back soon, his mom would definitely yell at him and possibly spank him even at his age. Regardless, they had to find the jingle dress dancer. Alan suggested they split up, he on the dance floor, Kevin in the parking lot. That way Alan wouldn't have to be near him.

Alan didn't spend much time looking. Kevin hadn't

given him much to work with. A pretty jingle dress dancer. Plenty of them. Pink dress. Okay. There were at least ten of them. It was also almost time for his group to dance. The older age group was dancing, and his division would come up in an hour and a half. His dad was probably on the floor right now.

He met back up with the guys at the dancing circle. They were stretching, and Alan slipped right in with them.

"Hey, guys," he started.

"What's up?" Jordan said.

"This guy from my school is here, and he has to find a jingle dress dancer," Alan said. "You wouldn't happen to have seen her, our age, pink jingle dress, apparently pretty?"

"Not around here," Jordan said. "Why?"

"She bought a pretty expensive bracelet for twenty bucks, and the seller wants it back," Alan said.

"That's a good deal," another dancer said.

"It was a mistake. I don't know. I said I'd help him," Alan said.

"Your friend—" Jordan started.

"He's not my friend," Alan interrupted. The mere thought of being Kevin's friend made him want to vomit.

"—should wait for the Jingle Dress competition," Jordan said.

"When is it?" Alan asked.

"Tomorrow," Jordan said.

That was good enough for Alan. Tomorrow, Kevin could see all the jingle dress dancers in one spot. Alan got up.

"Heading out already?" Jordan said.

"Yeah. I'm going to cash in on a favor," Alan said, smiling. Kevin now had to leave him alone for the rest of his life!

"Want us to spread the word?" Jordan shouted.

"Sure. Couldn't hurt." Alan said. Jordan and the guys began texting on their phones.

Somehow, Alan got dragged into helping Kevin tell his mom what had happened. Although he didn't want to go, Alan figured he could learn a few things about telling mothers devastating things by observing Kevin.

Alan followed Kevin back to the vendor area. He snuck a few looks here and there to see what was on sale. There was a handsome jacket that he really liked. It had geometric designs in black and gray leather. Later, he would tell his dad he wanted one for his birthday. He looked at a nearby stand and saw a dog wearing a shirt that said *Ancestor Approved*.

"All right, I just need you to smile and hang out for like—" Kevin started.

"Hang out? Man, I need to—" Alan said.

"Five minutes, max. By that time, she'll have absorbed most of the shock."

"I kind of want to see her freak out on you," Alan said. A slight smile crossed his face.

"Shut up, Braids," Kevin said, chuckling a little.

It sounded like Kevin was joking with him. Never in a million years had Alan thought that he would be joking with jerky Kevin. They approached his mom, who was reading a book.

"Ma, I got something to tell you," Kevin said. He extended his arms and held out a massive fry bread burger.

"Oh no, this burger has all the fixings. Must be bad." She sat upright, placing the book down. "Lay it on me."

"You tell her," Kevin said to Alan.

"What?" Alan felt bullets of sweat forming on his forearms and forehead. A flash of his own mom's face sprang to mind. He froze. Terror took the breath from his airway.

"Just tell her," Kevin said.

Alan shook himself and regained his senses. "She's your mom."

"Kevin?" his mom said. "Kevin. Look me in the eye."

Her expression turned sour. She folded her arms across her chest. His own mom wouldn't have this posture. She would collapse from the hurtful knowledge that Alan wanted to be Seneca-Cayuga and not Navajo. Alan's palms became sweaty just watching Kevin tell his mom what had happened.

". . . I just need a little more time! I'm sorry. I let you down." Kevin's head hung low like a lifeless puppet's. His mom looked mad and then, surprisingly, laughed. Still, her laughter had a note of anger.

"Oh! You're in trouble, little man," his mom said, through bits of sinister laughter. "You are in big trouble."

"She does this when she's about to lay the smackdown," Kevin whispered to Alan.

"Oh, this is much bigger than a smackdown," Kevin's mom said. Her laughter stopped and she got serious. "I'm talking chores all day, every day, twenty-four-seven. I'm talking no friends, no television! Now, first tell me why I punish you."

"You punish me because you love me," Kevin said.

"Now, get the bracelet back. Seriously. Go," Kevin's mom said. She opened her book again.

Kevin turned to Alan and patted his shoulder. "Man, I owe you one."

"Huh, what?" Alan said. "No problem." Maybe Kevin could give him tips on how to approach his own mother about tribal registration. "Hey, I need to tell my mom something, and I could use some help."

"What you gotta tell her?"

"A few weeks ago, they asked me if I want to—"

"I don't need backstory, just tell me what you gotta tell her."

"I have to tell her that I want to register with the Seneca-Cayuga Nation and not the Navajo Nation."

"What? Hold up. All right, I think I need the backstory on this one."

Alan explained his situation to Kevin while they walked to the main floor. In all the time that Alan had endured Kevin, he'd never thought he would be asking him for advice.

"And you can't enroll with both?" Kevin asked.

"Nope. Seneca-Cayuga Nation does do dual enrollment. But the Navajo Nation doesn't," Alan said. "I already know which one I want."

"Does that mean you can only be one?"

"What do you mean?"

"Like if you are Seneca, can you even go to Navajo ceremonies?" Kevin asked. He squeezed his chin.

"I don't know!" Alan hadn't even considered that. Were there other consequences he didn't know about?

"I don't know; you're the Senecavajo here, not me!" Kevin said.

"Senecavajo?"

"Half-Seneca-Cayuga. Half-Navajo."

"Never mind," Alan said. "I just need to tell my mom."

"I got it. Practice on me. Come on. Call me Mom and everything." Kevin smiled. He slapped Alan's shoulder playfully.

"What? Okay. Mother?"

"Yes, my baby boy?" Kevin said, forcing his voice to a higher octave. "I will love you no matter what you tell me." In his normal voice, "Go on."

"I want to enroll as Seneca-Cayuga."

"Oh, good heavens, no! My entire worldeth hath falleth apart!" Kevin yelled. Everyone glanced in his direction.

Hot blood flushed Alan's forehead. "Dude, shut up! My mom's not British!"

Kevin continued, "How couldeth you? I gaveth thee life and this is how you repayeth me!"

Alan looked to the ground, thoroughly embarrassed.

"How do you feel?" Kevin asked in his normal voice.

"Like getting away from you," Alan said.

"See! You're no longer scared!" Kevin said.

"Nope, still scared and also embarrassed by you," Alan said.

"Give your mom some credit, man. She's an adult," Kevin said.

Something clicked in Alan. His mom *was* an adult. It

was the stupidest and simplest realization he had. Thinking of his mom as an adult made telling her a little bit easier.

"Hey, Alan!" Jordan shouted in the middle of the floor. "Our section is up!"

"Let me know how it goes!" Kevin said.

"Okay. Thanks," Alan said, rushing to meet with Jordan and the others.

On the drive back from the airport to Navajo, New Mexico, Alan wasn't disappointed that he hadn't placed in any of the categories that he'd danced. He had made several new friends. While he felt great, a deep anxiety chewed on his happiness, threatening to swallow his newfound confidence. To get rid of this ugly feeling, he would have to tell his mother his decision.

When his father drove into their driveway, Alan's heart was beating so loud he was surprised his father didn't hear it. Sizzling beads of sweat rolled down his temples.

Then he got a text. It was from Kevin. **Don't chicken out! Speak up!** His heart slowed down and didn't bump up against his rib cage as hard.

At dinner, Alan tried to eat and be invisible. The weight of his decision thickened the atmosphere. His forehead grew hot and foggy, like he was in a sweat lodge. His mother sat in front of him with a wide smile, while his father told her what happened in Michigan. She wore her faded sweatshirt from Haskell Indian Nations University, where she and his father had met.

He looked down at the Hamburger Helper on his plate. It was his favorite, triple cheeseburger with diced green chili.

"So, is this something you want to get serious with?" his father said.

"Huh?" Alan said.

"Powwow. Is this something you want to do competitively?" his father said.

"Everything all right?" his mother asked.

"Yeah," Alan said. He sounded more annoyed than he intended.

"You don't sound fine," his mother said.

"Well, I am." Alan just couldn't tell her. Not when she was looking right into his eyes. He was going to break her heart.

"What's on your mind? You don't eat when you have something on your mind," his mother said, pointing at the barely touched plate in front of him.

Alan had been backed into a corner, betrayed by Hamburger Helper. If he said he wanted to enroll with the Seneca-Cayuga, would that mean he couldn't be Navajo? Would that mean he would be less like his mother? He looked at her. He hated that he would be the one to shatter her pretty smile. Even though it scared him, Alan had to speak up. He forced the bitter words out of his mouth. "I want to enroll with the Seneca-Cayuga Nation!"

That did it. Alan thought her smile melted into a deep frown. Meanwhile, his father stood up and started clapping.

His mother folded in half and held a hand over her lips. To him, it looked like she was going to cry.

"I'm sorry, Mom," Alan said.

She didn't smile, but she calmly looked at him. His father, completely unaware of the two of them, was too busy dancing around the kitchen.

"Honey, why are you apologizing?" she asked. She reached out and held his hand.

"Huh? You aren't devastated?" Alan said.

"Devastated! Jeez, no!" She squeezed his hand.

"But this means I'm not Navajo and won't be able to go to any ceremonies," Alan said.

His father stopped dancing and singing. His mother let go of his hand. She looked at his father and nodded.

"Son," his father said. "You are still Navajo. Enrolling with the Seneca-Cayuga Nation doesn't make you less Navajo. You're still allowed to go to Navajo ceremonies. And you still should. Because that's as much a part of you as the sweat lodge is."

"Honey," his mother said. "Understand this. You are Navajo. You are Seneca-Cayuga. But above everything, you are you."

"We love you, son, no matter which nation you enroll with. But thank the Creator you chose the best one!" his father said, laughing and dancing again.

"Oh, hush!" his mother said, playfully rolling her eyes.

Alan scooped some food into his mouth, and the Hamburger Helper tasted absolutely delicious!

SQUASH BLOSSOM BRACELET: KEVIN'S STORY

BRIAN YOUNG

The Tuesday of his spring break, Kevin was bored out of his mind. All his friends had gone away, and at home his mom was finishing the squash blossom bracelet that she was going to sell at the upcoming Michigan powwow. He walked to the only basketball court in his small northern New Mexico town, dribbling a smooth faded ball.

Someone was already on the concrete courts. He was powwow dancing. Kevin automatically knew he was going to annoy Alan, who was in his sixth-grade English class. Every single thing Alan did got on Kevin's nerves. For example, Alan breathed through his mouth and chewed gum like a goat. He didn't have any friends and sat alone during lunch. Kevin wasn't going to allow Alan to dance on the court. As far as he was concerned, basketball courts were for basketball. End of story.

"Move," Kevin said to Alan, stepping onto the crumbling concrete.

Alan pulled out his Bluetooth earpieces. "What?"

"Get lost," Kevin said, annoyed.

"Use the other side of the court. I'm using this one," Alan said, pointing.

It didn't matter that the other court had fewer cracks. Alan had to understand who was in charge. Kevin responded, "Tough break, Braids. I'm using this one." He shot his ball at the netless rim.

Alan went back to his dancing. Kevin, then, swung his elbows wide, hoping to whack Alan. Alan crouched low and held out his arms like a stupid bird.

Kevin knew very little of powwows, attending them only to help his mom sell jewelry. He didn't need powwows because he had Navajo ceremonies. Powwows were an "Indian" thing, and Kevin was no "Indian." He was Navajo.

Kevin launched the ball at the backboard. It rebounded with a thunderous clap. Just as planned, it bounced toward Alan, who was completely concentrating on his dancing. Kevin charged. Alan opened his eyes seconds before Kevin slammed his shoulder right into Alan's stomach.

"Seriously?" Alan said, in between loud gasps for breath.

"Ain't my fault you got in my way, Braids," Kevin said, smirking. "Oh, come on. You gonna cry?"

"No!" Alan said, his eyes red and wet.

"You gonna be a crybaby?" Kevin said.

"Man, forget you!" Alan said. He stood up and walked toward the nearby orange plateaus, where Navajo Housing Authority houses were. With Alan out of sight, Kevin shot a few hoops with a satisfied smile.

Kevin's mom woke him up when she parked their beat-up car outside Skyline High School, which was hosting the University of Michigan powwow. There were already hundreds of cars and trucks in the parking lot. There were old, busted Rez vehicles with doughnut spares and door panels that didn't match the color of the main car body. There were even Benzes that gleamed in the gentle spring sun. Kevin helped his mom carry the jewelry carts to their booth location. On their way, they passed a group of excited Elders taking pictures of the eagle statue in the rotunda. A bored-looking boy sighed, waiting for them to finish their photos.

After they set up their jewelry booth, his mom settled into reading while he scanned the powwow brochure. The front flap had a picture of the current and very pretty Miss Indian World, who was a guest judge. Grand Entry was scheduled in an hour.

He looked around. There were so many people it looked like an agitated anthill. Some people wore elaborate and colorful powwow regalia. He saw some pretty girls in jingle dresses; every step they took, the tiny jingles rang like little bells. A group of male dancers, some his age, wore enormous white hoops around their brown necks. Everyone was excited to be there.

Kevin felt a twinge of jealousy. He loved going to Navajo ceremonies, but his friends didn't.

He recognized one of the dancers in blue-and-green regalia. The familiarity came more from the way he walked and moved. The guy's feet shuffled like a duck's. His neck jutted forward like he was a T. rex. It was Alan.

Kevin lifted the brochure to shield him from Alan's stupid face. When he was sure that Alan had passed, he lowered the brochure. He hoped that was the last and only time he would have to see that face.

Dancing started. Sales slowed because everyone was watching the competitions. Kevin's mom had fallen asleep, her book over her eyes. Kevin was about to wake her up so he could go to the food court when a pretty girl, his age, in a pink jingle dress came to the booth.

Kevin lost his ability to speak. Two long braids pulled her hair apart. Silver cones on her dress twinkled with her steps. Her moccasins were sky turquoise, like the tiny feathers that adorned her dangling earrings. She looked at the squash blossom bracelet with the turquoise heart.

The pretty girl said some words that Kevin couldn't understand. So he said the only word he knew at that moment: "Sure." She smiled!

She then handed him a twenty-dollar bill, took the squash blossom bracelet, and walked away. She turned back to smile before disappearing around a corner. Kevin's cheeks cooled down and his head stopped spinning.

His mom woke and closed the book. Stretching, she noticed that the bracelet was gone.

"Oh, you sold the squash blossom heart?" she said.

"Yeah," Kevin said, his voice airy, wishing the pretty jingle dress dancer would return.

"This early?" She looked happily surprised. "Big pricers don't sell until after award money has been handed out."

Big pricers! Kevin looked at the price tag where the bracelet had been: $750.00! He crushed the twenty dollars that the jingle dancer had handed him. Hot guilt squeezed the air out of his lungs.

"Good job, shiyazhi," his mom said.

"Yeah, awesome job, me. Woo," Kevin said. He chuckled to hide his nerves. "Should make me your manager."

"Keep it up and I'll think about it. Hey, you hungry?"

"Starving," Kevin said, his thoughts far from food. He had to get the bracelet back!

"Why don't I go get us something from the food court?" his mom said, standing.

"I'll get it! You just sit here and, you know, sell the stuff, at the price they're listed at."

"Weirdo. Everything all right?"

"Everything's cool. Nothing's off."

"All right. What did you do?" She folded her arms and stared directly into his eyes. Her gaze could terrify a demon.

Despite his best efforts, Kevin looked at the empty space where the bracelet had been. "There was this girl . . ."

"You met a girl?" she asked. Her lips curved into a smirk.

That was way too close! He said, "Yes! She was a she. And I met her. She and I did the meeting while you were sleeping."

"You're a bit young for girls, mister." She shook her head. "We're having 'the talk' on our drive back."

Kevin sighed; anything to keep her distracted. His heart rate calmed and his body temperature chilled. "I'm not young anymore, Mom. I'm practically a teenager."

"My baby is growing up. If you run into her, buy her some food, too. Be all chivalrous and stuff."

"Yeah, I'll be 'shivyrus.'" Kevin took off, desperately scanning the crowd for pink jingle dresses and turquoise moccasins.

Kevin guessed he had a few minutes before his mom sus-pected something. He didn't want to tell her what had happened. But if he wasn't able to get the bracelet back, he would have to 'fess up. And if he didn't tell her, his punish-ment was going to be even worse when she found out. And she always found out.

He started at the food court. There weren't many peo-ple. He heard a jingling, like a ring full of keys. He turned, and immediately saw a jingle dress. However, it was green. His hope evaporated.

"Man, why can't all the jingle dress dancers just be in one place?" Kevin said. He ran his fingers through his hair. He decided to check the parking lot.

He jogged up and down the lanes and in between the vehicles. But there were no dancers. No fancy, no grass, no nothing.

Something jingled! He darted toward the noise. He sprinted down the row of vehicles. He caught a glimpse of blue moccasins stepping behind a tall van. Kevin dashed. There was more jingling. This was it! He had found her!

"Hey!" Kevin shouted as he rounded the corner. A cloud of pain exploded as he slammed his face into the back of someone. The person fell to the ground. Red flashes popped like fireworks in his vision. Slowly, they blurred away and he was able to see who was in front of him. "Braids! Seriously?"

"Ugh, it's just you," Alan scoffed.

"Watch where you're going!" Kevin snapped.

"Whatever." Alan grabbed a leather strip that had bells sewn into it. It jingled with every movement as he stood back up.

Kevin wanted to make Alan cry, but he didn't have much time. As much as he hated it, he would have to ask Alan for help.

"Hey, I'm sorry about running into you," Kevin said. The apology tasted like vinegar.

Alan raised an eyebrow, then said, "What do you want?"

"What are you talking about?" Kevin said, forcing a smile.

"I ain't helping you."

Kevin closed his eyes and summoned happy thoughts so he wouldn't push Alan back down. "I need your help, Braids. Please, you're the only person I know here."

Alan was considering.

"I'll do anything," Kevin said.

"Anything? Like leave me alone at school?"

"Won't even look at you," Kevin said. This actually wasn't that bad a deal. The less he dealt with Alan, the better for him, too.

"Fine. What do you need me to do?"

Kevin smiled and told Alan everything.

They searched different areas, Kevin outside, Alan on the dance floor. A good while passed, and Kevin was no closer to finding the pretty jingle dress dancer. Kevin stood in front of World's Best Fry Bread, which sold Navajo burgers, his mom's favorite. It was looking like he was going to have to tell his mom what had happened if Alan came back with nothing.

Maybe he could get Alan to stick around while he told his mom. Having him nearby would cool her rage.

Alan walked into view. From his question-mark posture, Kevin guessed that Alan hadn't been successful. He said, "I couldn't find her. The Jingle Dress competition is tomorrow. You can find her then."

"Tomorrow's no good," Kevin said. His mom counted profits at the end of every day. She'd find out then. It was time to bite the bullet and fess up. "You gotta be my wingman. Ain't no way I'm fessing up to my mom alone."

"I gotta get ready."

"You leave now and I'll punch you every day at school," Kevin said.

"Fine." Alan rolled his eyes. "I hope she gets really mad at you."

"Of course she'll be mad. I can handle that. What really gets me is when I disappoint her. She has this look." It was heartbreaking. "Same look she gave my dad when he left. Absolutely hate it. Know what I mean? Never mind, you can't."

"Why?" Alan said.

"Huh?" Kevin responded.

"Why can't I understand?"

"Dude, you have both your parents. They have steady jobs."

"Yeah, so?"

"You got it easy. You always have the cleanest and nicest clothes."

"Because I don't look a certain way doesn't mean I don't know how to work."

"You ever chop wood for winter?"

"No."

"Case in point. Hey," Kevin said to the vendor, an older woman with grease spots on her forearms. "One green chili Navajo cheeseburger."

"Oh, an Indian burger?" the vendor lady asked.

"Navajo burger," Kevin corrected her.

"I work," Alan said bitterly.

Alan was getting riled up. Kevin responded, "Did I say something?"

"Yeah. You think that I don't have my own issues that

I deal with," Alan said. "Think about what you say and try to be a little understanding. Some of what you say is hurtful."

Kevin had to really bite his tongue. If anything, Alan should toughen up! If something hurt his feelings, then tough luck for Alan. Not everything was happy-go-lucky. Kevin took a deep breath and instead said, "Speak up, then. If I say something you think isn't cool, say something."

Alan looked like he was deep in thought. Kevin gave the vendor the money. She, in turn, handed him a piping-hot green chili Navajo cheeseburger. It was now or never.

Kevin led Alan back to his mom's booth. The air in his lungs went cold when he saw his mom. He said to Alan, "All right, I just need you to smile and hang out for like—"

"Hang out? Man, I need to—"

"Five minutes, max. By that time, she'll have absorbed most of the shock."

"I kind of want to see her freak out on you," Alan said. A slight smile crossed his face.

"Shut up, Braids," Kevin said, chuckling a little. Had the two of them just joked? His mom saw him.

"Ma, I got something to tell you," Kevin said. He extended his arms and held out the massive plump fry bread burger.

"Oh no, this has all the fixings. Must be bad." She sat

upright. "Lay it on me."

"You tell her," Kevin said to Alan.

"What?"

"Just tell her," Kevin said.

"She's your mom."

"Kevin?" his mom said. "Kevin. Look me in the eye."

Slowly, Kevin looked in her eyes. Her expression was sour, her arms folded across her chest.

He took a big breath. "I sold the squash blossom heart for twenty dollars to this really pretty girl!" Kevin spoke so quickly that he was surprised the words were clear. "She just kept smiling and smiling and I got distracted and she gave me twenty for it. I've been trying to get it back! I just need a little more time! I'm sorry. I let you down."

She looked mad, then started laughing, something she did when she was super angry in public. "Oh! You're in trouble, little man. You are in big trouble," his mom said, through bursts of enraged laughter.

Alan looked really confused. Kevin whispered to him, "She does this when she's about to lay the smackdown."

"Oh, this is much bigger than a smackdown," Kevin's mom said. Her laughter stopped and she got serious. "I'm talking chores all day, every day, twenty-four-seven. I'm talking no friends, no television! Now, first tell me why I punish you."

"You punish me because you love me," Kevin said.

"Now, get the bracelet back. Seriously. Go," Kevin's mom said. She opened her book again.

Kevin turned to Alan and patted his shoulder. "Man, I owe you one."

"Huh, what?" Alan said. "No problem." He again looked like he was thinking, then said, "Hey, I need to tell my mom something, and I could use some help."

"What you gotta tell her?"

"A few weeks ago, they asked me if I want to—"

"I don't need backstory, just tell me what you gotta tell her."

"I have to tell her that I want to register with the Seneca-Cayuga Nation and not the Navajo Nation."

"What? Hold up. All right, I think I need the backstory on this one."

After Alan told him of his enrollment situation, he left for his dance division. Kevin searched through the crowd for jingle dresses by himself. His feet throbbed and ached from all his walking. He went to the outer rim of the main arena to scan the entire crowd. Down on the main floor, he saw Alan dancing with a grace that other dancers didn't have.

When Alan danced among the others, he was no longer a loner. The entire group swelled and shrank, rose and fell, paused and continued together. They weren't individuals, they were all a singular entity. And Alan fit right in.

The captivated audience members bobbed their heads and waved their feathers in beat with the drum. Kevin wished that he could see this same excitement for the traditional Navajo ceremonies. Often, he was the only youngster surrounded by Elders. He was the loner. Maybe that was why he didn't like Alan. Because by participating in pow-wow, Alan wasn't participating in the traditional Navajo ceremonies. Even if he was going to register with the Seneca-Cayuga Nation, Alan was still Navajo, too. Alan should still honor that part of himself.

Then again, where were Kevin's friends at the Ndaa' ceremonies, at the Ye'ii Bichei? At least Alan was honoring a part of himself.

Someone tapped his shoulder. Surprised, Kevin spun around. It was her! The pretty jingle dress dancer! She smiled and he lost all his senses again.

Her expression changed, like she was awaiting a response.

Kevin shook his head. "What?"

"You're looking for me, right?" she said. Her voice was lyrical and airy. "Jordan told me you're looking for me."

"Who? Never mind. I actually need the bracelet back."

"Oh." Her expression went from happy to sad. "I thought it was too good a deal. I actually left it back in my car."

"I just realized I used your twenty for a Navajo burger."

Kevin rubbed the back of his neck, smiled shyly. She blushed. Before his senses could go soft again, he said, "Hey, would you wanna meet up later? I can get money and we'll switch?"

"I don't know. I did buy it fair and square," she said in a playful tone.

"I'm sorry." Heat spread across his forehead and his cheeks tingled from smiling.

"Well, this sucks. It was going to be a gift for Elisi."

"I can ask my mom to make another one. One specifically for Alice-y."

She laughed. "Elisi. My grandma. Her birthday is in a week."

"Oh, yeah, it's gonna take more than a week. "

"All right. My section is coming up next. Here, text your number with my phone," she said, handing her phone to him.

Kevin wrote his name and number in her phone and texted himself. He felt his phone vibrate in his pocket.

"Kevin," she said.

"Yup, that's me."

"I'm Joyce." She twirled and walked away. With every step, the glimmering jingles on her dress chimed and twinkled.

❖

The week after the powwow, Kevin's mom had him doing chores every day and prohibited him from hanging out with his friends. Thankfully, she didn't take away his cell phone and he was able to chat with Joyce, who had returned to Oklahoma City.

Today, he had cleaned so well that his mom relaxed enough on his punishment to allow him to play basketball. She also wanted some space and silence while she made a new bracelet for an upcoming powwow. He was practicing his three-point shot when Alan approached the court. He stopped and watched Alan.

"How did the talk go?" Kevin asked.

"Better than I thought," Alan said.

"Nice." Kevin dribbled and shot again.

Alan stood on one foot and did ankle circles, warming up.

"Do you want this side of the court? Fewer pebbles."

"If you don't mind."

"No, I don't mind." Kevin dribbled the ball and moved to the other side of the court and shot again.

Alan put in his earphones and found his footing and rhythm. Every so often, the ball would rebound off the backboard and bounce to Alan. Alan would grab the ball and pass it back to Kevin.

JOEY READS THE SKY

Dawn Quigley

"Joey, pay attention to what you're doing!" some people say.

"Joey, stop staring out the window!" still others say.

Every day . . . well, most days, I hear people yelling things like this to me. At school, at home, and even at my mom's World's Best Fry Bread stand.

Why would the fry bread stand be any different?

Chop, chop, chop. That's my job at the fry bread stand. I don't get to make the dough or fry it. I don't get to take the customer orders. Don't even think I get to handle the money. I chop the fry bread toppings: lettuce and tomatoes. Sometimes, I even get to grate the cheese. Yep, you could say I have the most important job. But then you'd be lying.

Most weekends it costs my mom a couple hundred dollars to rent the vendor space on the powwow trail for our table, but, like I said, we're the World's Best Fry Bread, so we usually make that back within the first two hours.

"Joey, pay attention to what you're doing!"

"Joey, stop staring out the window!"

My big brothers are always yelling at me. But I sort of lose track of time a lot. Like when I'm looking out the windows at the sky instead of working. Which is why my brothers are yelling at me to get chopping again.

They're not all bad, my brothers. Listin, the oldest, will cuff Makwa when he gets too rough with me. Makwa's only two years older than me, but at school he's always looking out for me. So, they're okay. Just annoying most of the time. And usually I annoy Listin. And Makwa.

We got here to Ann Arbor Thursday night and set up our food stand at the powwow. It wasn't too bad of a drive from Minneapolis, but spending over ten hours in the car with my older brothers, who *love* to eat nacho cheese chips and drink Mountain Dew, well, let's just say the gas from them probably helped fuel half the trip. We only hit some snow driving around Chicago, but hey, it's March in the Midwest. It can be sunny and seventy here, or slippery, snowy, and six below zero. Only the strong make it here. Ayyyyyyyyyy!

The two things I love about road trips on the powwow trail are getting away from school for a few days (more on that next) and looking out my mom's old Chevy Equinox sunroof (more on that later). But most times my brothers make me shut the sunroof shade. I want to look out and up. They want it dark to nap. Guess who wins?

Yeah, getting out of school yesterday was awesome. It's not that I don't like school. It's that I *hate* it. I'm in the fourth grade at Four Winds Native American Magnet School. It's where my mom works as the lunch lady. Lunch Lady Lana.

Yep, that's my mom. She's raising me and my two older brothers alone after my dad died last year from cancer. My dad was really quiet, but he was our guiding star. Without him, we lost our way a bit. I think we'll always miss his way of showing us how to find where to go. And how to get there. I know I will.

I used to go to another school across town, but 'cause my dad's gone, my mom wanted us all to be closer to ride to and from school. At first, I was excited to go to a Native school, you know, me being Turtle Mountain Ojibwe and all, but then . . . well, then I got put in a remedial reading class.

You don't sign up for the remedial reading class. You're *sentenced* to it. Sentenced by the English teacher, the guidance counselor, the principal, or any adult in the school who feels you're not "achieving."

You got a D- in English? Off to the elephant graveyard of the remedial reading class! Hmm, a C- in science? To the far corners of the wasteland of the school for you!

To fit this class into a student's schedule, another class has to be dropped: gym, art, music, Native language. You know, the *good* classes. The only positive thing about the class is that I get to sit next to the window. Perfect spot to sky gaze.

It isn't that I *can't* read. No, it's that I can read the *wrong* things. The things that schools don't care about. Seems like there's only one way to read. Why?

Also, my school is not just a school Native kids go to. Anyone in the city can go to it. So there's mostly Native kids, but some non-Natives. This goes for teachers, too. Most are Native, but there's just not enough Indian teachers. Yet.

I guess I just don't match everyone's opinion of what a Native American is supposed to be. Some non-Natives think Indians are braid-wearing, feather-holding, horse-riding types. Of course, I'm . . . well, just Joey. My own self. I don't have an issue with how I'm being Native, but I don't think there's one way to be Native.

Being the youngest brother, I'm usually the butt of the jokes in my family (of course that's what my brothers say). And most of the punches, noogies, and pranks, too. I guess it doesn't help that I have a weird habit sometimes of tilting my head up sideways toward the sky—while squinting one eye. Okay, I do this most days.

It all sort of started two years ago when I came back from spending the summer with my relatives on the Reservation back in North Dakota and began using Ojibwe words in class and at home. I think I was good with the language. Really good.

I'd never been really good at anything, until then. The language made *sense* to me. I could even *feel* it in the air, and in the sky. Looking at the world through the Ojibwe language, things finally started to make sense.

But some of the other kids at school, and of course my brothers, didn't like this new knowledge I had. And they let me know it.

"Eya, *yes*, you punched me pretty hard in the gut this time!"

"Miigwech, *thank you*, for not throwing all my lunch in the garbage."

One of my teachers, Ms. Franken, didn't like the new Joey saying things she didn't understand. Yesterday, before we left for powwow, she asked if I'd finished my book report.

"Gaawiin, *no*, I didn't finish my homework."

"Humph, do you *ever* do it, Joey? *Can* you ever do it? Why are you even learning a foreign language, anyway?"

Ms. Franken huffed.

"Actually," I answered with a subtle sweet smile, "I'm speaking my foreign language *now*, English. The land we're standing on is Indigenous land, so which language is the foreign one?"

"Well, I, errr, humph!"

Kind of stinks that a teacher at our Native school acts this way about the language that was spoken on this land long before her people were here.

A Native school is usually a place to really be ourselves— to not have to explain every little thing about our history, language, and culture. Like, having to explain what "init?" means makes it lose its purpose. And that's bad. Init?

At my last school, well, I hated it. Not only was my dad sick, but I missed a lot of school so we could all be with him. But one prank still gets to me—when the biggest jock in the school spray-painted all over my locker: *CHIEF*.

And I read it (Joey-style), turned to him, smiled, and said, "Hey, how did you know I might want to cook when I grow up?"

That was what pretty much did me in. Everyone knew it right then. I couldn't read.

Of course my brothers heard about it, and . . . "Chief" is my new nickname. A Native chief is a leader of a tribe or band, someone to look up to. My brothers love me (or at least our mom says they *have* to), so I get that they're not being disrespectful to our leaders. But man! Being the youngest brother is tough sometimes.

Yet what they didn't know, what no one really knows, is that I *can* read. Just not the usual way.

We always stay at my uncle Mike's house in Ann Arbor. He's my mom's brother. Uncle Mike is the head custodian at Skyline High School, where the powwow is being held.

When we got there Thursday night, my mom and her brother stayed up all night laughing and talking. Pretty sure I heard my mom cry, too. My uncle came and lived with us after my dad died. He helped us all.

Back then, Uncle Mike taught me and my brothers how to shave. Of course, I don't even have peach fuzz on my chin, but I know how to shave now. He also taught our ma how to use the snowblower and clear our driveway. Ma now calls our snowblower "The Indian Vomiter." But my uncle reminded us that as Native people, we need to stay in community. Because some pain, like my dad dying, can slowly kill the living if we don't keep connected.

Not that we'll ever get over it, but it's good to have another person who remembers my dad and all the funny things he and Uncle Mike would do. If no one remembers a relative who passed, then it's too easy to forget the good times. Or that they even lived.

Uncle Mike is one of the only adults who doesn't care if I can read or not. Every time we visit him, he lets me tag along with him while he does custodian work. Uncle Mike is cool because he knows that there's more to reading than letters. More to life than test scores and grades.

On Friday morning, just as Uncle Mike was about to get another cup of coffee, I turned and held out something that was in my back pocket. Sometimes I get a feeling after looking at the sky. About what might happen in the future.

"Hey, Uncle Mike. Here, take this. And, well, just hold on to it for today, okay?"

He looked down at what I had placed in his hand, then looked back to me, confused.

"Just keep it, all right?" I asked.

Uncle Mike answered, "Sure, Joe. Not sure what this is, but I trust you." And my uncle slipped the metal object into the front pocket of his uniform.

Everyone moved to the kitchen to get things ready for our fry bread stand. I chopped the lettuce and tomatoes, and when I swung around too quickly, I collided into Listin.

"Joe, look out. You totally bumped into me."

"Hmm, pretty sure I didn't," I lied.

"Yeah? You want to knock it off?" Listin yelled.

"Nope, nothing wrong here. I didn't touch you." I knew where this was going. He gets kind of crabby when our mom makes him work on prepping the stand. He'd rather be playing basketball out back.

"Just watch it!" Listin pointed at me.

Ma said, "*Both* of you, just get back to work. Listin, you've gotta go run and get more ice down at the gas station for our sodas. Please, my boy."

Remembering what I read out the window earlier, I slipped something into Listin's jean jacket pocket while he bent down to grab the cooler to carry the ice bags in.

He didn't notice, but he would later. I knew it.

Early Friday afternoon we all drove to the school to set up our stand. Everyone else was getting the school ready for the upcoming powwow. I carried our supplies from the car to the school. I saw the sky turn from a clear blue to an ominous gray-green. And the sky rumbled loudly. Almost as if it were protesting my brothers' treatment of me.

I told you, this was the Midwest in the spring—never predictable. Out of the gray clouds came sleet with pelting ice shards, which covered the cars and buses in the parking lot. All of us ran for cover inside, but Listin ran back to the car for his cell phone. By then, everything was coated with a frosty glaze.

Listin tried to put the key in the door. The entire car door was coated with ice. He tried to scrape it, breathe on it, and rub his fingers over it. Yet nothing, nothing worked. Until, well, until . . .

He reached into his jacket pocket for gloves, but instead grabbed a thin plastic object and pulled it out. The thing *I* put in there: a slim white lighter with the words *Native Pride* on it. Listin looked confused as the ice rained down on him. I know Listin really well. I could just imagine what he was thinking: *Joey did this little prank! Wait till I tell Ma he's playing with lighters . . . I'll make sure he—*

He grabbed hold of the lighter, and suddenly he felt something like a warm breath cup his ear, whispering, "Mikwam." At the same time, Listin understood that mikwam meant "ice" in Ojibwe. He'd never heard that voice before, that calming voice.

He looked at the lighter, quickly flicked it on, and let the flame warm the door lock.

The ice melted enough so that Listin could put the key in and unlock the car door! He stayed in the car until the weather cleared.

I saw it all from the front door of the school.

Ice turned back into rain as it fell in sheets. Then along came a change in the color of the sky. It turned from gray to an ominous yellow-green color. Uncle Mike was heading outside to start clearing the ice from the sidewalks. But before even he finished scraping a few feet, the hair on the back of his neck felt like it was being electrified.

Slowly, a whining sound began to gather intensity. With fear, he turned around to look west of the school football fields. Quickly approaching was a small funnel cloud whirling from the sky, almost touching the ground.

Uncle Mike, who used to be a volunteer firefighter back when he lived in the Upper Peninsula, knew when danger was approaching. He grabbed his walkie-talkie to get ahold of the office to warn the school. Later Uncle Mike told me he was thinking: *Why isn't the siren going off? The siren is right there on top of the pole, only ten feet in front of the school.*

He continued to fumble with the walkie-talkie and reached into his shirt pocket to use his cell phone, when he grabbed a thin metal object. The thing I'd given him earlier that morning.

Just then, he felt a soft blast of warm air, almost like a breath, as he heard, in his ear, "Wese'an," said in an unfamiliar quiet voice. Instantly, as he held the small piece of metal, he understood this to be the Ojibwe word for "tornado." Uncle Mike ran to the pole just in front of the school. He climbed, using the metal ladder attached to the pole to guide his way up.

At the top of the pole, he saw the tornado siren's cover

was coated with rust, and on top of that, it was encased in ice from the day's storm. Its corrosion was preventing the sensor from connecting to the weather center's computer warning system!

Looking behind him, he saw what looked like funnel clouds almost touching the ground next to the school.

That's why it's not sounding off! People need to hear this to know to take cover as they're getting ready for powwow! Uncle Mike thought. He took the wirelike metal object that I'd given him, a large, straightened paper clip with a hook on the end, and shoved it under the plastic hood of the siren. The wire was able to punch perfectly through the rust and ice, into the hole on the siren cover, and freed it from being blocked.

Whir! The siren's great thundering alarm caused Uncle Mike to fall fifteen feet back down the pole. Just before he slammed into the ground, that warm, soft breath enveloped him and gently floated him safely down.

I, along with some other vendors setting up that afternoon, watched this all from the school. I held my ma's hand to calm her. But after a while, the green hazy sky seemed to clear, and I headed out the door to look around.

"Hey, Joey, where do you think you're going?" Listin yelled as he walked around the corner of the school.

After all, he wanted to know what I'd been doing with

a lighter. Seriously, I've never played around with fire, but Listin still didn't understand that I gave it to him because he'd need it later. And he did.

Makwa came out of the school too, and I sighed and signaled that I'd help carry the rest of our stuff in. He led me behind the school, where our car was parked. I twisted my head up again with my ear tilted toward the sky.

With one quick movement, I grabbed two garbage bin covers next to us.

"Makwa!" I hollered as I threw one of the covers to him. Suddenly, the skies opened again with a crack of booming thunder.

As Makwa reached out to grab the makeshift shield, he felt a warm breath of air coming from the ground, saying, "Mikwamiikaa." He'd never heard this peaceful but powerful voice before. Instantly, when he grabbed the garbage can cover coming at him, almost like a round plastic sled, he instantly knew that mikwamiikaa meant "hail."

Hail that pelted him and everything in sight just then.

He lifted the shield above his head to protect himself, looked over at me, and saw me doing the same. Makwa leveled his eyes at me, and at that second, a breath of warm wind surrounded him, keeping the hail from pummeling him again.

Well, that warm breath, and the shield I gave him.

Seconds later, the hail stopped, and the ground was

covered in an inch of pebble-size balls of ice. Makwa wasn't sure what had happened to him. His head felt a little lighter now. And his heart, too. But, after all, I was his little brother. The one who everyone knew wasn't "smart."

He looked up at me, only a few feet away, and started to ask, "So, how did you kn—"

But I lip-pointed down the little hill we stood on. My brother had no clue what had happened. I took the plastic cover from over my head, held it in front of him, took a run, jumped, and flipped the sled under my body. I sailed past Makwa!

Makwa laughed and followed me, cruising down the hill on his "sled" too. We both rode on top of the hail.

At the bottom of the hill we cracked up at the sheer fun of the ride. I fell off my sled. It was the first time since our dad died that we lost ourselves in laughter. It felt good.

Makwa stood up, put out his hand, and helped me up. "Man, really, I'm not sure what just happened up there, Chief—I mean, Joey, but I . . . I've been a complete jerk to you. I just—"

"Eya, *yes*, you have been," I responded, wiggling my eyebrows.

March can be warm and dry in the Midwest, or it can stink. The temperature outside can make you sweat buckets, or dump a blizzard on you with fifteen inches of snow. (And of course they *never* cancel school. Ever.)

On Saturday, the first day of powwow, it started out in the low thirties. Much better than the weather the day before.

So that morning, as we were unloading our stuff from the truck, I did it again. I stopped mid-step, turned my head, tilted an ear up toward the sky, and squinted my right eye.

I heard *it* again, but the sky was all clear now and told me all was safe. I stayed like this for a few seconds, then went to the school with my brothers.

My brothers asked me, "What'd you bring?" because they noticed my backpack slung over my shoulder. With some things inside. Just in case it happened *again*. Yet this time, instead of making fun of me, Makwa put me in a headlock (and *didn't* twist hard) and Listin carried my backpack for me. I guess this was their new way of being nice to me. I'd take it!

During the first hour, as we set up our food stand, no one was paying attention to me. Makwa was trying to act all cool as the dancers walked past to enter the gym. Listin made sure we were doing our jobs at the fry bread stations right. *And* he tried to be sure to carry the heavy stuff when the women dancers walked by.

"Joey, your ma said you can come help me with the

furnace right now." Uncle Mike winked, looking at my huge pile of uncut tomatoes.

As I took off my apron, I looked up at the window in front of me, to make sure all was calm outside.

Most of our time that morning with my uncle was spent on maintaining the seventy-five-year-old furnace and ancient electrical system at the high school. I held the flashlight while he tightened some wires. Dalton and his uncle, the assistant custodian, were helping, too. Dalton's parents' stand is next to ours. He's the only kid, but the youngest of all his cousins. He totally gets what it's like to try to dodge the teasing.

Uncle Mike tapped on the furnace. "Old boy, just hang on for the powwow this weekend."

After the lunch rush, my mom gave us some free time, so I wanted to watch the dancers. But I'd left my phone (my mom's old iPhone) in the car and wanted it to take some pictures. Really, I wanted to take pictures to tease Listin as he tried to talk to some of the girl dancers from South Dakota. He gets really nerdy when trying to talk to girls.

On my way out to the car I passed Maggie, and we smiled. I met her yesterday as we were setting up our fry bread stand. There was something about her eyes that had made me take a second look when we first met. I *knew* that look. That's the look of sadness.

She told me her dad had died, too. It's weird, but when you're around someone who knows the same pain as you, it somehow lightens yours. But only for a few minutes.

As I began to head to the parking lot, I passed another window. I thought about what happened yesterday, and what just might have turned my life around. Okay, maybe it helped some people realize that I can read, but just in a different way.

So now you know the story, the one from *that* day before the powwow. Not a single person was hurt—only my brothers' egos. The school and surrounding area only had a few small tree limbs scattered on roofs and driveways.

I told you about how I can't read the way most kids do, but also the way I *can* read.

Uncle Mike said to me as we packed up to leave after the powwow was done, "How'd the other food stands look today, Joe?"

I winked. "Meh, the meat loaf stand looks mushy, peas are putrid, and the applesauce is acidic. Remember, we're the World's Best Fry Bread."

Understanding how to read the sky is something nobody else can really do. And I can only do it knowing and learning my Native language. I get that I may never ace a big state standardized reading test in school. But it's okay.

Uncle Mike continued, "Son, you *can* do it. But 'it' doesn't mean a perfect report card in school. It means to keep following your path. Listen to what our language is teaching you. You did that, right? You could read the sky and helped all of us who *didn't* know how to read that way. My boy, I'm proud of you." Looking around at my mom and brothers, he tousled my hair. "We're *all* proud of you."

On the ride back to Minneapolis, Listin shut the sunroof cover. Fine. Whatever. Nap away, brothers. But then Makwa elbowed him, lip-pointed up, and flipped open the cover.

Smiling, I stretched my hand behind my head and looked up. At it. The thing I get. The sky I can read because of learning our language.

Miigwech, *thank you*, dear Creator. And miigwech, Ancestors, for keeping our Ojibwe language alive. Because of you, I can read . . . I can read the sky.

WHAT WE KNOW ABOUT GLACIERS

CHRISTINE DAY

Here's the thing about having an older sister in college: it isn't nearly as cool as it sounds. And that's coming from someone whose sister used to be the varsity cheerleading captain, the homecoming queen, the president of the Indigenous Peoples Club, and the leader of a canoe family called the Future.

Her name is Brooke. She was all these things and more, until she left for the University of Michigan. Now she lives far away. She can only Skype for twenty minutes at a time. And all she ever talks about is her classes, her exams, and *glaciers*.

"That's why recycling isn't enough on its own," Brooke tells our parents. The four of us are seated on the upper bleachers. The intertribal dancing is happening on the gym floor below in vivid, swirling colors. The dancers are smiling and stomping, straight-backed in their regalia. Brooke is raising her voice, shouting to be heard over the drums. "As a society, we *must* reduce our carbon emissions."

So, she isn't specifically talking about glaciers right now, but I promise, it's coming. And really, who talks about this stuff at a *powwow*? No one I know. Not until my sister went from the coolest, sweetest, most beautiful and popular girl in our hometown of La Conner, Washington, to this weird, ice-obsessed person who loves coffee too much.

She reaches for the thermos at her feet. It makes me want to scream and tell her, *It's eight p.m. on a Saturday night, Brooke. Why do you need coffee right now? Why?*

This is her fourth cup today. My parents and I flew in this morning, and she was drinking coffee when she met us at the airport. After we stopped by the hotel, she took us to the local café where she spends a lot of time studying. Then we came here, just in time for the Grand Entry. She filled her thermos once while I ate corn soup for lunch, and then again while our parents chatted with the Pendleton vendors.

Wait. Does my sister have an actual problem? What exactly does caffeine do to a person?

While Brooke continues her rant, I pull my cell phone out of my pocket. This caffeine question seems like the sort of thing Google was invented for.

And oh—

Increased heart rate? Insomnia? I'm scrolling and

scrolling, and I don't like this at all. One paragraph claims coffee can help to reduce headaches after "epidural anesthesia," and I don't know what that is, but I'm pretty sure Brooke doesn't have it. But the rest doesn't sound good. Does my sister know about these effects? Does she have any idea?

This is concerning. *This* is what happens when people move two thousand miles away from their friends and their family and their everything, for no real reason. This is what happens when you're forced to live in a closet-size dorm room, and use communal shower stalls, and eat Top Ramen for dinner every night.

Brooke has dark rings under her eyes. Acne on her forehead. Her long brown hair isn't as glossy or straight as usual. Like she forgot to brush it this morning. Her lips are chapped. And I don't want to be rude, but—her breath stinks. I first noticed it when she leaned close to share her program with me, and—whoa. What even happened in there?

I lower my phone and am about to speak up, but Mom is talking now, and apparently, I've missed something.

"This is excellent news, Brooke! We're so proud of you." Mom pulls her into a big hug. Their woven cedar hats crinkle and tilt on their heads, their brims butting up against each other. Our cedar hats are handmade, traditional. We only wear them at powwows now, but in the old days, our ancestors used cedar for everything: canoes, longhouses, summer clothes, fishing nets, bentwood boxes, even baby diapers. Imagine stripping the soft inner bark from a cedar tree, and weaving the fibers tight enough so that no pee will come out. Imagine doing all of that, instead of just buying diapers from Costco.

My ancestors were legendary, honestly.

Dad raises his arms, palms turned in a traditional Coast Salish gesture. He's murmuring words in Lushootseed, but his voice is deep and soft, and I can't hear any of it over the pounding drums. If I had to guess, though, I think he's telling my sister: *You lift us up. You make our hearts happy.*

Brooke smiles. She presses a hand over her chest. "Thank you. I'm so happy to have your support. I've applied for a scholarship; hopefully I'll get some kind of assistance—"

Mom waves her worries away. "Even if you don't get it, we'll make it work. We'll find a way to support you."

I frown. "What are you guys talking about?"

Everybody turns toward me. Like they just remembered I'm here.

Mom says, "Weren't you listening, Riley? Brooke's going to study abroad in Greenland this summer!"

"Only for a few weeks," Brooke says in a rush. "Summer semester is shorter than the others."

I exhale. Relax a little. "You'll be home for the canoe journey, right?"

"Well," she adds sheepishly. "Nothing is certain yet, but I might spend the rest of my summer here. I'm interested in a local environmental nonprofit. If I get the chance to intern there, I think I should take it."

Our parents are beaming and puffed up with pride. I know I should be, too. This is my sister, after all. The girl who was voted "Most Likely to Succeed" in her senior year hall of fame. The girl who wasn't popular for being rich or pretty or trendy, but because she is warm and kind and genuinely likable. She is the type of person who deserves everything good that happens to her. A real-life Cinderella. (If Cinderella wanted to pursue a double major in environmental science and sociology. She was a hard worker, so it's possible.)

I *want* to be happy about this announcement. I swear I do.

But when I ask, "What's in Greenland?" it doesn't come out super nice-sounding.

"A cutting-edge research facility," she says. "With a huge emphasis on local Indigenous leadership. Most of the faculty members come from Greenlandic Inuit societies. I'm going to contribute to an ongoing study, under their guidance."

"It sounds amazing," Mom gushes. "The perfect fit for you."

"What do people study there?" I ask. "Why can't you take summer classes online or—or something like that?"

"Because it wouldn't be the same. If I really want to learn and grow, I need to learn from the best. If I want to make a difference in the world, I need to show up and be present."

Wow. What an annoyingly Brooke-ish thing to say.

"We're going to examine the Greenland ice sheet," she continues. "It's the second largest ice body in the world."

Sure enough. There it is: *glaciers.*

Brooke is still talking. She's comparing the size of this glacier in Greenland to the big one in Antarctica. She's explaining the rates at which both are melting. She's saying this is a crisis, that it will somehow impact everybody eventually.

My gaze fixes on the drums and dancing. The jingle dresses *clink-clink-clink*, and the men around the drum circle change their rhythm, *thrum-thrum-thrum*. I can feel the music in my sternum.

Brooke leans in, breathing on me again. "Riley?" Her voice is gentle. Careful. "Are you okay?"

My throat feels clogged. If I say something now, there's a good chance it'll either come out mean, or I'll start to cry. I don't want either of those things. I don't know what else to do.

So, I rise shakily to my feet. And leave.

Here's another thing that bothers me: college is supposed to be *fun*. It's all about joining sororities, painting your face for football games, and meeting boys who are finally mature. Brooke and I should spend hours talking on Skype every night, as she tells me everything about her university experience.

But nothing like that has happened.

And it feels wrong, yet somehow, I'm the only person who has noticed. Mom and Dad think Brooke is thriving here, because her grades are good, and she keeps sharing all these smart-sounding articles on social media. *She's become so passionate and knowledgeable*, Mom often marvels.

Brooke has always been passionate and knowledgeable. But until she came here, I never saw her with acne breakouts. When I started going through puberty, she was the one who taught me all about skin-care products, aluminum-free deodorants, the importance of eating vegetables and staying hydrated. She gave me her old copy of *The Care and Keeping of You*, which had dog-eared pages and helpful notes in the margins. When I had my first period, she bought me chocolates and braided my hair and streamed my favorite movie on her laptop so I could watch it in bed. As I gritted my teeth and squirmed through the pain, she held me and whispered words of comfort that I still repeat to myself sometimes. Especially now that we no longer live together.

I push through the locker room doors and storm inside.

Two women are bent over a ribbon skirt, sewing a stray piece back into place. Another is reapplying lipstick in the mirror, a deep burgundy shade that matches the floral beadwork on her dress.

I go to the back and plop down on a bench, right by the locker Mom and I claimed earlier today. Then I pull my phone out of my pocket and search for photos of Greenland.

I find images of soaring glaciers and mountain peaks, clear blue seas and cloud-painted skies. Towns nestled between rolling hills, with buildings in shades of scarlet and royal blue and canary yellow. Icebergs rise from the water in jagged formations. It's beautiful, but it isn't home.

And I'm starting to think that Brooke *needs* to come home.

I close the internet browser, and my wallpaper photo makes my chest ache. Brooke and I are standing on the beach, beside the Future's canoe. A few girls from the family photobombed us, holding up bunny ears behind our heads in the background. Brooke's arms are circled tight around me, and her mouth is stretched wide as she laughs. I'm laughing too, but my mouth looks puckered.

It's not the best picture of me. Everyone who sees it points at my face and laughs. But I've never cared too much, because I love everything else about it.

After this photo was taken, Mom laughed and shook her head. "You girls are too much," she said. "The Future is silly."

We were giggling and falling over each other. I remember how lean and strong Brooke's arms were. How she smelled like vanilla perfume and sunscreen, clean and coconutty.

"Are you ready for this?" she asked. It was our first canoe journey of the season last year, and we were on our way to the Lummi Nation from our beach in Swinomish.

"I'm ready." I pulled away from her to flex my biceps as proof.

She laughed and nodded in approval. "The Future is *strong* with this one."

(See? My sister used to make double puns about our canoe family and Star Wars. How does someone go from epic puns to endless rants? Her freshman year of college has ruined her sense of humor.)

The adults helped us push our canoe into the water. It

was long and broad, with *The Future* painted along its side in bold white letters, its carved interior a bright shade of red. Even though this was my second year in the Future—a canoe family of Native girls, all between the ages of ten to nineteen—I was nervous as we bobbed into the channel. Like I was experiencing stage fright before a big performance.

"Paddles up!"

We lifted our paddles in response to Brooke's command. Mine was painted to resemble a blue orca whale, with thick swooping lines along its body, crescent-shaped eyes and flippers, and a row of gritted teeth. From the beach, our families cheered and whooped for us. Brooke sang out a single, joyful note and held it.

Then she stopped.

My lifejacket was snug around my torso. The sunlight warmed my skin. The sounds of the water flowed around us. The gentle waves lapping against the hull. The slight rocking as we sat with straight spines, our canoe pointed in the direction we wished to go.

"Remember our protocols," Brooke said. "We traverse these waters with good intentions. When we arrive at our neighbors' shores, we must seek their permission to land. We make this journey to honor our ancestors, and to celebrate our families and communities."

Brooke paused in her speech. A breeze swept over us,

swirling my hair around my shoulders, whipping strands across my face.

"I'm so proud of you all," Brooke continued. "I'm proud of your strength. I'm proud of your willingness to make this journey. This wouldn't be possible if we weren't here together. As we travel in this canoe, we are all dependent on one another. We must trust each other and work together. It's the only way we will reach our destination."

From there, Brooke launched into an ancient song. Her voice carried across the channel like a gathering wave, rich and throaty and building. Our paddles plunged back into the water, as we glided across the surface, surging forward. Deep in the background, our families roared from the shoreline, cheering us on like we were a team of astronauts on our way to the moon.

By the time Brooke finds me, I'm lying on the bench with my phone flat on my chest.

"There you are," she says. "You look . . . comfortable?"

I grunt in response. A group of Elders are chattering near the door, making predictions for the dance competitions. A mother is changing her baby's diaper somewhere nearby, entertaining him with tummy tickles and soft cooing sounds.

Brooke nudges my legs. I sit upright, so she can join me.

"Riley," she says softly. "I think we need to talk."

"Yep." My voice is flat and hard. "Probably."

"I owe you an apology. I should've told you about my plans for the summer. It wasn't fair, to keep it a secret from you. I wanted to surprise you and Mom and Dad, but—I don't think I went about it the right way. I'm sorry." A crease forms between her brows. "I've hurt your feelings."

I swallow the lump in my throat. There's no point in denying it. Her decision to study abroad feels a little like a betrayal. Like she hasn't missed me as much as I've missed her.

"Have I ever told you the old stories? The teachings our ancestors offered about—glaciers?"

I stare pointedly at the bank of lockers. Blink back the tears before they have a chance to gather.

Brooke reaches for me, brushing my shawl with her fingertips. This robe was a gift from our auntie Val, a traditional Coast Salish weaver with looms in her home office and graph-paper notebooks filled with sketches. Val prepared this regalia for me before my first canoe journey. She told me this robe would protect me and empower me.

This small gesture—my sister's gentle touch, this pause to acknowledge Auntie Val's work—helps me breathe. Helps me relax.

She says, "They compared them to our weavings. They

said that glaciers were like huge blankets covering the mountains."

Traditionally, our blankets were all white, so this makes sense to me. White snow; white wool. But this comparison is also significant, because our weavings are the foundation of our ceremonies. I glance down at myself, newly aware of the prayers Auntie Val whispered into this fabric for me.

Brooke says, "Our ancestors also compared glaciers to mothers. Because the freshwater rivers that run off from them nourish us, they sustain ecosystems for us, they provide a vital life force from their own bodies. Just as mothers nurture infants with breast milk. Glaciers are the exact same way."

I look up. The mother is leaving now, with her baby pressed against her chest, his cheek resting on her shoulder. She uses her diaper bag to push through the door, and as it opens, the emcee's amplified voice blasts through the gap. The contest and exhibition dancing is about to begin, and he is thanking the participants in advance. His voice becomes muffled as the door eases shut. The Elder ladies have also left to watch the competition; Brooke and I are alone.

"I know I've become . . . kind of obsessed. It feels like I'm constantly talking about glaciers, and climate change, and preservation politics. I know you and I haven't hung out in a long time. Our relationship has changed since I left home. And Riley, being away from you has been the hardest thing about being a college student. Which is saying a lot, because I feel like an overcaffeinated ghost most of the time." Brooke looks down at her lap. "I miss you so much. And I hate feeling like this—like I'm disappointing you."

The vulnerability in her voice and in her eyes breaks my heart open. I grasp both of her hands.

It's impossible to hold a grudge against my sister.

"You could never disappoint me," I tell her.

"Are you sure?" Brooke bites her bottom lip. It's her nervous habit, and it draws my attention again to how chapped her lips are—it looks like one of the dry scabs recently bled.

"*Never.*"

I pull her into a seated hug. Her arms come around me. Beneath her wool shawl, I can feel the angles of my sister's bones; she's too thin. I don't remember her ever being so thin. Our cedar hats scrape against each other, with a rasp like sandpaper. We hold each other for several seconds; I'm smoothing the tangled hairs down her back, and she's gripping my shoulders.

"But Brooke?"

"Hmm?" Her deep tone reverberates against my chest.

"Do you remember the advice you gave me? When I first joined the Future?"

She cocks her head. Pulls away slightly to meet my gaze.

"You told me to make my own well-being my first priority. And I asked you, 'Wouldn't that be selfish?' And you said, 'It's difficult to move the canoe forward, if you aren't taking care of yourself. You need to be strong. You need to be nourished. You need to be present and positive.' Remember?"

Her brown eyes move across my face. "Of course."

"You taught me all about self-care. You taught me what it means to paddle. If it weren't for you, I probably never would've made it out of the shallows."

She squeezes my hands. Her face transforms with a warm, beautiful smile.

"You've always known the right things to do. Which is why you're probably right about . . . this Greenland thing. If you need to go and join their study, instead of coming home and returning to the canoe journey, I can't stand in your way. I shouldn't guilt-trip you."

"Thank you, Riley."

"But"—I lift my eyebrows meaningfully—"I think *I'm* the one who needs to remind *you* about priorities now. Because no offense, Brooke, but you don't look so great."

She blinks. "Excuse me?"

"Girl." I release one of her hands and gesture at her face. "What happened to your nightly skin-care routine? And are you getting enough sleep? Are you drinking water?

Coffee really isn't good for you, you know. Unless you ever catch a case of ee-pee-dral anesthe-za."

She snorts. "Um, okay. Wow. I always appreciate your brutal honesty," she says with a snicker. "But hold on, *what* was that last part?"

"Doesn't matter. As long as you don't have it, there's no point to drinking coffee, which means you should probably start chugging some water. We also need to brush your hair. And get something for your chapped lips. As a matter of fact, here. One second."

I stand and turn to open our locker. I sift through our purchases from the powwow—T-shirts with the phrases *Ancestor Approved* and *Honor Native Land*, dentalium-shell necklaces, glass bottles of maple syrup—and grasp my cosmetics bag. Its starched fabric is light blue and patterned with strawberries. I unzip it and grab my brush, my apple-butter lip balm, and my small tin of breath mints. Then I turn to face Brooke.

"I'll work on your hair, you can use this, and—you can have a mint, if you want. They're winter-fresh. Kind of like your beloved glaciers."

Brooke laughs and opens her palm. "Thank you."

I pass her the tin and the balm, and stand behind her. "Let me know if I pull too hard, okay?"

"You're fine. Thanks."

"No problem." I lift a lock of her hair and ease the bristles through it, as gently as I can. "So," I say. "Tell me more about this trip to Greenland. What exactly will you do for the study? Are any of your friends going too? Will there be college boys?"

I can hear the smile in my sister's voice as she says, "Well, for starters . . ."

LITTLE FOX AND THE CASE OF THE MISSING REGALIA

Erika T. Wurth

"Wait. You're telling me you're missing regalia? Like, as in someone here at the powwow *stole* your stuff?" I couldn't believe it. No way. Just no way.

"I'm *telling* you, Tokala. Girl, it's true! And it's the not the first time something was stolen at a powwow either," Shana said. People sitting next to us at the powwow started staring. We had been sitting there, on the hard metal benches, taking a break from walking around to see what the vendors had for sale and watching the Fancy Shawl dancers. That's my favorite. I love to watch the girls swirl in the pit below us, their braided hair glossy. Plus, our friend Jenny was about to dance, and we promised we'd watch.

"At least we just happen to have a famous detective here. What-whaaaat?" Shana said, wiggling her eyebrows significantly at me.

"Oh well, I'm not like, famous or anything," I said, turning kind of red. Ever since I'd solved the mystery of my mom's disappearance, Native kids had been hiring me to solve crimes for them.

"Yeah, you are. You're totally famous. I'm just glad you're here." Shana looked down at her feet and sighed heavily. "I just never thought this kind of thing would happen to me."

I patted her back. I *was* happy I was here. I could help; I was good at solving mysteries and Shana had been my friend forever, ever since our parents had met at one of their Indian conferences, where they gave papers on Indian stuff. My parents were presenting at the University of Michigan. I was just glad there was a powwow at the same time and I could hang with Shana. Otherwise we'd be stuck running around the hallways of the university. Booorrrrriiiing. Though to be fair, whenever I was asked to solve a crime, one of my parents would come along, and then they were the ones stuck in a hotel grading papers, waiting for me.

"So let's go through what just happened. I like to be real specific," I said, getting my iPad Mini out. I'd gotten it with some of what I'd earned through crime solving. I didn't charge much 'cause it was only Indian kids who hired me, and they insisted on paying. My parents were making me put most of it in a college fund.

"I went to the locker room to change," Shana said. "I had the most lit regalia. I'm talking lit-as-heck, and that's what I was focused on."

I nodded. Shana was a Jingle Dress dancer. "Go on."

"And I went to pull my mocs out, you know, the fire ones my grandma helped make. The ones with the floral pattern, the pink-and-blue ones. And they were gone!"

"Like, twenty minutes ago?" I asked.

"Yeah! I searched all over the locker room, went to the car, and even asked my derpy brother to look for them at home," she said, pounding her fist into her palm.

That was why she'd been gone so long. I'd been starting to worry, had even texted Shana a few times after she didn't come back. Then, as soon as I was ready to go search for her, she came out looking really angry in her regular clothes, just her jeans and pink shirt with the words *Powwow Magic*.

"Do you think maybe your brother just didn't look hard enough?"

"No. He can be weak, but he knows how important this is to me. And honestly, I remember putting them in my bag. Like, I *really* remember because this is first time I was going to get to wear them, and I wrapped them in an old shirt and stuck them in my red-and-gray Pendleton bag that I got at Gathering of Nations, right under my clothes."

The Fancy Shawl dancers came on, swinging their arms, the green and white and red of their regalia bright, their shawls spinning out into the air to the thump of the drums. We stopped what we were talking about for a minute, so we could look for Jenny. She was toward the middle in yellow. I watched her move, her feet bouncing in time to the beat. She was such a good dancer. This powwow kinda reminded me of the ones my dad took me to, which made sense, since Anishinaabe and Lakota people were from around the same area—a long time ago they even used to fight. Of course, it was all so different from my mom's Nation. When I'd go home to the Chiricahua Reservation outside Deming, New Mexico, the ceremonies and dances, and the clothes—well, it was nothing like the Plains stuff here. It was cool, though: my parents liked to participate in each other's dances and such on their Reservations, with me along, of course. Like, I was preparing for my puberty ceremony on Mom's Rez, and Dad would have a part to play, even though he was Sicangu Lakota, 'cause he was my dad.

"And that's the *thing*, Tokala. That's when I remembered. And that's when I got pissed," Shana continued, shaking her head, her long braids swinging.

"What did you remember?"

"Well, that a bunch of regalia has gone missing at different powwows around here, you know, all Anishinaabe florals. First at White Earth—that's where Jenny had a pair of barrettes in that style go missing. We thought she'd just lost them. But then, at Mille Lacs, my home, hair ties *in the same style* went missing."

"Do you remember if you left your bag in a place where someone could get to your stuff?" I asked.

"Hmm," Shana said, putting her chin on her fist. "You know, I put it down behind me when we first came in. And you know what? I *did* leave it when we went to go look at the vendors. Remember, I pushed it kind of under the bench."

I nodded. That was definitely enough time to take stuff. Especially if someone had been watching Shana.

"Well . . . do you have any—I don't know another way to put this, but—enemies? Especially, you know, uh . . . girl cousins your age who might be kind of jealous of you? And also, maybe jealous of the other girls who had stuff stolen?"

"Heck yes, I do," Shana said. "Not to sound arrogant, but I'm a good dancer, and my regalia is straight fire."

I giggled. "Anyone specific, though? Like really, *really* jealous."

Shana wrinkled her brow and went quiet for a sec. Then she started nodding and said, "There are three girls that are like, you know, Indian cousins—and they are jealous of me. They've said things to me that were out-and-out mean. And I set them straight, you know me. I don't take anything from anyone. But let me think . . . which ones of them know all of us . . ."

"Well, I don't mean to interrupt you, but uh, my second question might help with that."

"Sure!"

"Which of those girls also does Jingle Dance or Fancy Shawl?"

"The only girl I can think of like that is a girl named Marisa Baudrillard," Shana said, scrunching her eyes thoughtfully. "You know, she used to bully all of us when we were kids. I mean all the time, girl. Steal our lunches, make fun of us. The only revenge we had on her was . . . oh man . . ."

"What?" I asked, really feeling like this was it.

"Winning at powwow against her," Shana finished, raising the turquoise necklace she'd just bought up from her neck and looking at it.

"Do you have any idea where this Marisa is now?"

Shana put the necklace down and got that same thinking expression on her face. Then she sighed and shook her head. "You know what? Never mind. I remember she told Jenny she couldn't come today 'cause she was sick."

It was my turn to sigh.

We watched Jenny dance, and then my phone went off, singing "Bread and Cheese" by A Tribe Called Red. I picked it up and talked to Mom for a minute, told her what was happening. My parents would be at the conference for a few more hours, so I had time to solve this crime. And I just had to!

"Wait a minute!" Shana said. "There is this one girl, she's super shy. Laura. I hate to say this, but . . . she's always eyeballing my regalia. And . . . ugh, this makes me feel crappy to say, but their family doesn't have a lot of money, and she really wants to dance; she's from my Rez, and daaaang, she can't bead. And doesn't have the money to buy any beads even if she did. But she's at *all* the powwows. She's definitely here. And you know what?"

My heart started to hammer.

"She was over at my house the other day. I was helping her with math, and she just kept looking at my mocs. Like staring all rude and asking if she could touch them. And then she was wearing these barrettes. And girl, they looked just like Jenny's! The ones that went missing! I thought I was just *thinking* that at the time, but now? Shoot. They looked just like them, Tokala."

"Okay. Okay, lemme think," I said. I watched the dancers finish up, my mind whirring like an engine, and after a while, the whole thing came to me. "Okay. This is what we're gonna do. Do you have pictures of the missing stuff?"

"Hmm, I think I could get them. From pics at powwows and old texts and stuff. Just give me a minute, f'real." Shana pulled her phone out and started going through it. After about five minutes, she looked up, her pretty brown face beaming with pride. "I got you!"

"What we need to do is find Laura," I said, chewing on my nails. I stopped. Mom was really trying to get me to cut that out, but it was an old habit, and I couldn't help doing it when there was a crime to solve.

"Then what?" Shana asked.

"Leave that to me."

We got up and started walking around, seeing a few friends here and there and telling them about the missing stuff, asking them if they knew anything, while at the same time looking for Laura. The hallways were crowded, and people were trying to push to get to the vendors. It was amazing to see all the Southwestern stuff: the silver, the turquoise, the Diné black pottery, the Pueblo white-and-red pottery—all next to the Lakota and Nish beadwork and quillwork, the earrings and necklaces in every color and design you could imagine. We looked in the bathrooms and the hallways where the vendors were, walked where we could see people sitting. We were just about to give up when Shana spotted Laura in line for fry bread.

As Laura left the line, we joined her while she walked back to the gym. She was kind of hunched over, and constantly pulling at her purple Minnie Mouse shirt.

She was wearing the beaded barrettes.

When we caught up to her, Shana introduced me, and I asked her if she could help me with something.

"Sure," Laura whispered, running her hands over her hair, which was up in braids. She had freckles and really did seem shy. I felt bad.

"So, we're trying to solve a crime," I said. She cocked her head, and I didn't see any flicker of guilt. Hmm. That was interesting. Laura seemed like the kind who'd wear her guilt on her face. "Some regalia is missing, and we're checking everyone's bags. Is it okay if we check yours?"

"Sure! Oh man, that's so sad. Who would steal regalia? That's just wrong, you know, to do to another Native," she said, shaking her head.

If she had taken those mocs, it was maybe forty-five minutes ago. There was no way she'd have had time to hide them. We walked back to the gym with her, and she let us go through her bags, and we talked and I told her how much I liked her barrettes. If Laura was guilty, there was *no way* she wouldn't reveal herself there.

"Thank you. My auntie gave them to me. She got them from the same lady that Jenny got hers from. You know how much I love hers," Laura said shyly. She didn't even hesitate when she said it. And there was nothing in her bags. Just nothing. We even showed her the pictures of the missing stuff, and she said she hadn't seen any of it, and again, she just didn't look guilty *at all*.

We thanked her and walked back over to where we'd been sitting down before.

"Shoot! I was just sure it was her!" I said, pulling my nail up to chew and then stopping. Gah, it was such a hard habit to break!

"Girl, I was totally sure," Shana said. We were quiet as the Jingle Dress dancers came on, and I could tell Shana was angry, not getting to dance.

"Wait—wait a dang minute!" Shana said. "That's Marisa." She leaned forward and squinted. "And those look just like my mocs!"

"I guess she wasn't sick after all," I said, shaking my head. The gall of her wearing mocs she'd just stolen!

"Are you sure? Like, *sure*?" I asked.

"I'm one hundred percent sure. And one hundred percent pissed off," she said, her eyes narrowing.

"Any idea what she's doing after she finishes dancing?" I asked.

"Helping her mom man her booth. They sell shell earrings. *'Cause they can't bead.*"

"Okay, let's go to the booth when she's done. We can ask to look through her bags. Show her the pictures. See what she says," I said.

We watched the Jingle Dress dancers finish up, the nice, rhythmic sound of their jingles something that otherwise would make me feel really good and cheerful.

"Let's go," I said.

We got off the benches and were silent as we made our

way to Marisa's mom's booth. I was thinking about my tactic. I had one way to go, and if it didn't work, I'd have to rethink.

I was used to this kind of thing by now, but I had to admit, my heart was hammering again as we made our way through the crowd and approached the booth, which was full of pink and white shell earrings and necklaces, all spread out on a small table, a paisley cloth covering the whole thing. Marisa *was* there, and she was a super-beautiful girl, tall, with long, thick hair and big black eyes. Though she'd changed out of her regalia, she'd kept her hair ties in. They were floral pattern but not pastel. Her mom was beautiful, too, and looked a lot like Marisa. They were staring at their phones, occasionally looking up to see if there was someone interested in the merchandise.

"Hang back," I told Shana, and she nodded and walked over to a nearby booth, one that was full of silver and coral jewelry, close enough to observe.

"Hi! My name is Tokala," I said, sticking my hand out to Marisa's mother. She looked up from her phone suspiciously and eyed me up and down.

"Marna," she said, without extending her own hand. I let mine drop. Marisa continued to look at her phone.

"So, there have been some crimes," I said, and suddenly, Marisa's head shot up.

Marna stared at me, silent.

"And before we call the police, a bunch of kids told me about it. They reported the crimes to the people in charge of all of the powwows that the stuff was stolen at, but nothing was done."

"You?" Marna said, smirking. "A kid? Why they tell you?"

Marisa gave an uncomfortable chuckle, though it sounded more like she was choking on mac 'n' cheese or something.

"Yeah, I know it's weird, but I'm good at this. And if we call the police"—and here I could see the panic on Marisa's face—"that could get someone who just made a small, bad decision in real trouble for the rest of their lives." It took all my willpower not to look right at Marisa.

Marna was silent for a long time. Then she set her phone down and crossed both her arms over her chest. She had one of those expressions on her face that adults have when they don't want you to question them. "What you want from me?" she finally asked.

"Oh, I'm hoping you can help. And not just you. The stuff that was stolen was girls' regalia. Hair ties and barrettes. And lastly, here, a pair of mocs. Boots. And all Anishinaabe florals. All pastel. So I'm just going around asking if people will let me look in their bags, and anything else they've got with them that's big enough to hold any of that stuff."

Marna snorted. "How you gonna know if it's the stuff you're looking for?"

"I have pictures of the stolen items. And, of course, I've narrowed it down to Anishinaabe girls who do Jingle or Fancy, though of course I could be wrong about that."

"You could be. Could be anyone stealing that stuff and selling it."

"You're totally right! The only reason I think maybe that's not the case is, like I said, that it's all Anishinaabe florals, and all pastel. If someone just wanted to make money from selling Indian stuff, they'd just steal the most valuable stuff they could get their hands on."

I was being *real* careful now not to look at Marisa, who was staring at me with her mouth fully open.

I thought Marna was going to refuse, but after a few minutes, she said, "Sure. I ain't got nothing to hide."

"*Mom*!" Marisa said, and then shut her mouth, hard.

"Enough!" Marna said. "You let that girl see your backpack, and show her the blanket you keep your regalia in. We got nothing to hide." She looked at me here and continued, "And we don't need the police up in our business."

Marisa sighed heavily, and reluctantly got up and placed her backpack and blanket on the table.

I searched through all of it but found nothing I was looking for. Maybe I was wrong? Maybe I should search through every Anishinaabe girl's stuff who was doing

Fancy and Jingle? If I could find the mocs, I would be able to prove that that person was the one who had stolen the rest.

I thanked both of them, and me and Shana went back to where we'd been sitting to talk over our game plan.

"I was sure it was her!" I said, shaking my head. "But then again, I was sure it was Laura."

"I *know* it's her, girl," Shana said. "I been thinking about it. Not only was she a dang bully, and not only did we beat her butt at competition, but she was always talking about our florals, always checking them out way close and criticizing them. And not only *that*, but I know she and her mom were trying to make some. They didn't know how, unlike me. I got skillz."

We got up and started marching back to Marisa's mom's booth. I was thinking about another tactic. But we stopped halfway there. Marisa was running, full-on running, down the hallway with what were clearly mocs with pastel floral regalia in her hands, toward the exit!

"Marisa!" Shana yelled, and started running after her with me following, barely avoiding knocking people over as they went.

"Where's the fire?" an old uncle said as we ran past him, and then down the stairs.

"Man, she's fast," I said, out of breath, and watched Marisa burst through the front doors.

We made it all the way to the parking lot, where Marisa was about to jump into a big ol' powwow van.

That's when I got really mad! Maybe madder than I ever have been in my whole life. I stopped in the parking lot, put my hands on my knees, and yelled, "Marisa, are you really going to get into that van and drive away with other people's stuff?"

Marisa scrambled to open the door.

"Aren't you embarrassed? JEEZ!" I yelled.

Marisa stopped. She hung her head, and though I could hear her friend yelling, "C'mon, get in, what are you waiting for?" Marisa turned around.

Me and Shana started walking toward her, and I could see how red her face was. And *wow* was I tired from running.

"What the heck, Marisa!" Shana said, when we caught up to her. "How would you like it if we stole your stuff?"

Marisa opened and closed her mouth a few times. "I just . . . your families were always better than mine, and always like, winning at everything and made the best beadwork and I just . . . got . . . jealous!" she said, bursting into tears. "I'm sorry." She handed the mocs back. Then she pulled the barrettes and hair ties out of her pocket and handed them back too, her long hands shaking.

"It's *okay*, Marisa, daaaang," Shana said, shaking her head. "We can teach you how to do beadwork, and even find out what kind of patterns your family does. We could meet at my house every other Saturday and bead together. It'll be fire."

Marisa's lip started trembling, and I pulled an old tissue out of my pocket, pulled some lint off it, and handed it to her. She used it to wipe her eyes and the rest of her face where the tears had run down. I felt really bad for her. All of her meanness was just 'cause she hadn't learned how to bead and wanted to. And Shana was being *so nice*.

"Thanks, you guys," Marisa said, only sniffling a little now. "I really am sorry. I shouldn't have done it, and I never will again."

"Girl, come and sit down with us," Shana said. "And why don't I get you some fry bread?"

We walked back to the auditorium, my thighs still burning from my run, while Shana and Marisa talked about beading, and boys, and school. A good feeling came over me, and I could see the sun right behind the auditorium, beaming light all around it. It was really beautiful. I sighed, feeling satisfied and proud. Another crime solved by Tokala! Yes!

THE BALLAD OF MAGGIE WILSON

ANDREA L. ROGERS

I sat down in a cold metal folding chair and opened my book. For the first time since before dawn, I had a moment to myself. My aunt Mabel's a nurse for Indian Health Service, and weekends are big community outreach days. Plus, my little sister, Virginia, was going to dance in a jingle dress for the first time, which was a pretty big deal. Me, I was just helping my aunt with the raffle at the IHS health booth.

My only plan was to read and watch the people I didn't know walk by. I liked to try to guess their tribes from what they wore. I hadn't danced in the year since my father had died.

We're Cherokee Nation—from Oklahoma. As my uncle Roy says, we are not a powwow people, but we're an adaptable people. There are loads of great Cherokee pow-wow dancers, though.

Uncle Roy got into powwow dancing when he roomed with a fancy dancer at Haskell Indian Nations University. Now he mostly emcees. He is funny. And sneaky smart. It's a job requirement. Uncle Roy and Virginia decided to go visit his friend Sheldon Sundown, who is the emcee for this weekend's powwow.

One of our tables was covered with pamphlets and health-related giveaway items. The other table featured three raffle prizes. A large purple shawl with pink ribbon work and white fringe took up half the table. A silver concho-style belt buckle sat in the middle of a donated Pendleton on the other half.

"How much for this?" A skinny Indian kid picked up the belt buckle. It was a rectangle stamped with geometric designs emanating from an oval reddish coral stone in the center.

"It's a raffle," I said. I pointed at the sign. I had scribbled it at five in the morning, but I was pretty sure *Raffle tickets $1* was readable.

The kid would have fit in great at a rodeo. That didn't mean he wasn't Indian. Not every boy can be a fancy dancer, I guess. I was leaning toward a Plains tribe. If we'd been in Oklahoma, I might have guessed Kiowa. Up here, maybe Dakota or Potawatomi or Odawa. Maybe one of the Ojibwe tribes. It was hard to say. There are a lot of tribes at these powwows.

He held the silver belt buckle in his hand the way you hold a kitten that's too small. I looked at him over the top of my book and took out my earbuds.

After the funeral, my sister and I moved here to Ann Arbor with my aunt. Mom stayed in Tulsa to focus on nursing school and work extra at the hospital. She's always at work or school, so she gave me my dad's old phone to stay in touch. There are recordings of him playing guitar and singing on it. His reedy voice had been singing "Wichita Lineman" when the kid got my attention. It was a song Glen Campbell made famous, about a man repairing and stringing power lines for Wichita County.

When my father died a year ago, he was electrocuted in a bucket truck while doing electrical work on the big power lines. He wasn't a lineman for anyone anymore. Listening to him sometimes still made me cry. Sometimes it made me happy.

I scanned the kid's clothes for a simple tribal identifier. My own T-shirt read *Siyo!* That's Cherokee for "hi." If I saw someone else wearing that shirt, I would guess they were Cherokee as well.

The kid was tall, with longish dark hair. He had it sandwiched between a cowboy hat and a sheepskin-lined denim jacket. He reminded me of photos I had seen of my dad when he was that age. He was studying the cover of the book I was reading. I couldn't tell if he had a tribally specific T-shirt. I tried to be sneaky with my observations.

"That book looks cool," he said. He talked like he'd grown up around people for whom English was a second language, maybe a Rez, maybe Texas, maybe Canada.

I shrugged. I was reading S. E. Hinton's *The Outsiders* for the umpteenth time. Before he'd died, my dad had bought it for me. It was one of the few books my dad had enjoyed in school, and it fit in my back pocket. Music, not books, had been my dad's thing. Nowadays, there are better books out there for girls, Indian kids, and other outsiders, several by Indian authors.

"Have you read *Tex*?" the boy asked.

I shook my head.

"She's an okay writer," he said.

Impressive. A lot of people assumed S. E. Hinton was a man, not a young woman who had written a book and published it when she was only eighteen. My dad hoped I'd be a writing prodigy, too. He'd had more faith in my writing than I did.

"This piece," he said, touching the buckle. "Who made it? What tribe?"

"Diné artist donated it."

"Nice." The kid whistled. He reached in his pocket and took out a twenty.

I frowned. The doors hadn't officially opened, and my aunt had gone to get change. I wondered if the kid's family was selling or dancing or both.

"I can't break that," I said, "unless you're buying twenty tickets." That quip was as close as I was going to get to trying to make a sale.

"What's the money going to be used for?" the kid asked.

I stood up, intending to point to another handwritten sign, but realized I had forgotten to make it.

I took a deep breath and recited, "The money will be used to make pamphlets addressing the prevention of diabetes and HIV and promoting elder care and early childhood development in our urban Indian community."

"All good causes," he said as he set the buckle down. "Well, I'll be back."

I picked the buckle up and polished the fingerprints smudged between the stamped indentations. It was warm from being held.

I wondered if I should make a sign that said *Don't touch*.

I smelled the fry bread before I saw it. I looked up and the Indian rodeo kid of undetermined tribal origin was back. He held a plate with a big Indian taco on it.

"I got change," he said.

"And the World's Greatest Fry Bread."

He laughed. "I'll let you know."

"My friend Joey's mom makes it. He brought me some earlier. It is the best."

The kid nodded and handed me a dollar. I pulled out the raffle tickets, gave him one, and handed him a pen. He wrote a phone number, but under the name and address he just wrote *Tex*.

I took it and squinted at him. The only tribes I knew with Reservations in Texas were the Tigua, the Kickapoo, and the Alabama-Coushatta. A lot of Lipan Apaches and the Texas Band of Yaquis, too. The Choctaws and Chickasaws in Oklahoma lived close to the border with Texas. I looked for some evidence pointing to one of those tribes.

Nothing.

"Long way from home," I said.

"Yeah." He looked around. "You finish that book?"

"Yeah."

"Want to trade?" He reached into his back pocket and pulled out a beat-up book with a motorcycle on the front. It was the one he had asked me about earlier. *Tex*. "I've read this one a bunch. I haven't read *The Outsiders*," he said, extending the book toward me.

I hesitated. It was silly to think giving a paperback book to someone was like giving away a piece of my father. My father'd be glad someone was reading a book he liked.

I got the book from my backpack.

The kid was touching the fringe on the donated shawl. I still hadn't made that *Don't touch* sign. "You dance?" he asked, as I handed him the book.

I shrugged. I didn't know yet, I guess.

"Yeah, me either. My stepdad's a fancy dancer, though." He paused. "When's the drawing?"

"Tomorrow at six p.m. When they announce all the contest winners. But you don't have to be present to win."

"I'll be there."

My aunt Mabel sent me to go take pictures of Grand Entry. My mom wanted to see Virginia in the jingle dress. I took one of her and Uncle Roy, portrait quality. I took another photo while they danced in with everyone else for Grand Entry. I sent them to my mom, and she texted back immediately two emojis, one happy, one crying. **Pic of you?** she added.

I ignored the message.

The first intertribal was at one thirty p.m. An intertribal is when everyone is invited to dance, all nations. I kept watching the clock.

At about one fifteen, my aunt asked me how I was going to wear my shawl. I could fold it and hang it over my arms in front of me, or I could wrap it around my shoulders. My aunt took the shawl off the hanger. "Come here, Maggie."

I stood. She wrapped the blue material around me. I stretched out my arms and grabbed the corners of the shawl. This was the first thing my mom had sewn in years.

Making time between work and classes probably cost her some sleep. But the stitches were straight and the fringe was evenly spaced. Knowing how many hours fringing it had taken, I wondered if she had found someone to help her with it so she could mail it in time for the powwow. I brought the corners up close under my chin, and it smelled like home. Strange how a smell put you back in your kitchen, talking to your parents at the dining table.

"Let me get a picture for your mom."

I slipped it off and felt like I was going to cry. "Maybe later," I said. "Why don't you go dance this time? I'll go tonight."

My aunt nodded. She got her shawl and went to find Uncle Roy and Virginia. I sat down and went back to reading *Tex*. I had no idea S. E. Hinton was so crazy about horses.

The Tiny Tots exhibition was set for three thirty p.m. My aunt and a nurse named Shawna were taking turns covering the booth. Shawna watched the table while we all went to watch Virginia dance for the first time. The exhibition was for children six and under. Virginia was five. If she kept up the jingle dancing, she would be competing in less than two years.

On the way to the arena, Virginia was unusually quiet. She turned and caught my eye and slid her hand into mine.

I knew she was nervous.

My uncle checked her braid and barrettes one last time, while my aunt adjusted the number pinned to her back. We found an opening in the circle to send her through. The singer started and when the drum began, Virginia danced away from us, into the circle.

When it was over, everyone cheered for the Tiny Tots. The emcee called all their names and their nations, encouraged them to keep dancing, and gave them each five dollars.

Virginia beamed. "I want to go buy fry bread with honey!"

We all looked at her in her beautiful jingle dress. I said what we were all thinking: "Not in that outfit, Virginia."

We got her into her street clothes, and she ate a giant piece of fry bread dripping with honey. The whole thing. She only got a little honey on her shirt. Most of it was on her fingers. Soon, Virginia crashed out, snoring softly on the blankets underneath our table.

Our booth was toward the back of the vending area. Occasionally, a swarm of people would show up because the emcee had reminded the crowd we were there, doing free and anonymous health screenings. We weren't getting as much traffic on our raffle as my aunt wanted.

At dinnertime, my aunt sent Uncle Roy and Virginia for plates of food and she told me to walk around selling raffle tickets. My sales strategy was to carry the jar of tickets and stand around and wait for an older person to ask me what I was raffling. It was pretty effective.

At one of the supper tables, I saw the rodeo kid with his family. He was eating slowly while reading. I couldn't tell what tribe his mom was, or if she was Indian at all. I assumed the man with them wearing a *Blackfoot Pride* T-shirt instead of his fancy dancer regalia was his stepdad. When I stopped at the crowded table they were sitting at, the kid looked up.

"Selling my belt buckle?" His mom looked at him, and he explained he'd bought a chance on the raffle. She bought him another ticket but put her name on it. I examined the ticket as I walked back to our booth, but I couldn't guess what tribe he was from her ticket, either.

Virginia and I had moved in with my aunt Mabel at the beginning of the school year, and I really hadn't made a lot of friends. My aunt said it was because I preferred books and my own company. Maybe. I had friends back in Tulsa who I texted occasionally. I didn't see any point in making a bunch of new friends temporarily.

Missing my dad kind of filled in the space where I should have been lonely. I mean, I already felt so full of sadness there didn't seem to be any room in my life to be lonely. Sometimes, I tried writing stories and poems about him, about us. When your dad dies, you might appreciate everything you can remember about him. And all the things you never got to do with him loom large.

Suddenly, I remembered that I had been using a poem I wrote about my dad as a bookmark. It was in the copy of *The Outsiders* I had loaned the kid. The poem was about grief and not dancing and the loss of my father. Would the kid read it? Worse, would he read it and think it was terrible?

My worry was interrupted by a group of rowdy Elders crowding around the table.

"Achukma! This looks good!" one shouted at another. They were Choctaw.

"Looky here, Amafo Billy! Aren't these colors the same as the college your granddaughter is going to?"

"They sure are. That shawl sure is pretty."

"Give me twenty tickets!" his wife said.

Her friends laughed. "Why don't you just buy all the tickets, Joanna?"

"I have a good feeling. Twenty is enough," Joanna said confidently.

Everyone laughed and helped her fill out her tickets. A few of them asked about the health screenings. They joked about getting their blood sugar measured after eating all that fry bread and disappeared into the crowd.

◈

Shawna had come back to take over the health screenings for the rest of the night. Uncle Roy went to talk to his friend the emcee. I managed to avoid the last intertribal of the night by offering to watch the raffle part of the booth while my aunt and Virginia went to dance.

My uncle showed up and helped me break down our booth. We walked out to the car to lock the prizes and raffle money in the trunk. We got into the car and turned the heater on high while we waited for Virginia and my aunt. Uncle Roy turned on the overhead light so I could read the book the kid had loaned me.

"Hey, Uncle Roy?"

"Yeah."

"I think I'm ready to return to the powwow circle. Could you help me with a giveaway basket?"

Uncle Roy smiled. "I already got everything."

We got to sleep in a little later the next morning because everything was all set up at the powwow. When we got there, Uncle Roy took Virginia and me to meet the powwow committee and tell them we were donating a basket in honor of our father. "Bring it with you at four thirty," Sheldon, the emcee, said.

When I went to our table, Shawna had my copy of *The Outsiders*. "Rosebud Sioux kid dropped this off for you.

And he bought another ticket for the raffle."

I looked at the ticket he had filled out. Once more it just said *Tex*. I didn't know if that was his name or address. I never would have guessed Rosebud Sioux from Texas. Then again, I was an Oklahoma Cherokee on Ojibwe land. Indians went wherever we wanted to, just like everyone else.

I wondered if the kid had finished reading my book as I flipped through it. The bookmark was missing. I felt more nervous again, the way you feel when you get called on in class. I hoped it hadn't fallen out and been read by some random stranger, or worse yet, someone who knew me. My name was on it. It was modeled on the pattern of "Nothing Gold Can Stay" by Robert Frost. It's an important poem in *The Outsiders*. I'd impressed a few English teachers by memorizing it.

The kid's copy of *Tex* was tucked into the back pocket of my jeans. I'd stayed up late reading it, so we could trade back. I hoped he still had my bookmark.

Uncle Roy and Virginia showed up in time to take me to dance during the intertribal. I was looking forward to it now. When you love someone and they die, you feel like the whole world should notice—all good things should stop. Not dancing for the year had been the only way I'd had to mark that, to silently tell the world around me this loss mattered. Around me the world had gone on, but I hadn't danced.

Before we went into the circle, Aunt Mabel took a picture of me wrapped in the shawl. She texted my mother immediately. I think she caught me smiling, even.

We joined the circle together. It felt good to follow my baby sister in the dancing, to know my aunt danced in the circle next to me. She gave me and Virginia some money to drop on the blanket in front of the drum. Now that I had finally joined the dancing, I was sad when it stopped.

Later that afternoon, we all attended the giveaway hosted by the powwow committee. Virginia and I carried a laundry basket full of groceries. Well, I carried the basket. She carried a jar of honey from home that tasted of Oklahoma clover.

I didn't have to hold it very long. The emcee announced to the crowd, "The Wilson family would like to return to the dance arena. They are presenting a basket in honor of a family member who passed a year ago."

I hadn't expected to find myself crying while I stood holding a basket of groceries. But there I was. One of the powwow committee members came and took it from me. She shook my hand and took the honey from Virginia and shook her hand. The jingles on Virginia's dress tinkled happily.

In some traditions, they don't say the names of the recently deceased because it is like calling them back to our world. I wondered if that would be such a bad thing.

Just before six we stopped selling raffle tickets and took the jar and the prizes to the emcee booth.

"Before we announce the winners for the dance competitions, we're going to pull tickets for the raffle. I'm going to let my friend from the Cherokee Nation, Roy Wilson, take over. I'm going to go see if I can have all the leftover fry bread," Sheldon finished.

The crowd laughed as Uncle Roy took the microphone. You could hear the smile on his face. I held the jar of tickets. You didn't have to be present to win, but it was always more exciting if you were.

"The first prize is this beautiful Pendleton, donated by Louis Stephenson. Virginia, can you draw a ticket?"

Virginia stuck her hand in the jar and pulled out five tickets. I noticed one of them clearly said, "Tex." I reached out and grabbed them, and handed Uncle Roy one of the others.

"The winner is Jack Headbird."

A cheer went up from the drum group, and they banged their drums in celebration.

"Looks like the drum group will be able to keep warm in their camp tonight."

Everyone laughed and the drums pounded.

"Let's give away the next prize, this beautiful belt buckle."

I gulped. I was still holding Tex's ticket in my hand with three others. Virginia had gotten them all sticky. I tried dropping them back in.

Uncle Roy put his hand in, and it came back out with one ticket pinched between his fingers and the one with "Tex" written on it stuck to the back of his hand.

He laughed. "Looks like I have the next two winners picked. The winner of the belt buckle is Joanna Tingle."

The group of Choctaw Elders roared with laughter. The Choctaw grandma got up and smiled. She walked toward us, took the buckle, and stood next to me.

"The winner of this beautiful shawl, donated by Elizabeth Wolfe, is . . ." He paused while everyone held their breath and then said loudly, "Tex!"

The kid's family erupted into cheers and laughter, too.

The kid looked sheepish and blushed. He waved at us and walked quickly up. Before he made it to us, the Choctaw grandma stopped him. He leaned down and she whispered to him. He smiled real big as she handed him the belt buckle. She stepped forward and took the shawl.

Everyone cheered. The Choctaw Elders were the loudest.

The kid stepped back where I was standing. He was

polishing the belt buckle with the corner of his shirt. Virginia may have gotten some honey on it, too.

"Is your name really 'Tex'?"

He laughed and shook his head. "Did you get your book back?"

I remembered his book in my back pocket. "Um, yeah, but—"

"Oh, man, I'm sorry. I took your bookmark out because I was afraid it would get lost." He pulled out his wallet and took out the folded paper I had used as a bookmark. On the outside of the wallet it said *Rosebud Sioux*. That was how Shawna knew what tribe he was.

"Rosebud Sioux aren't a Texas tribe," I said.

He smiled. "No, we're not. But it's home for now. Did you like the book?"

"Yeah. What about you?"

He smiled. "Needed more horses and some Indians. I really liked the poem, though."

I quoted the first two lines of Robert Frost's poem.

"I meant the other one. The one on the bookmark."

I froze.

"You're a good writer, Maggie Wilson," he said.

I smiled in spite of my blushing face. "Thanks, Tex."

We stood there quietly for a few minutes. He seemed to be admiring his new belt buckle, but then he said suddenly, quietly, "Sorry about your dad."

"Me too," I said.

And I was sorry. I was sorry there were stories he'd told me that I couldn't remember. I was sorry about the songs he'd sung but not recorded. Like I said, some tribes believe to say the names of the dead is to call them back.

I didn't have to call him back, though. The poem on the bookmark had been about loss and grief, but some of my stories were like a good dream. I got to be with him when I was writing, I got to say things to him I hadn't. I got to imagine another universe for him and me. In another time and place, the intertribal dancing would last as long as you wanted. The drummers would play a song about a lineman, and my father would join us in the circle.

BAD DOG

Joseph Bruchac

The pickup truck was standard powwow issue. An old
Ford with one broken headlight. Older than usual,
though. Maybe, with its rounded fenders, boxy shape, and
wooden bed, something from the fifties. The old man leaning against it fit right in with his truck. Indian, from the
look of him. Not in regalia, but in everyday dress like most
folks his age on the Rez. Black leather work boots, sort of
like the ones Uncle Charlie had favored when he was on a
job hanging iron. Levi's jeans that were worn, but clean,
maybe even pressed with an iron that morning before he
put them on. Not a hole in them, unlike the new designer
jeans that were full of strategic, fashionable ripped spaces.
Like the ones Wendell had seen the other kids from his
school wearing on the weekends. But not him, even if he
had the money. He hated jeans like that. Purchase one of -
those pairs of jeans, you were buying more air than cloth.

The old guy had topped it off with a plaid long-sleeved shirt that had a really well-beaded bolo tie fastened tight. So tight that it made the loose skin on his neck stand out, sort of like the wattles on a turkey. The clan animal on the bolo tie was a bear. Like the bear pendant carved out of bone on Wendell's necklace. The necklace Wendell could never wear to school back in Binghamton without having dumb remarks made about it by the non-Native kids, who made up 95 percent of the school population. The way he got treated for being Indian made him feel so bad sometimes he just wished he was dead.

"Hey," the old guy said, touching two fingers to the brim of his cowboy hat.

Just that one word, but said in a quiet, friendly way.

"Hey," Wendell said, putting down the big stainless-steel cooking pot. It was three-quarters full of the water that Aunt Maisie had told him to bring back to her portable kitchen. All set up to serve out the best corn soup in seven states, alongside her authentic Navajo tacos. And even though she was too polite to say it, her fry bread was at least as good as that at the food stand across from them labeled *World's Best Fry Bread*. Now, though, she'd needed more water from the RV, which hadn't been able to fit into their vending space and so was parked on the far side of the field.

Wendell's bright idea had been to avoid making two

quarter-mile-long trips by not bringing just half a pot full like he'd been told. Genius, right? Give him that much more time to change into his outfit for the smoke dance competition in one hour. Except it was breaking his thirteen-year-old back to lug that heavy a load.

"Water's heavy, innit?" the old man said.

Wendell smiled. It was okay to be teased that way. No malice or sarcasm in it, like when kids in school called him "Little Chief" or even "Tonto," meaning both as a put-down.

"Water's wet, too," Wendell said.

The old guy laughed. A nice, deep laugh that showed his teeth and made him look younger. Maybe he wasn't quite as old as Wendell had thought. Just worn—like leather gets from being left out in the sun.

"You got me there," he said. Then he spoke a phrase in Abenaki.

"Paakwenogwesian, nidoba."

The greeting that means "you appear new to me, my friend."

"Alnoba?" Wendell asked.

"Ôhô," the man replied. "Ta kia?"

"Ôhô, Alnoba nia. Ndelawezi Wendell."

"All right," the old guy replied. "Ndeliwizi Ktsi Mdawela."

Ktsi Mdawela. *Big Loon*, Wendell thought. *Cool. Maybe*

I should have told him my Indian name. Too late for that now.

"So, Wendell," the old guy said, "I bet your mom or your auntie is waiting for that pot and that water, right?"

Wendell nodded.

Big Loon pointed with his lips at the bed of his truck. There was something dark and alive in there. Wendell could see through a gap in the wooden side that it moved just a tad as he looked there.

"Come back later and I'll introduce you to Bad Dog. Now go dance. You'll do good."

Wendell picked up the cooking pot. It seemed lighter now. He was able to walk faster with it. Maybe because he was anxious to reach Aunt Maisie so he could get into his regalia for the competition. Or maybe because he was curious about who Bad Dog was. And also how the old guy who called himself Big Loon knew Wendell was going to dance.

The man who was the smoke dance singer was from Onondaga. And he was good. Wendell had heard him singing before, drum held firm in his left hand as he tapped out the rhythm, voice high and strong. Wendell spun, dipped, his feet moving fast and perfectly in time. And when the song stopped, he ended up right with it, bent way over at the waist, balanced on one foot. He didn't win, but he was in the top three in his age group. Which was his best showing yet.

"Oh man, their feet were just about breaking the sound barrier," Sheldon Sundown, the Seneca emcee, exclaimed over the PA. "You all give it up for these three young warriors." And Wendell couldn't help but smile as all the people gathered around the dance circle applauded.

Wendell changed back into his T-shirt and jeans, putting his regalia carefully into the closet space Aunt Maisie had cleared for him in their big Winnebago RV.

"We need you, nephew," Aunt Maisie called from outside.

And that was true for sure. Now that there was a break in the dancing, people were lining up in droves to buy the best food at the powwow. No time to check out whatever was in the back of that vintage pickup. Throwing on his apron, he took over the grill from his cousin Eddie, who moved over to start ladling out corn soup.

The rush lasted a solid hour and a half. It only calmed down when the drums started again and people began heading back to the circle to watch the fancy dancers. Aunt Maisie rapped her big spoon against the empty steel pot and looked at Wendell, who slipped off his apron and picked it up without saying a word.

"You doin' good, nephew," his aunt said. "Take your time."

◈

"Don't miss your water, till your well goes dry," Big Loon said as Wendell put down the pot—filled higher than the last trip. Then the old man laughed—a laugh just as warm and friendly as the first time he'd spoken to Wendell. He was sitting now in one of a pair of old-fashioned folding canvas camp chairs that he'd set up along the sunny side of his one-eyed pickup. Even though it was about 45 degrees outside, it was comfortable there.

"I got extra here," Wendell said. "Thought you might want some for . . ." He nodded toward the back of the truck.

"Right thoughtful of you," Big Loon said. "He will be thirsty." He stood up, reached in through the open window of the truck, and pulled out a clean-looking clay pot with curlicue designs on its sides. "Want to dip it out with this?"

Wendell nodded and took the clay pot. It felt good in his hands. It was more than just smooth and cool. It felt almost as if it was saying something to him. He dipped it into the water and lifted it up. Hardly a drop ran down the side. It was as if the pot drank the water up.

Big Loon motioned with his chin toward the back of the truck, then held out one hand for Wendell to stay back before opening the gate.

"Bad Dog," the old man said in a soft voice. "You thirsty?"

A deep rumble of a growl that seemed to shake the

ground around them answered that question. But it wasn't threatening. Somehow Wendell could sense that. Big Loon unhooked the gate, lowered it, and spoke over his shoulder to Wendell.

"Give it to him slow, Grandson," he said. "And don't be trying to pet him. He's not like that happy-go-lucky dog wearing a *Rez Dawg* T-shirt been wandering around all day." Then he stepped aside so that Wendell could see into the bed of the truck.

What Wendell saw surprised him. He'd been expecting something the size of a bear, especially after that growl. But what looked up at him was a stocky, muscular little canine no bigger than a beagle, though its head and body and tail were wolflike. Its fur was jet black except for two white spots over its eyes. Those eyes—which looked up at him with a calm, knowing gaze—one was black and one was as blue as the sky.

Wendell put the clay pot full of water down in front of the animal. It looked up and then seemed to nod approvingly at him before stepping forward to drink.

"Good enough, Grandson." Big Loon gently moved Wendell back as he closed and hooked up the tailgate. "Now come sit a spell."

Wendell eased gingerly down into one of the brown camp chairs.

"Don't worry," Big Loon chuckled, as he sat next to

him. "These chairs been through more campaigns than you can count. Got 'em right after leaving Carlisle. Now want t' hear 'bout Bad Dog?"

"You bet!"

"Nope, not me. Never go near a casino."

Wendell looked down at his feet and shook his head. Big Loon was like so many other Elders he knew—totally in love with their own corny sense of humor. But he had to smile because, once again, it was so different from the kind of mean-spirited crap he had to deal with at school just about every day. Thinking of that made his smile disappear.

"School's rough, innit?"

Wendell looked up. "How'd you know that?"

"Can't say for sure. Maybe just that I know that look on your face, Grandson. Had that same look on mine when I was your age. But at least these days you don't have boarding-school teachers that beat you, chain you in the cellar, and feed you on bread and water, if you speak a word in Indian. But, hey, enough about that. You want to hear about Bad Dog."

"Uh-huh."

The old man spread his arms wide.

"A *long* time ago," he said, stretching out that second word for what felt like a half hour, "there was a boy like you. His parents were gone and he was living with someone who said she was his aunt." Big Loon paused. "But not like your aunt, who is a right decent person. This aunt lived with him in a cave and kept her face covered up. And all she ate was raw meat from the things that boy hunted for her. Every evening she'd feel his arm and then growl, 'Not fat enough yet.'

"It had been like that since he was real little. Life was hard for him and he thought he'd never get away. Then, one night, when she thought he was asleep, that boy looked through a hole in his deerskin blanket and saw her face as she ate some birds he'd caught for her. She had teeth like a wolf and big staring eyes. That's when he realized she was not his aunt at all. She was one of them cannibal monsters called Chenoos. She was just waiting till he was big enough and then she'd eat him.

"Well, he knew what he had to do. He waited till she was asleep and then took off running. He ran and ran, even faster when he heard her chasing him and howling behind him. Finally, he came to a small longhouse where an old man was standing outside with a little black dog right next to him.

"'Nosis!' that old man said. 'Grandchild! I'm so glad t' see you. You've been missing so long.'

"And just then that Chenoo caught up. 'Old man,' she howled, 'I'm a-going to eat your grandson and then I'm a-going to eat you.'

"That's when Bad Dog growled, and the old man smiled.

"'Bad Dog,' he said. 'Get bigger.' And just like that, the dog got twice as big. 'Get bigger,' he said again, and that dog doubled its size once more. He kept on saying 'Get bigger' till that dog was taller than the trees. The Chenoo tried to run, but Bad Dog just grabbed that monster and swallowed her with one gulp. And that boy and his grandfather went back to their people and lived a long time happily. Amen."

Wendell blinked his eyes. "What's it mean? That story?"

Big Loon shook his head. "Can't say for sure. Maybe it means something for you. Like big as your troubles might be, something might come along one day and take 'em away. "

"How come you told me that story?"

Big Loon laughed. "Grandson, easy to tell you been in a white man school. All they teach you is to ask questions and expect one of them cut-and-dried answers, eh? Well, I can't say for sure. So. Let's just say it was because you happened to come along."

He nodded toward the steel pot. "And right about now I expect your aunt is waiting for you to come along with that water."

Wendell stood and lifted the water pot. It didn't feel near as heavy as before, and it wasn't because he'd dipped some of the water out for Bad Dog. He just felt stronger.

"Wliwini, n'mahom. Thank you, Grandfather."

"Nda kagwi, nosis. Now get going."

When he got back to the food booth, the fancy dancing was still going on.

"Wendell," Aunt Maisie said. "How'd you do that?'

Wendell put down the pot. "Do what?"

"Get back so fast with that water. Last time it took you half an hour."

Wendell felt confused. "Can't say for sure," he said.

Aunt Maisie stared at him, a funny look on her face. "What did you say?"

"Can't say for sure?"

Aunt Maisie put one hand up to her chin. "Lord, nephew, not only is that what he used to say, you even sound like him."

Wendell started to ask who she was talking about. But before he could open his mouth, someone else lifted the back flap of the tent and slipped into the booth. It was his uncle Charlie.

"Lookit this," he said to them, holding up two familiar-looking canvas chairs. "Real antiques. Even got the date printed on them."

US GOV'T 1918 was stamped in faded letters on the back of each chair.

"This old fella in a truck older'n him just sold 'em

to me. Ten bucks each." Uncle Charlie grinned. "Some bargain, eh? Just like the chairs you told me your great-grampa, who lived to be a hundred and three, had from his time in World War I. Wendell Washington, wasn't it? But what was his Indian name?"

Wendell could feel the smile on his own face getting bigger.

"Big Loon," he said.

"How'd you know that?" his aunt and uncle said at the same time.

Wendell shook his head. "Can't say for sure."

BETWEEN THE LINES

Cynthia Leitich Smith

Electric colors and pulsating song beckoned from inside the high school.

Near the busy entrance, Mel leaned against a pillar, clutching a worn paperback novel. Wind felt chilly. Her stomach, hollow. She glanced toward the video shoot on the lawn, where her mom was still—*still*—talking about her time in the coast guard.

That boy on the other side of the doors, the one seated against the wall on the concrete walk . . . was he using his phone to take a picture of her? Why? She wasn't dressed in regalia or doing anything interesting. "Hey, you! Stop that!"

The boy, Ray, froze at the warning in her voice. In the parking lot, he'd noticed her arriving with her mom, who was being interviewed along with his grampa Halfmoon for a documentary on Native veterans.

Earlier that afternoon, Ray had been wandering around the powwow, sketching and using his hand-me-down cell phone to take reference photos for future sketches. He'd come outside to get some fresh air. The way Mel had gripped her book had caught his eye.

"Don't you have somewhere to be?" she asked him.

He opened his mouth and closed it again. He felt embarrassed, unsure what to say.

Right then, a couple of Elder ladies, approaching the entrance, stopped in their tracks.

"You all right?" asked the Elder in long beaded earrings and a long denim coat.

"Yeah." Mel pointed in the general direction of the shoot. "My mom's over there."

"Hmm." The other Elder was sporting a Detroit Pistons jacket and a fuzzy blue scarf. "Looks like they'll be busy for a while." She gestured to invite Mel inside. "You'd best come along. The weather's all over the place this week. We had sleet—"

"More like rain," her companion replied.

"No, it was sleet, and a twister, too."

"It was *not* a twister, Priscilla!"

"Was so! I told you—I heard about it on the radio."

Mel liked them right off, and she was tired of waiting outside.

With a friendly grin, Priscilla added, "This sourpuss

is my sister, Laurel. We drove in earlier this week to visit our niece. She's a student in the architecture school at the college."

Nodding, Mel texted her mom that she was heading back to the powwow. Mel was about to introduce herself when Laurel asked, "Where're your people from?"

Meanwhile, Ray had tucked his phone into his clear backpack and gathered up his colored pencils and sketchbook. The girl was already gone.

What a mess that had been! Maybe he should've asked her permission before taking the photo. He definitely should've. He'd even thought about it, but Ray had a shy streak.

Even if he'd been back home at Chicago's annual powwow or splitting deep-dish pizza with his baseball buddies, Ray wasn't a big talker. But he was always doing something, and today he was mostly focused on drawing. His art teacher had told him that hands and feet were among the hardest subjects to draw. "If you can master hands, you'll be able to do anything."

Ray took off jogging across the school lawn. The documentary maker, Marita, had mentioned the importance of natural light and sound quality. That was why she'd set up the shoot outside, but Ray hadn't expected it to take so long. He should've known that Grampa, who was the social one in the family, would get caught up in all the excitement and make a bunch of new friends. In any case, Grampa wasn't being filmed at that very moment, so Ray said, "Okay if I go inside to check out the vendor booths?"

"You go and find that Carly," Grampa Halfmoon said. "Offer to help out at their booth."

Marita paused what she was doing, waved hello at Ray, and raised her camera again. She hailed from the Tigua people of Ysleta del Sur Pueblo, near El Paso.

While working on the film, she was traveling from coast to coast with family, including her cousin-in-law Carly, who sold books and maps at powwows and other Native events.

That morning at the hotel, over bacon and waffles, Grampa Halfmoon and Carly—who was Muscogee Creek and Cherokee—had really hit it off. Carly had shown a real interest when Ray opened his sketchbook and flipped through a few drawings he'd created on the train ride into Ann Arbor. Ray had appreciated the attention. His buddies back home were a lot of fun, but they mostly talked about sports, not art.

In the vendor area, Ray spotted a T-shirt that said *Ancestor Approved*. He studied beadwork and bought a beaded key chain to give his grandfather. Finally, Carly waved Ray over and made space on the display table. "Good to see you again, kiddo. Want to draw right here?"

"Sure thing, wado!" Settling in, Ray reached for a big

coffee-table book on beadwork. He turned to a glossy, close-up color photo of an artist's hands at work. Ray began sketching.

In the concession stands area, Mel had slipped her paperback novel into her puffy purple coat pocket. She was maybe halfway through the story. She'd spent babysitting money on it. Mel felt obligated to push on through, but it was tough going.

The Elder ladies were telling her all about their soon-to-be-architect niece's plans to study abroad in Shanghai, about their visit to a fancy local delicatessen in Ann Arbor, about the station wagon they'd named "Maud," about their car troubles, and about how Sheldon Sundown, the "dashing emcee," had rescued them with jumper cables last night in the hotel parking lot.

Mel listened and listened and listened and listened, and finally, she happened to mention that the documentary being filmed outside was about Native military vets.

"You don't say!" Priscilla exclaimed. "Isn't that interesting, Laurel?"

"She served in the navy," Laurel said, handing Mel an orange pop.

"I served in the navy," Priscilla echoed. "Do I ever have stories to tell!"

Sipping her icy drink, Mel could only imagine. A few

minutes later, the sisters excused themselves to go talk to Marita the filmmaker and . . . Mel felt better.

A hearty dose of caring Elders had done her good.

Mel wandered into the gym, figuring that by now her mom *had* to be done with the filming and probably got caught up chatting. With Laurel and Priscilla in the mix, she might be outside socializing until dinner. Mel grinned at the thought. Her first real smile of the day.

Scanning the bleachers, Mel made her way to a spot in the top corner to sit. She'd tied the padded coat around her waist and had to twist a bit to fish the novel out of the pocket.

Mel opened the paperback, closed it again. She tapped the novel against her knee. It was a fantasy story, and Mel loved fantasy. It had the word "Indian" in the title, and she'd wanted to read a story with a Native character. But it was chock-full of old-timey Hollywood Indian speak. Mel regretted the five bucks she'd spent on it at her local used bookstore.

About halfway down the bleachers, a girl about her age with cropped dark hair was using a real camera (not a phone app) to photograph an adorable, chubby baby wearing a beaded headband. What with the music of the drum and a gym full of people, Mel couldn't hear their laughter—the baby's or the girl's—but she could feel it.

She considered making her way over to them and

introducing herself, but what would she say? Mel had felt lost—more anxious than usual—since her best friend Emma had moved to Lansing over winter break. Mel's counselor had encouraged her to come to the powwow today instead of staying home with her auntie and little cousins. "Maybe you'll make a new friend." But it was always hard for Mel, talking to new people. She got nervous, froze up. What if she made a fool of herself?

The photographer girl looked so happy, confident.

Mel opened her book once more and tried again.

For the first time, Ray's sketch of beading hands, the sketch that poured from his colored pencils, resembled actual human hands. Sort of. Close enough. What a day!

It had helped to begin by breaking the palms and finger joints into basic shapes and paying more attention to the spaces between the fingers. He'd made real progress, and along the way, he'd also helped sell four copies of the pricey coffee-table book on beading.

Passersby were drawn in, curious to watch his artistic process.

"Kiddo, you've got a real future in bookselling," Carly said with a chuckle.

Ray ducked his head, embarrassed, and excused himself to get some fry bread.

"Hang on." Carly handed over some cash and waved

him on. "Get me a Navajo taco and a drink, too." As Ray went searching for lunch, Carly considered the available options.

Where to show off Ray's terrific new sketch? Table space was at a premium.

Being a Black Indian cowboy and a two-spirit activist, Carly proudly stocked nonfiction and poetry on both subjects, along with Native-created novels and a handful of picture books. Carly liked poetry the best, the way the words could light up a heartbeat, a misread signal, a careful stitch, or a sudden shift from strangers to friends.

After reconfiguring the book arrangement twice, Carly finally decided to display Ray's artwork in front alongside the bookmarks and business cards. They propped it up at an angle.

In the concessions area, Ray had more than one option for the World's Best Fry Bread, but he chose the stand where a boy who was about his age was chopping lettuce. Those would be interesting hands to draw. But then Ray remembered the girl with the book who'd hollered at him outside. Should he risk distracting the boy with the knife in his hand or interrupting while the stand was so busy? Probably not. *Okay*, Ray thought, *back to the camera app.* Only this time he'd be stealthier.

Joey, a Turtle Mountain Band Ojibwe, set the kitchen

knife down. "Hey, there. Uh, what's so exciting about lettuce?"

Ray had been caught in the act again. He shrugged. "I . . . I wasn't taking a picture of the lettuce. I was taking a picture of your hands chopping it." He held out his phone to show Joey all his photos of hands. "I use the pics as models to draw different positions."

"Huh. Good for you, man," Joey said, reaching for a ripe tomato.

Ray glanced down at his phone screen. It might be interesting to do a collage with all the photos of the hands in addition to drawing them. "You really sell the world's best fry bread?"

Joey tossed up the tomato, caught it one-handed. "We've all got our talents."

Appreciating the pose, Ray grinned and took a picture.

Carly took off a straw cowboy hat. "I've got just the book for you."

Mel brightened at the cover of *Skeleton Man*. She liked spooky stories.

"There's a sequel, too," Carly added, reaching. "I've got it right here."

Mel set her orange pop on the display table so she could flip through *Skeleton Man*, not realizing her drink was resting unevenly on Carly's business cards. Then she set her purse on the foldout table next to it and peeked inside her wallet.

"I'll take the first one." Mel frowned. "Don't have enough money for both."

"You don't say." Carly arched a brow. "What's that sticking out of your pocket?"

Mel pulled out the book she'd given up on. "I couldn't get into it."

"Uh-huh." Carly glanced at the cover, read the description on the back, and nodded thoughtfully. "I understand. How's about I trade you this for *The Return of Skeleton Man*?"

What a deal! In the exchange, Mel bumped into her purse, which bumped into her cup, which was already a tiny bit tilted, and *ka-splash!* The orange pop went *everywhere*. Inside Mel's purse, onto her puffy coat, onto her new books, and all over Ray's drawing.

Ray was walking up when he saw the accident. He hurried over, handing the food and drinks to Carly, who quickly turned to set it all on a cardboard box on the floor. Then Ray lifted Mel's purse out of the way.

"Give that back!" she exclaimed, yanking her purse back. A second later, Mel recognized him. "It's you, from outside. Why are you following me?"

"I am *not* following you!" Ray exclaimed. His voice bottomed out. "My sketch . . ."

"What?" She glanced down. "Oh." She realized that had been his drawing. Biting her lip, she appreciated the time it must've taken. The skill it must've taken. Orange soda pop was already staining the paper. The bookmarks and business cards were ruined, too.

"I'll run and get napkins," Ray said as fizzy liquid dripped off the table to the floor.

"Take it easy, kids," Carly began, clearing a stack of books out of the way. "It's a shame, but these things hap—" Ray had already disappeared in the crowd.

Mel began to back away, hugging her new books. "Sorry, sorry," she said to Carly. "I'm so sorry. I, um, my mom just texted me. I've got to go."

Before long, Ray returned with a whole roll of paper towels—donated by Joey—to sop up the spill. By then, Mel was gone. Ray thought about trying to find her, to tell her that there were no hard feelings. But, he figured, if she'd wanted to be friends, she wouldn't have rushed off like that. Besides, his fry bread was calling to him.

That evening, settling in on the Amtrak Wolverine train, Grampa Halfmoon was admiring his new beaded key chain and telling Ray all about the film shoot. ". . . Grand Traverse Band, they said. This lady, Priscilla was her name—she was there with her sister, Laurel. Real friendly, both of them. I sure do like folks who like to talk."

"Me too," Ray said, distracted. Right then a familiar-looking girl carrying a new, slightly orange paperback novel was walking toward them with a grown-up woman.

Grampa smiled at the woman. "Good to see you again! This is my grandson, Ray."

"You too! This is my daughter, Melanie."

As the two kids traded awkward hellos, their respective grown-ups picked up their conversation from earlier that day, discussing the Cubs baseball team. Which was all well and good, except that other passengers, standing behind mother and daughter, needed to get seated.

"Ray, how 'bout you sit over there with Melanie while we visit," Grampa suggested.

Lacking any excuse not to, Ray grabbed his clear backpack and relocated across the aisle.

For nearly an hour, he and Mel sat side by side on the train in absolute silence. She began reading *Skeleton Man*. He opened his sketch pad and—studying a photo on his phone—began drawing Joey's hand, modeling the tomato from the World's Best Fry Bread stand.

Mel liked her new book *much* better than the one she'd traded away, but she couldn't help sneaking the occasional peek at what Ray was doing. He caught her looking and offered a wan smile. Was he still mad at her? she wondered. He didn't seem mad.

"I'm sorry I spilled pop all over your drawing this

afternoon," she said in a quiet rush. "I didn't do it on purpose. I didn't even notice the picture until . . ." That hadn't sounded right. "I'm not saying it wasn't a good picture," she went on. "It was really pretty." Was he one of those boys who hated anything to do with himself being called "pretty"? She hoped not.

Mel pursed her lips. She still wasn't happy about him randomly taking pictures of her, but she didn't want him to think that she'd ruined his work on purpose either.

Ray took a breath. She was talking to him. Least he could do was reciprocate. "It's okay, Melanie." He said her name slowly, like he was trying out the word. "Really, my ferret has eaten some of my best artwork. He's spilled watery paint on it, shredded it, stolen it."

Was that insulting, comparing her to his pet? Ray didn't mean it that way. "Not that you're like a ferret. You're definitely a person."

At Mel's quizzical, vaguely amused expression, he reached for his phone and tapped his camera app a couple of times to show her a photo of Bandit.

Mel grinned at the image. "He's cute. Lots of personality?"

"*So* much personality," Ray agreed. "My grampa calls him 'ornery.'"

Ray tapped his screen a couple more times to get back to the grid of photos. He tapped the image of Mel's hands, holding the paperback novel she'd traded away at Carly's booth. He'd done his best to zoom in, but the photo wasn't as good as those he'd taken from a closer distance.

"Sorry, I should've asked first." There, he'd said it. Ray had been tempted to explain away the mistake by saying he didn't want to interrupt her reading—like he hadn't wanted to interrupt Joey chopping lettuce at the fry bread stand. But truth was, it was never easy for Ray to talk to new people. So he handed her the phone instead.

Mel scrolled and studied his images. A lot of pics of Grampa Halfmoon and Bandit, a handful of Wrigley Field and sparkling lake views. So many hands—young and old, shaded in a range of beiges and browns. She glanced at his open notebook again.

Returning the phone, she said, "You're an artist."

The whole train seemed to shimmer. The stars shone brighter out the window.

Ray knew Grampa and his art teacher believed in him, but nobody had ever said, "You're an artist." Just like that. Let alone someone his own age. Maybe Mel wasn't easy to get to know, but she sure did have a kind heart. "I'm trying to learn how to draw people," he said. "Hands—they're hard. So are feet. I haven't even tried feet yet."

Then they were chatting away. Mel said she was Muscogee Creek and Odawa, that her friends called her "Mel," and that she lived with her mom and a tabby cat named

Dragon in Kalamazoo. Ray said he was Cherokee and Seminole, that his friends called him Ray, and that he lived with Bandit and Grampa Halfmoon in the Albany Park neighborhood of Chicago.

"Maybe you and your mom could meet up with me and Grampa for a Cubs game," Ray suggested, ducking his head a little. "Would you like that, Mel?"

He wanted to see her again? "Yeah," Mel said. "I mean, I'd have to check with my mom, but I think she'd really go for it."

Earlier that day, Mel had been in a bad mood. She hadn't liked that one book. She'd hardly paid attention to the Fancy Shawl dancers, and they were her favorite. Sure, she'd had some nice moments, hanging out with her mom, talking to Priscilla, Laurel, and Carly.

But mostly, even though she'd been surrounded by so many people, Mel had felt alone and tight in her skin. She and Ray had gotten off to a rough start. Make that "starts"—plural. Who would've guessed that she'd end up with a new friend?

"Can you draw my hands reading *this* book instead?" Mel opened *Skeleton Man*. "I'm sitting right here beside you. You won't even have to take a picture."

"Glad to," Ray replied, breaking out his colored pencils.

CIRCLES

CAROLE LINDSTROM

First powwow.
First plane ride—Detroit!
Arriving at high school,
Nations are gathering.
Mom met Dad
and moved far away.
Raised apart
and distant from
our ways.

Want to remember
everything.
Trusty camera—check!
Show and share with friends
back in DC.

Not during honor songs
or sacred moments.
Ask first outside arena.
And don't touch regalia.
Ready!

Drum pounds
BOOM BOOM BOOM BOOM.
Ground under my feet
sounds
boom boom boom boom.
It feels like home.

Like a circle
joining together,
a line heading
in opposite
directions.

We come together
Like a circle.
Like we
never left.
Because we are
all related.

Women in their jingle dresses,
straight and tall,
glide across the floor in their
soft moccasins—barely touching,
leather, wood,
leather, air,
making circles as they float.

Circles
In the jingles
In the skirts
In the drum
In the turns
In the lives

Fancy dancers in bright regalia
spin and dip.
Colorful ribbons adorn,
feathers flying
in the sky,
making whirling circles.

Circles
In the feathers
In the footwork

In the beadwork
In the drum
In the lives.

Auntie Rose
bouncing grandbabies
on her round knees.
Baby Savannah wearing her
beaded headband.
Beads, circles,
touched by
aunties, kokums,
and me.

Bleachers filled with relatives,
some seeing each other
for the first time.
Is that Cousin Charlie
at the big drum?
I've only seen him in photos.
And Cousin Wanda
lining up for the Shawl Dance?

We are all related,
no matter how far apart.

Raised with powwows, or not.
We are all connected.
Coming together,
like circles.

GLOSSARY

"Fancy Dancer" by Monique Gray Smith

Cree glossary

kisâkihitin: I love you.

kinânskomitin: Thank you. I'm grateful to you.

"Warriors of Forgiveness" by Tim Tingle

Choctaw glossary

pashofa (pa-SHO-fa): traditional and still popular Choctaw corn chowder, a thick soup served as an appetizer or main dish

yakoke (ya-ko-KE): thank you

halito (ha-li-TO): hello

hoke (ho-KE): all right, okay

luksi (LUK-si): turtle

achukma (a-CHUK-ma): good

Luksi Achukma (LUK-si a-CHUK-ma): Good Turtle, a traditional Choctaw name

"Brothers" by David A. Robertson

Cree glossary

tansi (TAHN-sih): hello

"Secrets and Surprises" by Traci Sorell

Ojibwe glossary. Readers can go to this site for pronunci-
ation guidelines: www.ojibwe.lib.umn.edu.

nimaamaa (nee-mah-mah): mother

imbaabaa (em-bah-bah): father

makwa (muh-KWAH): bear

makoons (mah-coonz): bear cub

nizigos (nee-zee-goos): paternal aunt

nookomis (no-koo-miss): my grandmother

boozhoo (boo-jhew): hello

aanii (ah-nee): greetings, hello, hi

mikinaak mnishenh (mee-kee-nak me-neeshen): Mackinac Island

noozhishenh (noo-zhah-shen): my grandchild

niibin (nee-bin): summer

nimishoome (nim-shwhoa-may): paternal uncle

miigwech (mee-gwetch): thank you

Gchi-Manidoo (gitch-chee mahn-eh-doo): the Creator

"Wendigos Don't Dance" by Art Coulson

Cherokee glossary. Cherokee phonetics don't generally use
uppercase letters. Cherokee sentences also rarely use

punctuation, since a native speaker will know when the thought is complete.

ᎣᏏᎩ (hawa, ha-WAH): a common exclamation meaning "okay" or "all right!"

skoden: a shortened version of "let's go, then," an expression used by Native people of many tribal nations

ᎣᏏᏲ (osiyo, oh-SEE-yoh): hello, often shortened to "siyo" in informal conversation

ᏩᏦᎦ (totsuwa, toh-JOO-hwa): redbird or cardinal

ᎡᎵᏏ (elisi, ay-LEE-see): my grandmother

ᎠᏦᏣ (atsutsa, ah-JOO-jah): boy or young man, often shortened to "chooch" or "choogie" as a nickname

ᎬᎵ (gvli, GUH-lee): raccoon

ii (vv, unh-unh): yes

ᎣᎵᏍᏕᎳ (halisdela, hals-DAY-la): help!

"INDIAN PRICE" BY ERIC GANSWORTH

Tuscarora/Haudenosaunee glossary. The six Haudenosaunee languages have no written versions of our languages, beyond linguistic diacritical symbols. "Nyah-wheh" is one phrase consistent among the six. The spelling here is my invention, an attempt to make pronunciation easy. The first syllable is tough. English does not seem to have the sound "nyah" as it is used here. It is close to the Russian word for "no" (nyet), with the end sound of "law" instead. For the

second syllable, the sound is like the word "when" but
with no hard "n" at the end. It is more like the word
trails off: "when . . ."

nyah-wheh: thank you

"Senecavajo: Alan's Story" and "Squash Blossom Bracelet: Kevin's Story" by Brian Young

Navajo glossary

shiyazhi (she-YAZH-ih): my little one

ndaa' (IN-daw): Enemy Way Ceremony

ye'ii bichei (YEH-ee bih-CHAY): literally "maternal
grandfather of the Holy Beings." In context of this
story, refers to the Night Chant Ceremony.

Cherokee glossary

ᎡᏟᏏ (elisi, ay-LEE-see): my grandmother

"Joey Reads the Sky" by Dawn Quigley

Ojibwe glossary. Readers can go to this site for pronunci-
ation guidelines: www.ojibwe.lib.umn.edu.

eya (EE-yuh): yes

gaawiin (GAH-ween): no

miigwech (mee-GWECH): thank you

makwa (muh-KWAH): bear

mikwam (mi-KWUM): ice

mikwamiikaa (mi-kwum-EE-kah): hail

wese'an (way-say-UN): tornado

"The Ballad of Maggie Wilson" by Andrea L. Rogers

Cherokee glossary

ᎣᏏᏲ (osiyo, oh-SEE-yoh): hello, often shortened to "siyo" in informal conversation

Choctaw glossary

achukma (a-CHUK-ma): good

amafo (a-MA-fo): grandfather

"Bad Dog" by Joseph Bruchac

Abenaki glossary

alnoba (AHL-no-bah): a person

kagwi (kah-GWEE): that

kia (kee-YAH): you

ktsi (ket-SEE): big

mdawela (me-DAH-wi-HLAH): loon

n'mahom (UN-ma-hom): my grandfather

nda (un-DAH): no

nda kagwi (un-DAH kah-GWEE): literally "not that"; used to mean "don't mention it" or "you're welcome"

ndeliwizi (in-de-LEE-wee-zee): I am called

nidoba (nee-dun-ba): my friend

nosis (no-SES): my grandchild

ôhô (unh-hunh): yes

paakwenogwesian (paA-ha-KWI-nun-GWE-see-AN):
You appear new to me

ta (dah): and

wliwini (Oo-lee-oo-NEE): thanks (literally, "good
returning")

"BETWEEN THE LINES" BY CYNTHIA LEITICH SMITH
Cherokee glossary

ᎬᏩ (wado, wa-do): thank you

"CIRCLES" BY CAROLE LINDSTROM
Cree Glossary

kokum (kôhkom, KOOH-gom): grandmother

NOTES AND ACKNOWLEDGMENTS

"What Is a Powwow?" and "Flying Together" by Kim Rogers

I am honored to be a part of this groundbreaking anthology alongside amazing authors and friends. Cynthia Leitich Smith, I am forever grateful for your mentorship and friendship. Your kindness and generosity never cease to amaze me. You've paved the way for many of us. Kris Kuykendall, Nalini Krishnankutty, and Christine Evans, I truly appreciate your thoughtful critiques. You've helped me become a better writer. Rosemary Brosnan, I'm thrilled to work with you and am excited about my debut picture book coming soon with Heartdrum/HarperCollins. Tricia Lawrence, I'm so happy you are my agent and friend. My husband and children, I couldn't have followed my dreams without your love and support. My gratitude to those who've served, including family members. So:ti:c?a to you all!

"FANCY DANCER" BY MONIQUE GRAY SMITH

This story is dedicated to all the children and young people who are learning about their ancestry and culture. May you be watched over, guided, and protected. May you be kept safe from inner and outer harm, and may you know immense joy and pride. And may you always remember to be kind, especially to yourselves.

I'd like to thank Cynthia Leitich Smith. This story would not be what it is without your questions, curiosity, and feedback. I raise my hands to you out of respect and gratitude.

"WARRIORS OF FORGIVENESS" BY TIM TINGLE

Hollywood movies would have you think that *every* Native man was a "warrior," one who chased wagon trains and engaged in battle whenever possible. In this story I would like to socially redefine the word. In addition to our highly respected professional Native soldiers and veterans, we also have citizens who fight to preserve our traditional human values in day-to-day life. As demonstrated in the narrative, these values include forgiveness—thus "Warriors of Forgiveness."

I send my immense gratitude to Choctaw friends Susan Feller and Jay MacAlvain, whose helpful spirits are honored in "Warriors of Forgiveness."

"REZ DOG RULES" BY REBECCA ROANHORSE

Thanks to Pernell Begay for suggesting *Ancestor Approved* as a T-shirt, and to all the many Rez dogs I've known throughout my life for the inspiration. May we all strive to be as free.

"SECRETS AND SURPRISES" BY TRACI SORELL

This story could not have been written without the aid of others. I want to acknowledge those who educated me about the University of Michigan's powwow, its present and past, especially Hector Galvan, Program Manager, Office of Academic Multicultural Initiatives; and Gabrielle May and Maitland Bowen, both with the Native American Student Association; as well as Native UM law school alumnae Cami Fraser, Kirsten Carlson, and Elise McGowan-Cuellar. Angeline Boulley, Colleen Medicine, Debra-Ann Pine, and Melissa Montoya Isaac offered invaluable feedback on the story, Jingle Dress dancing, and the Ojibwe culture and language. Dr. Margaret Noodin also helped me with the Ojibwe language. Miigwech to all for the assistance they provided. All errors in the story or Ojibwe language usage are mine alone. I dedicate this story to my longtime friends in the Turtle Mountains and the Soo, two of my favorite places in Indian Country.

"INDIAN PRICE" BY ERIC GANSWORTH

Nyah-wheh, thank you to Cynthia Leitich Smith for her

Jedi Council–like passionate and organized support of Indigenous writers in myriad fun and interesting ways, and to Rosemary Brosnan, for recognizing the necessity of such a volume and committing to its success. Thanks to my friend Graham Stowe for clarifying some organizational nuances I didn't understand. In particular, nyah-wheh/miigwech to my niece, Kristi Leora Gansworth, for sharing her experiences from the powwow vendor circuit to help me get some things right to the best of my abilities. All mistakes my own, as always.

"Joey Reads the Sky" by Dawn Quigley

I taught English/reading in seventh through ninth grades for most of my teaching career. I saw kids who "failed" in standardized reading tests—and these students are the ones who stole my heart. One of my earliest memories is of being teased for not knowing how to read. I know this pain of not being "smart." Yet, like my Joey character, these students of mine brilliantly "read" in other realms. "Joey Reads the Sky" was inspired by one student in particular, who struggled to "read" English texts, but each week would regale us with stories of "reading nature" (e.g., when the Minnesota lakes would be safe to walk on in the winter, when deer would look for mates and mark trees as they scraped trunks in the process). He taught *us* how to read nature.

I have issues with the tumult of testing in our P–12 schools. This story is my introverted activist way to say: I'm grateful to be able to honor them here, the ones who can read the world in ways that are not respected—the ways we desperately need of "knowing" in this world.

"WHAT WE KNOW ABOUT GLACIERS" BY CHRISTINE DAY

Brooke's lesson about glaciers being like mothers comes from an ancestral teaching described in *Salish Blankets: Robes of Protection and Transformation, Symbols of Wealth* (University of Nebraska Press), written by Leslie H. Tepper, Chief Janice George, and Willard Joseph. This teaching was attributed to Chief Ian Campbell of the Squamish Nation, who says, "I've heard of our glaciers being referred to as big blankets that are also sacred because the waters that flow from them are like a mother nursing a child." These words were the inspiration behind this short story.

I'd like to dedicate "What We Know About Glaciers" to my sister, who is best known as "Miss Jen" to her preschool students.

"THE BALLAD OF MAGGIE WILSON" BY ANDREA L. ROGERS

Though I loved *The Outsiders* as a twelve-year-old in 1981, I always wondered where the Indians were. The book's take on history, gender roles, class, representation, and language about Native people would not resonate with Maggie. There are better books for girls, Native people, and other outsiders. "The Ballad of Maggie Wilson" is written in honor of my father and my uncles. My dad's eldest brother died a lineman. My uncle Roy took me to my first powwow when I was a kid and my first Stomp as an adult. Thanks to Alice Barrientez, who gave my daughters and me guidance regarding powwow etiquette and reentering the circle after the death of my father. Wado to my critique group, Native Writes, for putting eyes on this, especially Ruby Hansen Murray, Traci Sorell, Erika T. Wurth, and Stacy Wells. Also, Rebecca Roanhorse, Dawn Quigley, Art Coulson, and Stephen Graham Jones generously answered random questions. Thank you, Rosemary Brosnan, for liking my story. Additional thanks to Cynthia Leitich Smith, who never fails to encourage me. Wado to Cherokee Nation and their fantastic employees, who always support my attempts to get things right. Finally, wado to my family for making my life and writing better and real.

"BETWEEN THE LINES" BY CYNTHIA LEITICH SMITH

The characters Ray and Grampa Halfmoon first appeared in my book *Indian Shoes*. I'm a Muscogee Creek citizen, and I'm also a Cherokee descendent and have beloved family members who are citizens of the Cherokee Nation of Oklahoma. The Halfmoon family stories are a sort of wink and love letter to them, especially Cousin Elizabeth. I originally conceived of Ray and Grampa in my early days as a children's writer, living in Chicago. My time in the Great Lakes also included a few years in Ann Arbor, where I earned a J.D. from the University of Michigan Law School. Mvto (thank you) to Joe Bruchac for his permission to mention his books *Skeleton Man* and *The Return of Skeleton Man*.

"CIRCLES" BY CAROLE LINDSTROM

I would like to say aaniin to Cynthia for asking me to be part of this anthology. And to Dan and Sam, my constant lights. And to all ancestors who have gone before me who are part of my eternal circle. Aapiji go miigwech.

EDITOR'S ACKNOWLEDGMENTS

A shout-out to the Native students—past, present, and *future*—at the University of Michigan. As a graduate of the law school, I feel compelled to say, "Go Blue!"

My thanks to the wonderful contributors of artwork, stories, and poems to this anthology. Both individually and as a collective, I appreciate your skill, professionalism, generosity, and cooperation in crafting this book. I'm especially grateful to Traci Sorell for compiling and sharing information crucial to our world-building efforts. We all owe a debt to the many U of M folks (listed in her note) who graciously responded to Traci's thoughtful queries.

Thanks also to our Heartdrum editor, Rosemary Brosnan, and my agent, Ginger Knowlton, for their faith, brilliance, expertise, and guidance.

ABOUT THE CONTRIBUTORS

An enrolled member of the Nulhegan Abenaki Nation, **JOSEPH BRUCHAC** has been attending, performing at, vending at, and even putting on powwows for over forty years. Author of over 170 books, his newest titles are *Peacemaker* (Dial), a novel about an Onondaga boy's encounter with the founder of the Iroquois League of Peace; *One Real American* (Abrams), a biography of Ely Parker, a Seneca "Grand Sachem" and Union general in the Civil War; and *The Powwow Dog* (Reycraft), a contemporary graphic novel illustrated by Dale DeForest.

ART COULSON is Cherokee from Oklahoma and comes from a family of storytellers. Some of his earliest memories are of listening to stories on his grandmother's lap. He has been a writer his whole life and published his first two books in elementary school (he was a self-publishing early adopter). Art served as the first executive director of the Wilma Mankiller Foundation in the Cherokee Nation of Oklahoma after a twenty-five-year career in journalism. Art is the author of *The Creator's Game* (Minnesota Historical Society Press), *Unstoppable* (Capstone), and *The Reluctant Storyteller* (Benchmark). He lives in Minneapolis.

CHRISTINE DAY (Upper Skagit) is the author of *I Can Make This Promise* and *The Sea in Winter*. *I Can Make This Promise* was an American Indian Youth Literature Award Honor Book, a Charlotte Huck Award Honor Book, and a best book of the year from *Kirkus Reviews*, *School Library Journal*, NPR, and the Chicago Public Library. Christine lives in the Pacific Northwest with her family.

ERIC GANSWORTH, Sʼha-weñ na-saeʼ (enrolled Onondaga), writer and visual artist, was raised at the Tuscarora Nation. He is Lowery Writer-in-Residence at Canisius College. His most recent book is *Apple: Skin to the Core*, a memoir in words and images. His YA novels include *Give Me Some Truth* (Whippoorwill Award) and *If I Ever Get Out of Here* (YALSA Best Fiction for YA, AILA Honor Award), for both of which he also recorded audiobook performances. His others include *Extra Indians* (American Book Award) and *Mending Skins* (PEN Oakland Award). He's had numerous visual art shows, and his work has been widely published.

CAROLE LINDSTROM is an Anishinaabe/Métis author, and an enrolled member of the Turtle Mountain Band of Ojibwe Indians. She writes books for children and young adults. Her debut picture book, *Girls Dance, Boys Fiddle*, based on Métis culture, was published by Pemmican Publishers. "Drops of Gratitude" is included in the anthology *Thank U: Poems of Gratitude* (Lerner/Millbrook), edited by Miranda Paul and illustrated by Marlena Myles. *We Are Water Protectors*, inspired by Standing Rock as well as the fight of all Indigenous peoples for clean water, was illustrated by Michaela Goade and published by Roaring Brook Press. Carole lives with her family in Maryland.

NICOLE NEIDHARDT (cover illustration) is Diné (Navajo) of Kiiyaa'áanii clan on her mother's side and a blend of European ancestry on her father's side, and is from Santa Fe, New Mexico. She has a bachelor of fine arts from the University of Victoria and is currently working on her master of fine arts at OCAD University in Toronto, Ontario. Nicole's Diné identity is the heart of her practice, which encompasses Mylar stenciling, installation, digital art, painting, illustration, and large-scale murals.

DAWN QUIGLEY, PhD, is a citizen of the Turtle Mountain Band of Ojibwe and an assistant professor of education. She taught English and reading for eighteen years in K–12 schools along with being an Indian Education program codirector. In addition to her coming-of-age novel, *Apple in the Middle* (NDSU Press), and nonfiction picture book, *Native American Heroes* (Scholastic Press), she has a Native American chapter book series with Heartdrum/Harper-Collins about lovable and quirky Ojibwe first grader Jo Jo Makoons. Quigley also has published more than twenty-eight articles, essays, and poems. She lives in Minnesota with her family.

REBECCA ROANHORSE is a speculative fiction writer of Black and Indigenous (Ohkay Owingeh) descent. She is a *New York Times* best-selling author and has won multiple awards, including the Nebula, Hugo, and Locus Awards. Her middle grade work includes *Race to the Sun* and a short story in the *Star Wars: Clone Wars* anthology. Her adult novels include *Trail of Lightning, Storm of Locusts, Star Wars: Resistance Reborn*, and *Black Sun*. She lives with her husband and daughter in northern New Mexico.

DAVID A. ROBERTSON is the author of numerous books for young readers, including *When We Were Alone*, which won the Governor General's Literary Award and was nominated for the TD Canadian Children's Literature Award. *Strangers*, the first book in his Reckoner trilogy, a young adult supernatural mystery series, won the Michael Van

Rooy Award for Genre Fiction (Manitoba Book Awards). A sought-after speaker and educator, Dave is a member of the Norway House Cree Nation and currently lives in Winnipeg.

ANDREA L. ROGERS writes in a variety of genres, centering Cherokee people. She is the author of the book *Mary and the Trail of Tears: A Cherokee Removal Survival Story* and an essay titled "My Oklahoma History" in *You Too? 25 Voices Share Their #MeToo Stories* (edited by Janet Gurtler). She is an enrolled citizen of the Cherokee Nation and grew up in Tulsa, Oklahoma, in the former Indian Territory. She graduated from the Institute of American Indian Art in Santa Fe, New Mexico, with an MFA in creative writing. She currently commutes between Fort Worth, Texas, and Fayetteville, Arkansas.

KIM ROGERS writes books, short stories, and poems across all children's literature age groups. Her work has been published in *Highlights for Children*, the Chicken Soup for the Soul series, and many other publications. Kim is an enrolled member of Wichita and Affiliated Tribes and the National Native American Boarding School Healing Coalition. Much of her current writing highlights her Wichita heritage. She lives in Oklahoma with her husband, two boys, and one ornery but very cute Chiweenie dog named Lucky.

CYNTHIA LEITICH SMITH is a *New York Times* best-selling author of books for young readers. Her debut book, *Jingle Dancer,* is widely considered a modern classic. She was named Writer of the Year by Wordcraft Circle of Native Writers and Storytellers for *Rain Is Not My Indian Name* and won the American Indian Youth Literature Award (young adult category) for *Hearts Unbroken.* She also serves as the Katherine Paterson Chair on the faculty of the Vermont College of Fine Arts MFA program in Writing for Children and Young Adults. Cynthia is a citizen of the Muscogee Creek Nation. She holds a bachelor's degree in journalism from the University of Kansas and a JD from the University of Michigan Law School in Ann Arbor, where she served as president of the Native American Law Students Association.

MONIQUE GRAY SMITH is a proud mom of Cree, Lakota, and Scottish ancestry. She is an award-winning and best-selling author of both children's books and adult novels. Her works include *My Heart Fills with Happiness, You Hold Me Up, When We Are Kind,* and *Tilly and the Crazy Eights.* Monique is well known for her storytelling and spirit of generosity and believes love is medicine. She is blessed to live with her family on the traditional territory of the W̱SÁNEĆ people, also known as Victoria, Canada.

TRACI SORELL writes fiction and nonfiction books as well as poems for children. Her debut nonfiction picture book, *We Are Grateful: Otsaliheliga*, won an American Indian Youth Literature (AIYLA) Honor, a Sibert Honor, a Boston-Globe–Horn Book Honor, and an Orbis Pictus Honor. The audiobook edition won an Odyssey Honor. *At the Mountain's Base*, her first fiction picture book, won an AIYLA Honor. *Indian No More*, her middle grade novel with Charlene Willing McManis, won the AIYLA Middle School Book Award. Traci is an enrolled citizen of the Cherokee Nation and lives in northeastern Oklahoma, where her tribe is located.

TIM TINGLE is a member of the Choctaw Nation of Oklahoma and an award-winning author and storyteller. His great-great-grandfather John Carnes survived the Trail of Tears, and in 1993 Tingle returned to Choctaw homelands in Mississippi and began recording stories of tribal Elders. The author of twenty books, he was awarded the Ariel Gibson Lifetime Achievement Award for his contribution to literature in the state of Oklahoma. Tingle was a featured speaker at the National Book Festival, based on critical acclaim for *How I Became a Ghost*. His YA novel *House of Purple Cedar* won the American Indian Youth Literature Award.

Erika T. Wurth's publications include two novels, two collections of poetry, and a collection of short stories. A writer of fiction, nonfiction, and poetry, she teaches creative writing at Western Illinois University and was a guest writer at the Institute of American Indian Arts. Her work has appeared or is forthcoming in publications including Buzzfeed, *Boulevard*, the *Writer's Chronicle*, *Waxwing*, and the *Kenyon Review*. She has been on the faculty at Breadloaf, is a Kenyon Review Writers Scholar, attended the Tin House Summer Workshop, and has been chosen as a narrative artist for the Meow Wolf Denver installation. She is Apache/Chickasaw/Cherokee and was raised outside of Denver.

Author and filmmaker **Brian Young** is a recipient of the prestigious Sundance Ford Foundation Fellowship (2008) and is a graduate of Yale University with a degree in film studies and Columbia University with a master's in creative writing (fiction). An enrolled member of the Navajo Nation, Brian co-directed *A Conversation with Native Americans on Race* with the *New York Times*. He is currently working on two middle grade novels for Heartdrum; the first is *Healer of the Water Monster*.

Dear Reader,

Images of graceful dancers in powwow regalia—a blur of color, light, and motion—are often widely shared to reflect Native people today. Those vibrant photos and videos evoke culture, tradition, and community—celebrating a moment in time. Yet the Native dancers depicted and the intertribal powwows that surround them live well beyond that moment.

They are multifaceted people and gatherings, each representing thousands of stories.

A powwow is a terrific opportunity to highlight the diversity of the intertribal Native and First Nations community, of individual Indigenous Nations within it, and of young Native heroes.

I'm so grateful to the contributing writers, poets, and artists in this book for embracing my invitation to bring a powwow to life on the page and for working together to create a resonant, page-turning, and fictionalized cultural experience for you.

It's been a joy to introduce those of you who are Native and First Nations readers to stories that hopefully feel both familiar and new. It's been a joy to introduce those of you who are non-Native readers to them, too, connecting you with Indigenous characters and points of view.

Have you read many stories by and about Native people? I hope that *Ancestor Approved: Intertribal Stories for Kids* inspires you to read more. This anthology is published by Heartdrum, a Native-focused imprint of HarperCollins Children's Books. I'm delighted to include the book on our first list for so many reasons: because it embodies and raises up Native voices and visions . . . because the art, poems, and stories are so wonderful . . . and because it beautifully reflects our commitment to the intertribal community while centering heroes who are young like you.

Mvto,
Cynthia Leitich Smith

In 2014, We Need Diverse Books (WNDB) began as a simple hashtag on Twitter. The social media campaign soon grew into a 501(c)(3) nonprofit with a team that spans the globe. WNDB is supported by a network of writers, illustrators, agents, editors, teachers, librarians, and book lovers, all united under the same goal—to create a world where every child can see themselves in the pages of a book. You can learn more about WNDB programs at www.diversebooks.org.